WARBO

BONITA HUNT

Outskirts Press, Inc.
http://www.outskirtspress.com

Paperback ISBN: 978-1-9772-2849-9
Hardback ISBN:978-1-9772-2856-7

Cover Image by Alexis Durbin

Outskirts Press and the "OP" logo are trademarks belonging to Outskirts Press, Inc.

PRINTED IN THE UNITED STATES OF AMERICA

CHAPTER ONE

It had been three days since the Crowder party had left the wagon train on the Oregon Trail headed for Fort Kearney, the headquarters of the Nebraska Calvary. From there, they had been assured of a Calvary escort to Chimney Rock, where they would join a larger wagon train headed to California.

It was a beautiful day, the morning dew still clinging to the tall grass and painting the trees in the distance a shining silver. As far as the eye could see the vast country stretched endlessly ahead. Clumps of cactus dotted the scenery and prairie dogs stuck their brown little heads from their holes to watch the intrusion of their private playground.

Janie West had walked beside the wagon for many hours that day and she was hot and tired and so relieved to see Doctor Crowder and his wife, Marie, pull under some big shade trees beside the Platte River for the night. She helped Doctor Max gather some wood and soon he had a nice little fire going to warm their dinner. As soon as Janie finished eating, she grabbed a big towel and some clean clothes and declared, "I am going to take a bath." She headed to the river and stripped out of clothes and went to the bank.

She swam out into the water and then came back and grabbed the bar of lavender soap and started shampooing her hair. She was trying to untangle the massive amount of hair when she heard Marie scream. She stood up in the water and waded close to the bank. The sun was in her eyes and she did not see the tall Indian standing by the rock by her clothes until she was almost upon him. She screamed, "Go away, go away now! What is going on?" He stopped and stared. Never had he ever seen a creature this lovely. She stood naked in the water, and he felt his breath sucked out of him and he felt a strange burning in his loins.

He did not move as Janie ran past him and grabbed her towel and wrapped it around her as she ran to her clothes. She pulled the dress over her head and took the underwear with her. The big Indian did not move. He was staring at this creature before him. What is she doing in my world? She wrapped her hair in the towel and took off, and she screamed when she bent down to see if she could help. She gasped for air as the bile started up into her throat. She moved to the wagon to steady herself and lost what little dinner she had just eaten. Tears welled up in her eyes and she yelled at the Indian following close behind. "Oh what brave men you are. Just two old people and you had to kill them."

Some of the Indians started to get into the wagon to see what they could steal for their camp. Janie yelled at them and pushed the big guy back and crawled into the wagon. The Indian was so surprised that this little woman would defy him, he just stopped and watched. She grabbed her small bag and stuffing her pantaloons along with the doctor's bag of tools and then she felt the gun that the Doc always left with his bag. She turned and shot the first brave that was coming into the wagon. He fell out screaming and lay still on the ground.

Janie immediately thought of the words that their scout had told her. Save the last bullet for yourself, because it would be better than living with the savages. Janie contemplated killing herself, but the courage never came. "I'll make them savages kill me now," she declared as she stepped from the wagon. She fired point-blank at the first brave as he pulled up to the wagon. He fell as the horse bolted. He pulled himself up but only made a few steps and collapsed on the ground. As she trained her gun on the next victim, the gun was taken from her by a big ugly man, sneaking up behind her. He grabbed her arm and reached for the towel that encircled her head. The bright auburn hair fell and cascaded down her back like a flowing river of red. She lowered her eyes and waited for the blow that would end her life. Then nothing. The hatchet stopped in mid-air and the brave let go of her like she was poison.

The move surprised Janie and she regained a little of her confidence. No one advanced, they stood there speaking in tongue and motioning to her hair.

"Well, come on you dirty filthy savages!" she yelled. "What's the matter, you afraid of one little woman?" Another Indian came through the crowd and walked up to her. She lashed out with her long fingernails and raked them across his chest. She caught him off guard, but without a word, he grabbed her wrist and pushed her toward the brave next to him. He mounted his pony in one quick leap and motioned for her to ride with the brave standing next to her. As the big Indian pushed her to his horse she let out a blood-curdling yell and waved her arms at the horse. The animal bolted and the brave fell to the ground still clutching the reins. The pony ran dragging the brave through the rough bed of stones and cactus.

The other Indians stood around not daring to go near her. They all mounted their ponies each unwilling to try their skill at taming her. They did not want to lose face as the others had. They looked to their Chief for his next order.

Warbo, chief of the Pawnees, sensed that it was up to him and, without hesitation, he rode up to the woman and swept her up onto his horse. He carried her in front of him like a sack of flour. Janie kicked and screamed, "Let me up you filthy Indian."

He grunted and kicked the horse into a trot and then into a gallop. Janie gasped for air and clutched out for something to hang onto. She grabbed the naked leg of the Indian. It was all she could do, so she hung on. The pony ran fast, his long legs covering the ground with increasing speed. A solid blur of green, brown, and gold was all she could see as she bounced along holding on for her life. The dust from the pony's hoofs choked her and she coughed for air. They had only gone a short distance, for Janie it had been miles when the chief stopped his horse and spoke in perfect English. "you want ride like squaw should ride?"

"I'll ride, I'll ride, she groaned.

"Wild One will not make Chief lose face," he said.

"Just let me up," she begged.

He let the reins lay for a moment and lifted her in position in front of him. Janie had a hard time getting her feet to straddle the pony with her long skirt. He tried to move the long material, but his hand felt the smooth soft skin of her leg and he stiffened. He pulled his arm back swiftly and Janie looked at him a small giggle came out. Mercy, she thought. I don't have my pantaloons on and she realized that she was naked beneath her dress. She pulled the dress down and smiled sweetly at him. She swore his face looked redder than before and she grinned. Half afraid to face him she turned and looked into his painted face and his eyes. The hair on her arms slowly began to rise. They were so cold. Blue and penetrating. So blue they almost looked black. He sensed her looking at him and he returned the look, unfeeling and piercing.

He slowed the horse as they approached the hill on the far side of the prairie. She turned and asked, "who taught you to speak English?"

"My Mother, Morning Star," he answered keeping his eyes on the climb ahead.

"Who taught your Mother?"

"She was once white."

"What do you mean, she was once white? Once you are white, you don't change."

"She was captured like you and turned Indian."

"Well, I am not turning Indian, you understand. I AM NOT GOING TO BECOME AN INDIAN." She shouted at him. She grabbed his brown arm and squeezed it to show her resistance.

"What will your leader say?" she asked.

"I am Warbo, Chief of the Pawnee, he stated and she felt his shoulders stiffen like a proud peacock.

"Why didn't you let them kill me back there, or do you want to watch me die slowly?"

"You fight hard, kill two brave warriors. You earn the right to be wife of Pawnee."

"Wife of Pawnee, me? Never!"

He didn't answer and they reached the crest of the hill. He stopped for a moment and surveyed the countryside. The burning wagon smoldered in the distance.

"Well, are you proud of what you've done? Brave men you Indians, twenty men against one man and two women." She looked at him now her courage coming back.

"You won't be so brave when "Dark Eagle takes you," he said.

"Who's Dark Eagle?"

"Wild One make Dark Eagle lose face, you be Dark Eagle's wife."

Oh, he must be the one the horse drug, she thought. Her pulse quickened. I must remain calm. I can't let them know I'm scared. As they crossed another meadow, the grass grew taller and the countryside greener. Janie tried to remember the direction that they were going in case she ever did a get a chance to escape she would know what direction she should go. Escape some chance of that, she thought as she made a mental drawing of the terrain.

She thought of Dark Eagle and she shuttered to think that she could be touched by that evil-looking-man. Watching the Chief, she decided that he definably would be preferable to Dark Eagle. At least he could speak English and she could communicate with this frightening and irritating man. Her mind worked fast, a plan forming in her head.

They approached a water hole and Warbo stopped to water the horse after the long ride. He released his grip and kept scooting as far back on the pony as he could. She realized that she made him very nervous the closer she got to him. "Why am I not to be the wife of the Chief?"

"Warbo has wife, no want another."

"Doesn't Dark Eagle have a wife?"

"Dark Eagle have many wives."

"So Dark Eagle can handle many wives, but Chief can only handle one?"

That remark hit home and Warbo jerked on the reins and pulled the horse from the water and grabbing Janie to him, he took off like a shooting arrow. They rode at breakneck speed and Janie held on tight to the naked leg beside her. When at last the horse was winded, he slowed to a crawl and slowly made his way towards the camp lying in the meadow below. Janie knew her time was running out and although she was worried about his reaction, she pressed him farther.

"What if one of the other braves will want me, what will Dark Eagle say to that?"

"Dark Eagle, strongest warrior in camp. He will fight for you and he will take you. He will teach you respect for our people or he will kill you?"

Quick to take advantage of that remark she said, "If Dark Eagle is the strongest warrior in camp, why is he not chief?"

"I am strongest. Warbo is Chief."

"You do not want to fight Dark Eagle for me?"

Warbo guided the horse down towards the camp and ignored her question.

She persisted, "Is Warbo afraid he cannot please me because I am a white woman?"

The anger flared in his eyes and not realizing he tightened his grip on her so tight she could hardly breathe. "Warbo is not afraid of any squaw."

"I am not a squaw, and I never will be. Even the mighty chief of the Pawnees will not please me."

"Dark Eagle take Wild One and tame her. Warbo not want woman with hair of fire."

"You do not like my hair?" She taunted as she tossed her head to make it blow in his face.

As he felt her hair slip through his fingers, he saw her coming out of the water with her hair blowing in a rosy glow and he felt like a young boy going into battle for the first time.

Suddenly Janie felt an uncontrollable desire to laugh. Her Janie West, who never had to compete for any man, suddenly trying desperately to get and Indian interested enough in her to fight for her. It was funny and she laughed aloud. Her laughter filled the air and this time it was Warbo's turn to have the hair on his neck rise slowly. The horse pranced at the sudden noise and he tightened his grip to control the animal. She laughed louder and looked at him as though she were laughing at him. Something about this woman riled him and he suddenly stopped the horse and pushed her to the ground. "You walk," he yelled.

Janie lay there for a moment but whenever she was truly frightened she didn't cry she laughed. It was senseless but as she rolled over in the grass and looked up at the menacing Indian she giggled again. He let her laugh, watching her and admiring her courage. What a strange beautiful young woman, he thought to himself.

Dark Eagle rode up and when he saw her sitting there, he ran his horse so close he nearly ran over her. It made her stop laughing for a moment and she scurried to her feet picking up a rock as she rose and throwing it after the departing brave. "I'll never be your wife, you ugly pig."

Warbo stayed close by to make sure she didn't try to escape. The other braves rode by tense with the excitement the captive had brought them.

As Janie approached the camp, she could see the squaws coming to meet their men, the children and dogs close behind. She sent a prayer saying. "God, give me the strength to endure this nightmare."

CHAPTER TWO

The small party of braves entered the camp. Squaws, children and dogs formed a line to watch as the fire-haired captive walked proudly, her head held high, showing no fear. She could feel a deadly cold moving slowly through her body. The old braves stared at her and she returned their look, cold and unblinking.

The two dead warriors were brought to the center of the camp and the squaws came forward to claim the bodies.

The older squaw showed no sign of empathy, but the young girl muffled a cry as she led the horse toward the long row of tepees. Janie watched and seeing the composure of the other Indians she wondered if they were cable of feeling anything. She shivered with this revelation.

Her bags were dropped in front of her, not knowing where this captive was going to be placed. She stood for a moment and surveyed her surroundings. Tepees, large tepees stretched as far as she could see. They were placed in a circle. Janie noticed some had large poles at the back with shields and other articles hanging from them. She was to learn later these poles were called tripods.

Smoke rose from the campfires that were placed a short distance from each tepee. Small pieces of meat were impaled on forked sticks hanging directly over the coals. The smell of scorched meat penetrated the air and a thought crossed Janie's mind. "I wonder what's for dinner?"

Warbo had dismounted and a young brave had taken his horse and led it away. He stood there now and looked at the bags she had wanted so badly. Picking up the doctor's bag, he opened it and casually brought out some of the bandages and gauze. Among the pills, he found the doctor's scalpel. He flashed the knife at Janie as if he knew it was there all the time. "Wild One not need knife."

"Keep it. Maybe you can protect yourself from Dark Eagle with it."

She could see his immense hatred strong in his eyes as he looked at her. After making sure there was nothing of value left in the bag, he opened the cloth bag containing her clothes. The squaws gathered in a tight circle to satisfy their curiosity. The pantaloons came out first and he looked at Janie with a look of bewilderment and waited for her answer. Not missing an opportunity to best this man she stepped forward and pulled up her dress. "See, this is where I wear them."

The deep tan in his face turned to a darker red and it was evident he was embarrassed. The squaws giggled and Janie smiled broadly, enjoying every minute she could rattle this big man. He dropped them quickly and brought out many dresses. The women were excited and made odd noises as they examined the stitches and designs of these foreign clothes. They wanted to get a better look at the clothes and began crowding closer, each picking up one to look at, their wrinkled faces lighting up. Never had they seen cloth as fine or thread so small.

"Oh, no you don't, I'll burn them before I let a bunch of savages wear them!" She went down the line jerking the dresses from their gnarled hands.

As she grabbed for the last dress, the squaw didn't let go. She held tightly and looked Janie in the eye. Janie returned the dresses to her bag and began stuffing them in. Warbo had satisfied his curiosity and stood watching her from the shade of a big cottonwood some distance away, admiring her courage.

She returned to the stubborn squaw and reaching for the dress she yelled. "Let go or I'll pull your mangy hair out!" Her temper was up and her confidence building. "I've never been afraid of any woman, and that goes for squaws too." She pulled hard on the dress and then let go suddenly and sent the squaw over backwards in the dirt. She was a large-boned woman and a few inches taller than Janie. She had a mean face and if Janie had ever seen anyone uglier she could not recall. She wore a mangy dress of deerskin. Her high moccasins covered her brown ankles. Her hair was knotted into long braids flowing down her back.

She dropped the dress and picked herself up. She circled for a moment and then her foot flew through the air and catching Janie in the midriff. Janie grabbed her stomach, gasping for air. The squaw had the advantage now and stood waiting for Janie to get up. All the time she was getting her breath back, Janie was thinking. As she got to her feet she pretended to stumble bringing herself within range of her opponent. She took the squaw by surprise and they fell to the ground in a tight grip.

The other squaws yelled and cheered their fellow tribeswoman on. They formed a tight circle, their faces bright with excitement. Janie used her long fingernails to advantage as she clawed the squaws face. She thought she would pull the hair from her head and then she felt the strong hands go around her throat. The sun faded and the clouds swirled above her. Darkness came and Janie awoke she could see Warbo standing over her, his hands crossed in front of him and, a smug smile on his face.

"Wild One make many enemies. Dark Eagle will teach you to respect the Pawnees."

"Maybe so, maybe so, still trying to get her breath back. I shall look forward to that." She reached out her hand to him for help. He automatically took her hand and pulled her up. His hand felt like he had thrust it into the fire, and he stepped back from her.

"If he fails, then the great Chief of the Pawnees will not lose face. Does Dark Eagle do all the hard jobs?" She knew for some reason she deliberately enjoying making him squirm.

"Warbo can do anything Dark Eagle can," he said in self-defense.

"Oh, I'm, sure of that", she remarked in disgust.

A young Indian maid was standing nearby and Warbo instructed her to take the Wild One to the lodge. She picked up the bags and spoke softly to Janie, "Come, I will take you to our Lodge."

"Wow, another savage who speaks English," she said aloud. She followed the girl down the row of tepees. She saw Warbo enter a large tepee and the young girl entered the smaller one next to it. As they stepped inside, Janie stared in amazement. She hadn't given any thought to what an Indian tepee would be like but this she hadn't expected.

"I am Little Dove, wife of Warbo. You rest until the council meets." She went to a pallet of buffalo furs and rolled them out. She arranged the pillows decorated with beads and porcupine quills, then left quickly.

Janie dropped to the bed of furs and felt the weariness come over her. She lay there staring at the tilted cone that formed the tepee. The back of the tepee was steeper with the front sloping to the ground. A smoke hole had been made farther down. Smoke flaps were on both sides of the door. She estimated the tepee to be at least ten feet in diameter. As her eyes scanned the lodge, all she could think of was, "am I going to live in a tepee the rest of my life with a bunch of Indians. She moved to the back of the tepee and saw two willow rod backrests. They looked like chairs with no legs.

"Mercy, I bet that's comfortable she said half out loud. More pillows, beautifully decorated bags, rawhide cases and, wood boxes lined the north wall. A small bag hung about shoulder high beside the door.

Crude looking bowls and other articles made from bones were placed by the fire. Janie assumed these to be cooking utensils. A good size pile of wood was stacked neatly beside the door. Her eyes came to rest on a small medicine bag that Doctor Crowder had always carried and she felt her throat grow tight. The awful recollection of their deaths came vividly back to her and she realized that she was weak and frightened beyond her control. So much for being brave, she thought. Marie's face came to her and what they had done to her brought waves of nausea to her stomach.

The tears came slowly down her cheeks. She cried for the woman who had been her friend for so long and the doctor who had practically been her father during the last four years. She cried for the fear of not knowing what was going to happen to her. Knowing there was no chance of escape in the immediate future and the Indians had only gained a little respect for her and she had a feeling that it would be short-lived when Dark Eagle took possession of her. She wiped her eyes on the dusty hem of her dress. Lying back on one of the pillows, her eyes filled with hot scalding tears.

She remembered the first time she had met Dr. Crowder and later his wife, Maria. Her mother had died when Janie was only five and her Father had left her in the care of her maiden aunt. Dear old Aunt Agatha, if she could only see me now. She had done her best trying to raise this little hellion, but Janie had always proved too much for anyone who tried to tell her what to do. From the time she was old enough to walk, she did things her way and no one could get the best of her. Aunt Agatha was plagued with respiratory problems and was sick most of the time. The little tyrant proved too much for her and she was placed in a boarding school. It was nothing more than an orphanage and it was here that Janie learned to look out for herself as no one else would.

She fought her way through those last five years and when she turned eighteen, she was allowed to look for a job. In her spare time, she worked at the orphanage with the younger children to earn her keep. It was on one of these days while she was looking after one of the sick kids that Doctor Crowder was called. As she worked with the doctor to make the child comfortable he admired her ability to handle children.

"You are a fine young assistant, Miss West," he told her as he packed his bag.

"Thank you, doctor, I love working with children."

"Have you ever thought of becoming a nurse?"

"Not much chance of that in these parts, I'm afraid. I doubt if I'll ever find a job, much less go back east to study medicine."

It wasn't too long after that when Dr. Crowder returned to the orphanage and explained to her that he was thinking of hiring an assistant. He told her he couldn't pay much but he would teach her the skills of nursing as she went along.

At this point, anything was better than this place and she readily agreed to his offer. She felt a sense of freedom as she left the school and moved in with the Crowders. She smiled when she thought of Marie, such a kind gentle woman who did not enjoy good health. She was a jolly person and she embraced Janie like the daughter she never had. Marie would sit in that old rocker by the pot-bellied stove reading her tattered and worn bible. Her hair was worn tightly about her head in a huge knot. Her brown eyes had a certain glow in them and Janie lived in contentment for several years. She learned the skills of nursing and how to sew and make her clothes. Marie was the mother she never had.

Now bitterness tore at her heart and she swore revenge on these murdering savages who had snuffed out the lives of the only two people who had loved and cared for her. I will get my revenge, she vowed.

A tear escaped down her cheek and as she brushed it away, she felt the ring on her finger. She twisted it a little and then smiled. No, they hadn't killed everyone. She still had Carl, her fiancé and he was waiting for her in California.

Carl Downer was a young cowboy from one of the larger spreads of the Ohio Valley. His father was a big rancher and now his son wanted to have a small place of his own. He took his share of the cattle money and headed to the land of sunshine and promise. He wrote as soon as he had settled on a small piece of land. When he described the rich valley and the booming town of Sacramento and how badly they needed a doctor, she read the letter to the Crowders. After much debate, they decided to make the trip. The Doctor convinced Marie it would be better for her health to move to a warmer climate.

And now look where we are, as she brought herself back to her predicament. Both dead and me in the middle of an Indian village fighting to stay alive. Oh, Carl, I will try so hard to get back to you she promised herself.

Her train of thoughts was interrupted as a shadow filled the doorway. Little Dove entered followed by an old woman and another squaw that looked to be in her late thirties. "This is my Mother called Prairie Breeze and my sister known as Running Deer." They stared in curiosity at their visitor and then knelt on their knees as little Dove brought the supper. She placed a large bowl hewn from wood in the center of the lodge. She handed each of them a large dipper made from a buffalo horn and made signs for them to eat.

The two women dipped into the bowl and brought out chunks of meat and corn. They ate, sipping and, sucking their food as they did. The liquid ran down the old woman's chin and dripped onto the worn dress of skins.

Janie felt her stomach grow weak as Little Dove handed her a dipper. "What is it?" she asked. "It is the tongue of the buffalo with corn and roots."

"Sorry I asked," Janie answered. By the time she mustered her courage to take a bite, It was gone. Little Dove left the lodge and soon returned with another bowl. The two women ate again and Janie was astonished at their enormous appetite. When they finished they retired to the back of the tepee and Janie could tell they were discussing her as they talked.

She eyed the bowl and decided it had been a long time since she had eaten and she wasn't likely to get anything else tonight. She swallowed fast and tried not to taste it. The broth tasted like the one they served in the orphanage. As her stomach accepted the liquid she nibbled on a small piece of meat. It was tough and hard to chew. She could not recall ever having chewed one morsel of food for so long before she finally forced it down her throat.

After chewing until her jaws ached she filled up on the corn and roots left in the bottom. She watched as Little Dove pressing her lips to the small round bag she had seen by the door. The young girl wiped her mouth and then realized Janie was watching her.

"Wild One want drink?" she motioned to the bag.

Janie stood up and stretched. After that soup she was thirsty. She nodded and moved to the bag. She could see no opening so she asked," How do you get the water to come out?"

Little Dove stepped to the bag and pressed her mouth to the opening concealed at the top. She pushed gently on the pouch between her palms to bring the water. She made it look easy and Janie stepped confidently to the bag. She wiped the opening and the thought of drinking after these Indians and she nearly stopped but the craving for water won her over and she pressed her mouth to the opening and pushed too hard and water squirted up into her face and ran down her neck and onto her dress. She sputtered, "Of all the stupid ways to drink." She wiped her mouth and face with the hem of her dress. She could taste the sweat from her body as she did. She tried the bag once more and gently squeezed and the water-filled her mouth. It was cool and pleasing. Amazing she thought.

She was watching the women at the back of the lodge and they were talking and motioning to her. Little Dove was indeed little and her features were soft and delicate. It was hard to believe that she was the daughter of the old woman who sat toothless and grinning as Janie stared. Her skin was wrinkled with age and her hands were thin and gnarled. It reminded Janie of a skeleton with fingers so thin they looked like tiny bones.

The older girl called Running Deer was more than pleasingly plump and Janie determined that she was just plain fat. Her teeth were still intact, but they looked like she had chewed tobacco because of the brown lining her gums. She giggled occasionally as they talked on in their endless chatter, Janie felt her nerves grow tighter by the minute.

Little Dove came and sat down by Janie, sensing her loneliness and she could tell this woman was certainly a little frightened by what was to come. Her long braids hung down her back. They were neatly combed and she wore a band of colored beads about her head. Her dress of softened deerskin was clean and the fringe combed about the bottom. Janie thought she was the prettiest Indian she had ever seen. The friendly ones they had encountered along the trail all resembled each other with their high cheekbones and wrinkled skin.

"You are the wife of the great chief?" she asked as she eyed the young girl.

She nodded. Janie continued, "You have no children?"

She hesitated and then with eyes downcast she answered, "no, my shame is great."

"Shame! Why should you be ashamed? How long have you been married?

"Many, many moons. I have failed to give Warbo a son to follow in his footsteps."

"Does that mean years or months?"

She was silent for a moment as if she were thinking about how to answer in white man's tongue. "We have two long winters since I became Warbos' wife."

Janie assumed she meant two years and then probed for more information on the tribe.

"Did Warbo's mother teach you to speak English?

"Morning Star teach us the ways of the white man and their language so Warbo can council with our enemies."

"He certainly doesn't do a very good job of counseling going around killing the white people and taking captives, she said bitterly.

"White men have killed many of our braves and even our women and children, she said in defense of her people."

"Warbo said, his mother became an Indian and I want to know how she turned into an Indian? Did they torture her?"

Morning Star was never tortured. She married chief Sly Fox and gave him a son. She is proud of Warbo, he is fine Chief. She smiled and said, "you will bear Dark Eagle a son to be proud of too." Janie felt like hitting her but the sound of drums broke the silence.

Janie felt the hair on the back of her neck rise and she trembled and felt a coward jerk of her heart. Little Dove quickly rose and said, " Come it is time for the council."

"Now, tonight? I'm not ready. I must change my dress." The thoughts raced through her mind of Indians fighting for her and suddenly she knew she must look her best to lure the big dumb Indian into fighting for her. She reached into the cloth bag and took out her prettiest dress. A white gown with a black velveteen ribbon running in a V-shape down her bodice and her back. The bodice was cut low and showed off her abundant breasts to perfection. She ran a comb through her hair and let it flow free and long over her shoulders. A vision of loveliness and Janie thought I hope this gets you to thinking big guy!

The three women watched in fascination as she transformed herself into a sultry young woman. Never had they seen such finery and their eyes were bright with the excitement of the evening. I'd think I was going to a grand ball the way I am fussing around. But I must make that half-breed, English speaking Indian fight for me. The thought of that mean-looking Dark Eagle putting his hands on her made her skin crawl. Not that Warbo was such a catch but better than the alternative. He was certainly the lesser of two evils.

The flap was pulled open now and the two braves stood motioning for her to come out. She braced herself and stepped proudly through the opening.

CHAPTER THREE

A short fat warrior dressed in buckskins grabbed her arm and started pulling her towards the campfire. She stopped short and pulled backward and he looked at her to urge her along. The look she gave him must have given him second thoughts. He did not want this person to shame him as she had the others. He motioned to the campfire and she followed, walking tall and straight, without emotion.

The fire leaped high in the cool night air as the squaws and children sat on the outer edge of the circle and their mates stood huddled together and Janie knew they were they weren't discussing the weather.

They took their places and began beating on the drums and shaking their rattles. They were joined by several braves dancing and screeching as they pranced around the fire. As they passed in front of their captive, she felt a cold shiver creep down her back and fear took its place in her mind.

As they chanted, Warbo entered the circle supporting a large headdress of feathers. Around his neck hung a necklace, made from the claws and teeth of an eagle. The war paint was gone and his face was clean and tanned. He wore long tanned breeches with fringe and the muscles of his body were very prominent. Even with the warpaint gone from his body, he was a formidable-looking man. Only his skin showed the Indian. His Mother's traits came through with the blue eyes and his nose was not flat like the Pawnees.

The squaws and even children showed their respect as they bowed low, some with their arms up in salute. As he circled, Janie compared him to a King with his faithful followers on their knees before him. He thinks he is a God, Janie thought. She stood still at the post where they had placed her and did not move.

When Warbo finished parading around the circle, he came and stopped in front of her. He said nothing but with arms crossed in front of him, he stood waiting for her recognition.

"All squaws honor their chief," he said sternly.

"And do I look like a squaw to you?" she said tartly.

She did not know the deadly game she was played as his anger flared and he stepped forward and planted his strong hand on her bare shoulder. As his fingernails bit into her skin, Janie winced and stiffed a cry. She looked up at him and said, "Fight for me Warbo, please, please!"

His fingers trembling ever so slightly as he held her there, but her words caused him to release his grip, "You will learn to respect the mighty chief of the Pawnees." She grabbed his arm and pulled herself up as proudly as she had gone down. "Not unless you fight for me". She showed no sign of pain although her shoulder felt like she had been stabbed. She kept her eyes on his to increase his nervousness.

"I am not afraid of any of my warriors including Dark Eagle," he stated.

"Perhaps you are only afraid of the Wild One?"

He avoided looking at her as he turned to the group of warriors waiting outside the circle. As he seated himself and Little Dove arranged his headdress, he nodded to the braves and the song took up once more. No one moved among the Indians until Dark Eagle leaped into the circle. It was his turn to have the attention and he strutted around like a proud peacock and then shouting to the crowd he proclaimed. " I am Dark Eagle, and I claim the captive as mine." He continued his prancing and with a zig-zag step and continually uttering a loud guttural "Ugh" and a rattling sound from deep in his lungs.

After completing three circles around the fire, a second warrior left the group and sprang forward in the dance. Each, in turn, followed until about fifteen half-naked bodies loomed in the firelight.

Janie had never seen a more savage bunch of men in her life. Just looking at the faces and bodies begrimed with paint, their fierce features reflecting the flame, made her shutter. They stood with their teeth bared and every brow knotted into fierce anticipation of the night.

When the dancing finally came to an end, the drums beat a low roll. Warbo stood tall and proud. He spoke in Pawnee and Dark Eagle answered in a loud boisterous manner. Dark Eagle flexed his muscles and started pointing to her. Janie didn't have to understand what he was saying as he came closer to her.

For a moment Janie thought he would go unchallenged, but then a man about Dark Eagles size entered the ring. He wore only the loincloth and carried no weapon. They circled each other for a minute and then Dark Eagle grabbed his arm and pulled the man against his body. They struggled against each other and for a moment it looked as if Dark Eagle was going down but then he lifted the brave off the ground and sent him rolling from the circle.

The spectators cheered and applauded and another warrior entered the ring and this match ended as quickly as the first. It was plain they were no match for this brute of a man. The rest of the warriors backed off and Dark Eagle had won his prize.

He moved to the post and Janie shrank back avoiding his touch. He grabbed her and taking his knife from its sheath he slid it across Janie's throat, just light enough to avoid hurting her but giving her a sickening idea of what was to come. Fear was in her every bone and she looked to Warbo for another chance. She could see no emotion in the man.

Dark Eagle grasped her hair in his hand and pulled it high above her head like he was claiming a prize turkey. Her hair felt like it was being pulled out by the roots. She twisted in his grip, frantic with terror. In hopeless desperation, she lashed out at the sweaty and lathered body of her predator. As her foot met his skin bone, he backhanded her so hard, he sent her sprawling to the feet of Warbo. As the blood trickled from her mouth and dropped onto her white breast, she spit at Warbo "At least I am not to belong to a half breed."

Warbo could contain himself no longer. A rush of blood filled his head and he felt like he was rushing into a burning fire. As Dark Eagle dragged her to her feet and prepared to hit her again, Warbo spoke.

What was said, Janie couldn't tell, but she could tell that it pleased Dark Eagle. He let go of her and sent her sprawling outside the circle. As Warbo lifted the headdress from his head, he shot a look of hatred at the red-haired captive.

Little Dove took the headdress and spoke to Janie.

"Wild One bring much trouble. Warbo is good Chief. If Dark Eagle win fight many of the tribe will suffer."

"Why, they're only fighting over me."

"They fight for you, but not like before. They will fight to the death. There is no love between these two and whoever wins, will take you and become chief. She stood watching and Janie felt like she had been slapped in the face. Even as she spoke, Janie could see the knives flash in the firelight. A sharp cold chill slithered through her body. She watched in horror as the fight got underway.

They began circling, each a little wary of the other, both sure-footed and searching for a chance to drive the knife into the heart of the other. Dark Eagle lunged forward and Warbo side-stepped to avoid a swift chop to his throat. Dark Eagle's foot came up in his groin and Warbo sank to his knees. Once again, the savage footwork and the knife was knocked from his hand. Janie held her breath as Warbo slowly regained his footing. The crowd yelled for their Chief and Janie could tell they knew the seriousness of the fight.

Warbo doubled over and went into a fast roll and knocked the big man to the ground. The dirt and dust created a thick haze and it was hard to see what was happening. Janie heard Warbo groan and as he staggered to his feet, blood dripped slowly from his side, she knew Dark Eagles knife had found its mark.

"Come on Warbo, I'm sorry, get up! You can do it!' she yelled.

As though she had given him strength, he straightened and

plummeted down on his foe. The angry men crashed to the ground. Warbo rolled clear and Dark Eagle was thrown so near the fire that the distinct smell of burning flesh filled the air. He omitted a small moan and his desire to kill was renewed more than ever and Janie could tell it was a fight he had relished for a long time. Before he could regain his footing, Warbo was upon him, knocking him to the ground, clutching his throat in his hands. As he exerted himself, the muscles on his arms stood out tight and drawn. Blood spurted from the wound in his side, causing him to weaken.

Dark Eagle's fingers dug into Warbos' eyes and he lost his grip. Dark Eagle was on his feet. An appalling kick to the groin sent Warbo back to the ground and his opponent running in search of the fallen knife. Warbo felt the cold steel beneath him and raising himself on one knee, sent the knife sailing through the night and, embedding itself in the back of its intended victim. A cry of anguish pierced the night, the fight had ended. Dark Eagle was dead and Warbo was not far from it. He pulled himself up and walked to his fallen warrior and pulled the knife from his back. He walked toward Janie, and the hatred for this woman was evident. He took the bloody knife and wiped it across her cheek and then finished cleaning it on the bodice of her white dress.

Janie stood still, too scared to move. She could smell the sweat pouring from his body and the wound in his side gaping wide with dirt starting to crust. His face was dusty and bloody. His mouth twisted into a cruel grin. "You belong to me now and before the moon rises three times you will wish Dark Eagle had won. Great is my hatred of the white men." He turned and walked slowly from the circle.

As she watched him leave, she knew one enemy was dead but an even greater one now owned her and she dreaded the thought of what was to come. Her eyes dropped and she saw the blood vivid on her dress and the shock of the day came upon her and she knew she was going to be sick. She found the nearest tree and clung to it.

CHAPTER FOUR

When she returned to her lodge, she saw the Doctors' bag sitting there close to the door. She thought about Dr. Crowder and wished he was here. His words came to her now as she stood there contemplating what to do next. His words came back to her now, "Janie, you are a good nurse. Always put your hands to good deeds."

"My God, what if he dies? The tribe will believe that I killed him. I must go to him and see if I can help, she exclaimed." She grabbed the bag and ran to his lodge, bursting in the door as if she lived there.

Little Dove was bending over him on the bed of furs and tending to his wound. She didn't know the other woman who was heating some water. Little Dove looked up to her and asked, "What are you doing here?" You will only upset him."

"I have come to help. I am a nurse and I know a lot about medicine. I can help him if you will let me. She hurried to his side and looked at the wound. She could tell by the amount of blood that he was losing, that the knife must have severed an artery. "We must stop the bleeding now, or he will die." She stood and pulled up her dress and pulled the long white slip down around her ankles and stepped out of the garment. She grabbed some scissors from the bag and began cutting the material into long strips.

She dipped the rags in the hot water and began cleaning the wound. Warbo opened his eyes and spoke. "Leave my lodge, now!" he ordered.

"You will die if we can't stop the bleeding now. Trust me, Warbo, I can help you. I don't want you to die."

The woman from the fire spoke, "I am Praire Breeze, Warbo's Mother. I will watch to make certain that you do not harm my son any further."

It was not hard to spot the bleeding artery as she could see where the blood was coming from. She pinched the artery shut and held it tight while her other hand searched for the other end. "I need your help, Little Dove. Pat the blood away so I can find the other end. "

She started patting the blood away and soon Janie grabbed the other end of the artery. She pulled them together and tried to put one end into the other. To no avail, she told Prairie Breeze to find the needle and thread in the doctors' bag and give it to her. Warbos' mother quickly found the needle and threaded it and handed it to Janie. Janie pushed the needle through one vein to the next and wrapped the thread around to hold it in place, all the time praying that it would hold. The blood seemed to stop flowing rapidly but you could still see blood seeping from the veins. She sewed again and stopped the leak and then pulled the skin back in place and stitched it up as well. Next, she took the long strips from Little Dove and together they poked the material from one side of Warbo to the other. Warbo was still conscious and kept his eyes on her as she leaned over his chest to reach the strips on the other side. When he felt her hands against his chest, his breath came in long gasps. Janie's face flushed and she too felt the blood rush in her veins.

"Almost done Warbo, just relax and let me finish." Her voice seemed to take his mind off of whatever he was feeling and he let out a long sigh and looked at the woman who had caused him so much trouble. Even in his weakened state, his eyes roamed her body and he suddenly turned his head when his eyes came to rest on her rising and falling chest. Devil woman, he thought.

Janie finished dressing the wound and picked up her tools and washed them in the hot water that still simmered on the fire. "Make him stay quiet and not get up until that wound starts to heal." The two women shook their heads in accordance and assured her that they would not let him up.

"Come and get me, if he starts to bleed again. Keep all that moss and leaves off him until he is better." The body will heal itself, she told them. She gave him one last glance as she left the tepee. He turned his head away from her as though to dismiss her.

She washed her body and removed the blood-stained dress and soaked it in water. As she fell onto the pile of furs, she thought, this day has been a very long nightmare. She had lost her companions, watched men fight over her and, then tried to save the big muscled man they called Warbo. It was simply too much and she fell into a much-needed reprieve.

The other women were still sleeping when Janie awoke. She knew she was being watched but she found a tree and squatted behind it. She washed her face in the cold water of the river and made her way back to her lodge. She brought out a dress and put it on and decided she needed to check on her patient. Not that she wanted to see him, she just wanted to make sure that the women were following her orders and to see how his wound was healing. As she got to the opening of the lodge, she could hear LittleDove and Prairie Breeze talking. She opened the flap and peaked in. Both were sitting at a close distance from the bed.

"May I come in?" she asked.

Little Dove nodded and Janie came to his bed. His face was red and she knew he must have a fever. She crouched down and laid her hand on his forehead. It was burning up. "Oh God, we need to cool him off." She started pulling the many covers away and leaving him bare except for the loincloth. It was bloody as well and she instructed Little Dove to clean him and replace it with a clean one. She reached into the doctor's bag and pulled out the thermometer and pushed it between his slips.

"What is that for?" Little Dove asked.

"It will tell me if his fever is too high. It won't hurt him, I promise."

Not completely trusting her, they both moved closer to make sure that Warbo was alright. Finally, she pulled the instrument from his mouth and studied it. "Wow, he has a fever and it is very high. We must remove some of these covers."

Little Dove protested, "He will catch a cold if you take his covers away."

Janie answered, "He will catch more than a cold if you keep all those blankets on him. What we need right now is cold water. They both looked at her like she was going crazy.

"Cold water?" replied Little Dove.

"Yes, I need something to carry it in?

"Use pouch to carry water said Prairie Breeze, I will help you." She got up and together they carried the pouch to the river and filled it up. Janie was surprised how heavy it was and how much it held.

When they returned to the lodge, Little Dove handed her a large bowl and Janie poured the water in it. She soaked the towels in cold water and laid them on his chest. He did not move and this was of concern to the young nurse. Taking a cloth she wiped his forehead and shoulders and all of his body. She felt a little squeamish when she lifted the remaining blankets off him. Only the small loincloth covered him and she started washing his legs, feet, and up to his privates.

His mother watched her and smiled at her when she hesitated to go further. "We need to turn him on his side, so I can wash his back". Both women knelt on his side and gently pulled him to his side. Janie took the wet cloth and washed his back and down his behind to his legs. He was hot and feverish to the touch.

"We will keep him covered in cool wet towels and if that doesn't work, we will take him to the river and cool him off".

Janie sat down beside him and continued to drop water onto the towels, to keep them wet. After several hours, she took his temperature again and still the fever raged on. She remembered how Dr. Crowder had placed children in the bathtub and held them there until their fever broke.

"You two go and find two strong warriors to help us carry Warbo to the river. I want him on a travois or something for him to lie on. I don't want his stitches to come loose. Prairie Breeze scurried off and came back with Broken Arrow and another brave called no name. Janie thought that was odd, but put it to the back of her mind. She was concentrating on getting Warbo well. I must get rid of the fever. Tell them I want them to carry their chief to the river, but do not want to break his stitches.

Brave Arrow told Little Dove to bring strong blanket and they would place him on it and carry him to the water. They all went into the tepee and laid the blanket beside their chief. Very carefully they lifted him to the blanket. He groaned but did not open his eyes. Janie said, "Follow me to the river."

The two braves did as they were told, but when they got to the river, they stopped and spoke to Little Dove. "Is Wild One going to drown our chief?" They all looked to Janie and she waded out into the shallow part of the river. She used her foot to make sure no rocks or jagged sticks were sticking out. "Bring him to me but do not drop him"

They waded out and held on carefully to Warbo.

"Just lower him into the water gently but do not get his face in the water. I only want to cool his body." Slowly she steadied him as his body sank into the water. Brave Arrow kept his head up and Janie poured water over his entire body. She could tell the braves were getting tired of holding him, so she ran her hand over his body and was relieved that it was indeed getting cold.

"We can take him back now, she told the braves. Slowly now, Warbos' hand fell off the blanket and she picked it up and held it while they carried him back to the lodge. Little Dove cleaned the bedding and straighten the pillows and they carefully lowered him onto the bed, taking the wet blanket off as they did.

She took his temperature again and was relieved that his fever was not gone, but it had come down to a safe level. She touched his forehead and was wiping his face when he opened his eyes. She didn't move and he looked at her and started shaking. She jumped back and said, "I'm sorry, Warbo, I was just checking to see if your fever had gone down."

He looked down at his body and could see the bandages on his chest and he started to get up. "Don't move, Warbo", Janie said.

"You were badly injured and I don't want the stitches to break loose. I will leave if you will promise to just lay still for a few more days."

"Go", was all he said.

Janie looked at his mother and wife and said, "Keep him quiet. Not a lot of blankets keep him cool. Any changes and you come and get me, okay?"

Little Dove nodded and went to sit by her husband. "Why did you allow her to come in here?" he asked. She answered, "You would have died. She sewed up your insides and stopped the bleeding. She Is good medicine for you."

CHAPTER FIVE

Janie was amazed to find the front of Warbo's lodge covered in wildflowers, gifts of food and, presents of value. The medicine man was continually walking up and down in front of the lodge. He wore the sacred robe of the buffalo. On his head was a large hat with the horns of the buffalo sticking from the top. His face was always covered in paint, and he would stop and start chanting. His fierce face would scare any evil spirits away that might enter the lodge.

He carried a small bundle of bones and skin. Great medicine of the tribe. He rattled the bones so long and loud, Janie thought her bones were rattling. When she entered the lodge, Warbo was standing up and when he saw her he said, "Go, Warbo is well. I do not need you anymore."

"I need to check your stitches, she said, as she walked up to him."

He turned away from her and said, "I do not need you, I am well. I ride today to burial grounds."

"You must not ride until the wound is healed. It might break open and you will surely die".

He replied, "You walk, I ride. We must bury the warriors that you and I killed. I must go," he stated. He moved slowly to the door and pushed her out of the lodge. His horse was brought to him and he led the animal to a large rock and slowly climbed on.

Janie just shook her head, giving him a frown," suit yourself oh mighty chief."

The bodies of the fallen Indians were wrapped in their best robes and blankets and were carried by horseback to the burial grounds of the Pawnee. The relatives of the fallen warriors, as well as those of Dark Eagle, followed in mournful procession across the prairie.

Janie was forced to witness the ceremony and walk with the procession. They must have walked several miles into the hills where the burial grounds were located. The bodies were placed on wooden platforms high off the ground, to prevent animals from disturbing their grave.

Warbo passed Janie on the way back to camp and the hatred was evident in his face. His eyes stared cold and filled with vengeance. No one could see the pain; this woman had brought to him. She will pay, he thought to himself.

Janie was amazed at the strength of Warbo, Little Dove and, Running Deer. They had gone to represent the lodge of the Chief. They showed no sign of fatigue and Janie could tell they enjoyed the state of exhaustion that she was in.

On the third day of her capture, Little Dove brought a dress of brown, softened deerskin and, handed it to her and, told her to put it on. Long fringe decorated the hem; the neckline was covered with colored beadwork. It was not ugly but the thought of wearing Indian clothes brought out the fury in her.

"And I suppose that I am to wear this? She asked.

"It is the dress of our people. You will wear it tonight when Warbo takes you for his wife."

"Tonight!" She recalled the words he had spoken to her just two nights ago. "When the sun rises three times, you will wish Dark Eagle had won."

She shuddered. "He certainly doesn't waste time, does he? I mean, the least he could do is court me awhile." She smiled as she said it and Little Dove looked puzzled. She assumed that the Wild One was mocking their customs, as she always did. As she picked up the dress, she could smell a faint odor of the cooking fat; they used to soften the leather. "I won't wear it, I just won't". She picked up the dress and band and stormed out of the tepee. She headed straight for Warbo's lodge and throwing the flap aside, she stepped in. He was sitting on one of the willow rod backrests, his feet tucked under him. "I am not a squaw and I'll not look like one. Do you understand, Big Man?"

A very much surprised Indian looked back at her, for never had anyone dared enter the tepee of the chief without asking permission. He just sat looking at her, the brown eyes blazing, her small white fists clenched at her side.

When he finally realized what was happening, that this pale-faced white woman was once again defying him, he came to his senses. He picked up the dress and threw it back at her. "You wear." His voice was commanding and Janie knew he meant what he said but still, she fought to outdo him.

She let the dress fall to the ground, not bothering to catch it. "Can't you stand to look at me in my clothes?" Do I have to look like a squaw before you make me marry you?" her voice was loud and clear.

He was calmer now. He didn't want their voices to carry to the curious women waiting around to see what the Wild One would do next. "Great honor to be wife of chief. When the sun sets and rises again, you will wear the mark of Warbo, dress like Pawnees, and show much respect for your husband."

"Mark, what mark? I suppose you're going to use your watercolors and tattoo me." The thought amused her and the smile played on her lips and her eyes spitfire. Warbo went to the back wall of the lodge. He took a short stick from the wall and held it up.

It was short, and at the end was the carving of a snake. It was smooth and the snake was only about two inches long.

"I must say it's fitting. A snake for a snake. And just how do you put this on me?" He was slow to reply, watching for her reaction when he told her. "I burn it on."

Janie's face suddenly turned pale as she looked at the stick which grew larger before her eyes. From the look on Warbo's face, she knew he meant what he said.

Her temper cooled considerably and now all she could think of, was why? She looked at Warbo "Why, why must you do this to me?"

"You wear the mark of Warbo, so you not want to return to your people."

The shock of being branded overcame Janie and she pictured Warbo standing over her as a cowboy brands a calf. "I suppose you'll put the brand on my hip like you brand the rest of your animals."

His face grew darker as he knew what she had been thinking. "You will wear the mark on your face, where all can see." He could tell she was terrified and he wished she would leave.

"My face, my face, she exclaimed, horrified. The hatred for this man raged in Janie and she felt the fury of desperate need. "You rotten, primitive savage. You pig!" She started to kick at him to take some of the spite out on him, but he quickly sidestepped and caught her in his arms.

"You're a coward, Warbo."

The nearness of her body bothered him but he didn't let go. You watch me kill Dark Eagle, and you say I am coward?"

"Are you not man enough to keep me here without scaring my face? Must you make me look hideous and ugly before you can stand to sleep with me?"

"Warbo not want to sleep with white woman." Their faces were close now and their lips nearly touched as they shouted at each other. His body contradicted him as he pulled her even tighter.

Her heart was racing and she looked deep into his eyes and said, "If you scar my face, I will kill myself. Then who will lose face? You are right about one thing, I would not want to return to my people and that is the only thing that is keeping me alive now.

"We will see, Wild One. Now go." He let her down and pushed her toward the door. As Janie started to go she deliberately went out of her way to step on the deerskin dress and band that still lay crumpled in the middle of the tepee.

Warbo stood staring at the dress and the open flap of his lodge. Once again he felt the sting of defeat. He wanted to be alone, he needed to think. The high, shrill voices of the children at play reached his ears and suddenly he knew he must get away. He left the camp and struggling to get on his pony, he took off for the mountains.

There in the mountain seclusion, with the tall pines towering above him and the sound of the waterfall close by, he sat and recalled the words of the angry young captive.

"If you scar my cheeks, I will kill myself." He wondered at the words but there was a gnawing fear in his stomach that told him his fears might be justified. Why should one small woman turn his world upside down?. Maybe it was the fact that from the first time that he laid eyes on her, the scene flashing back to him, he wanted her and for the first time, he admitted it to himself. What would it be like to make love to a woman like Janie?

He recalled other captives that had come into the hands of his people. He remembered seeing grown men beg for mercy. Of these, he recalled no one to match the fight of this hot-tempered woman. Other women had submitted to the ways of the Pawnee and in time were traded to friendly tribes for horses.

He thought of the effect it would have on his tribe if she did kill herself. The laughter and ridicule of the young braves already seemed to whistle through the trees around him. He knew that his honor was on trial if this young woman outwitted him. My first mistake, he thought, was letting her push him into a fight with a fellow tribesman. He cursed himself for fighting for such an evil woman.

After tonight she would be his wife in every sense of the word, bear him a son, and prove his manhood. He had failed with Little Dove; will I fail with the Wild One? He wondered. For the first time in his life, Warbo was unsure of himself.

For some reason, he didn't relish the thought of scaring that lovely face and yet he told himself that he hated this woman. He contemplated putting his knife through her heart and ending his problems now. He still hadn't reached a decision that night as he stood with the snake-like mark in his hand waiting for Janie to be prepared.

Even before she entered the circle he could feel her presence and the feeling of uncertainty came over him. She walked tall and proud as he knew she would, the fear well hidden. She wore a dark green dress, cut low and revealing. It hugged her tiny waist and the curves of her hips swayed as he walked. Her fiery red hair was piled high on her head.

He had never seen a woman's dress that showed the curves of her body and his senses came alive. He couldn't take his eyes from her. A blanket was stretched on the ground with four crude wooden stakes to hold it in place. Warbo motioned for her to lie down.

"I'll stand. I don't have to be roped and tied like an animal." She did not tremble and she thought, there comes a time when calmness replaces fear.

Warbo didn't argue but kept his eyes from meeting hers. He thrust the stick into the fire and then the drums took up a low roll. The young braves danced and howled like animals. Their screams pierced the stillness of the night. To Janie, the sounds were weird and horrifying. Even the trees echoed the barbaric noises. Head rose behind head and gleaming eyes were seen peering through the darkness to watch as Warbo claimed his bride.

As Janie watched their fierce earnest faces, their forms wrapped in shaggy robes, she could tell they relished this fiendish revelry. Warbo took the stick from the fire. As it cooled, it glows red in the darkness. The dancing stopped and all was quiet. Janie felt her blood run faster and surge through her veins until she thought her heart would burst. He spoke to Twisted Hair and Brave Arrow to hold her. She braced herself as he approached. Their hands were hot on her arms and she cringed beneath their touch. As Twisted Hair held her close to his sweaty body she could smell the rank odor of his flesh.

As Warbo came close, she made the first attempt to stop him. Her voice was low and pleading. "Warbo, look at me. If you want me to bear you a son, then don't do this to me. Not my face, anywhere but not my face."

Warbo hesitated only a moment and his eyes quickly covered her body as they always did each time he was near her. Then he stepped closer and taking the stick tightly in his hand he pressed it to her pale white flesh.

The braves let go and stood back waiting for her to fight. She swayed for a moment trying to regain her senses after the biting sting of fire. Her hands flew to her face. They were smooth and untouched. Then the slow sting took her eyes to her chest. She could see the mutilated flesh and the bubbles already forming.

"My God, My God, my chest" she screamed. The smell of the seared flesh came to her and she dropped to the blanket, the blackness settling over her.

CHAPTER SIX

When Janie sank to the ground, the curious onlookers stood watching and some grinned to see the fight drain from the Wild One. The reluctant bridegroom stood back waiting for her to move. She didn't and he finally gathered his courage and lifted her gently in his arms and carried her down the long row of tepees. Little Dove followed and fixed a pallet for her.

She pulled the dress away from the burn and from Janie's shoulders and exposed the burn. He watched her white breasts rise quickly and looked at the damage he had done to her lovely white skin. He quickly averted his eyes and left the tepee.

"Make the Wild One well," it was more of a command than a statement.

Little Dove knew she must keep the Wild One alive for Warbo's sake. Not for fear of losing face, but she had noticed the change in her husband since the white woman had come to live with the Pawnees. As she applied a wet rag to Janie's forehead and left to gather wet leaves and moss to make a compress for the wound. Janie could hardly move for several days and she moaned and tossed when she slept. Running Deer did nothing to help and chided her for bothering with the white slave. Morning Star helped with her care and she remembered that she had not been this tough when she was taken. Warbo came every day to see how she was healing and Janie knew the hatred he had in his body would soon slip away. When Little Dove told him that the Wild One would soon be healed and her body had finally accepted the burn. He stooped to the pallet of furs and his hand hovered above her forehead for a moment and then he touched her brow, Janie stirred and opened her eyes.

She looked at him for a minute and the memory of the wedding ceremony came slowly and vividly to her mind. She pushed his hand away and tried to rise from the pillow. The stabbing pain in her chest sent her moaning to the pallet. The sight of him renewed her anger and she forced herself up on one elbow. "What are you doing here? First, you burn your women and then sit and watch them suffer."

She winced as she stared down at the contours of her bosom. The burn stood clear and vivid where a large crust had formed. There were no puss bubbles as she had seen on so many burns during her time as a nurse. She laid back, still and quiet.

"You be very grateful to Little Dove. She has taken care of you for many moons. You owe her your life," he said as he stood looming over her.

"My life! ha! What good is my life? I'd rather be dead than live the rest of my life in your miserable lodge. I may be your slave, but I will never be your woman. Now get out of my sight." She turned her face away and said no more.

"Wild One is full of evil spirits, maybe it better you die?." he said angrily as he stormed out of the lodge.

Little Dove applied the compress once more and Janie did not stop her, as the compress relieved her pain. Janie wondered why this woman would nurse her so faithfully. Was it her duty or did Little Dove like her and wanted to help. She didn't want to admit the latter, so she convinced herself it was duty and her love of Warbo.

After recovering from her dreadful wedding, she decided she needed to talk to Warbo's Mother, Morning Star. She wondered why she had stayed and if she loved her husband. She found the Lodge where Morning Star lived with her dead husbands' relatives. She asked permission to enter and said, "I came to thank you for coming and making your son let me help."

"Come in. You are welcome in our lodge." She motioned for Janie to sit down on one of the short chairs. "Thank you for saving my son. You are a very good nurse."

Janie studied the woman and found it hard to believe that she had ever really been white. She wore the clothes of the Pawnee and her hair was almost silver and only a few strands of brown remained. Her eyes were blue and her features were soft. The years had tanned her skin and she was nearly as brown as the Pawnees. Still, something in her voice and manner made Janie relax and some of the tension in her subsided.

"My sons' wife is welcome." She said.

"At least my Mother–in–law is white," she said bitterly.

Morning Star threaded the many-colored beads one by one onto a small pillow. She smiled at Janie as if to reassure her that everything would be alright.

"Didn't you ever try to escape? I mean, you didn't want to stay, did you?

"When I came to live with the Pawnees, I had a young girl child. I had to think of her and escape was impossible with a small baby."

"But they killed your family. How could you stay? It seemed incredible to Janie. Here sat a white woman talking as though her people never existed.

"My family was on a small wagon train when we were attacked by the Indians. I ran to the trees and hid in the bushes. When they were gone, I returned to the train and everyone was dead, the wagons burned and no food was left. I wandered around for several days and then the Pawnees found me. They were good to me and I learned later that it was the Delaware tribe that had attacked the wagon.

"Then you have no family among the white people?" she asked.

"No, soon after I became the wife of Tall Oak. A big man and was good to my little girl, who was frail and sickly. She died that winter and soon after, I was with child. I had a son and we named him Warbo. He became my life and I could not leave him even if I could escape. I knew it would be impossible to raise him in the white man's world, so I stayed."

"But I do not love your son. Will you tell him to let me go? Will you help me?"

"Warbo is a fine man. He is not mean like Dark Eagle was. You are a lucky woman. In time you will care for my son."

Janie knew she would get no help with Morning Star and the only thing she had left of the white race was her blue eyes and soft features.

Janie soon learned that she was expected to do her share in providing food for the lodges of Warbo. Women were rated highly for their skills in domestic arts. They raised corn, beans, pumpkins, squashes, melons, and tobacco. The corn and broccoli were ground in huge wooden bowls and preserved for winter. She was surprised when she found some asparagus growing along the creek bank. She worked with Little Dove, for companionship, but more than that, she was gaining their trust and confidence. Running Deer took the advantage of the white slave doing her work; she got lazier by the day.

They roamed the woods, picking berries and dried these in the sun. More days were spent wading in the river to the smaller islands in search of wood for the fires. Her dresses were getting thinner by the day. She soon cut them to below her knees. It won't be long before I am going to have to submit to wearing the dress of the Pawnees.

She lived in fear that each night she would be summoned to the tepee of her husband. She knew he hated her as much as she hated him but he was expected to provide his tribe with a son. Warbo avoided her and deliberately went out of his way not to encounter her. Her curiosity could stand it no longer and she finally confronted Little Dove.

"If I am to be the wife of Warbo, why has he not made me visit his lodge?"

Little Dove's face reddened and she realized Janie didn't know the shame she was bearing. "You are being punished for your failure to recognize your husband. Warbo waits for Wild One to visit his tepee and ask for permission to be his wife."

"Waits for me, to ask him?" Janie chuckled and then the laughter rang out loud and clear and filled the quiet evening. The longer she thought about it the harder she laughed. "I hope he doesn't hold his breath waiting for me," she said between chuckles. She pictured him now sitting there in his tepee hoping she would come and confident that she couldn't stand the ridicule of the camp any longer. He says he hates me. Ha!" The laughter subsided and now the fury boiled in her. "Are you telling me the truth?"

"Warbo has shamed you in front of his people. It is disgrace to be treated as he is treating you. My people wait for you to make peace with their leader."

Janie knew she was sincere and inwardly she fumed. Imagine that big savage waiting for me, Janie West, to come and sleep with him. I'll die first, she vowed. To be denied the pleasure of his company, pleased Janie, and she hoped his patience would not wear thin.

Throughout the coming weeks, it was Janie's turn to sidestep her husband. Whenever they met he would avoid looking at her, but she could feel his piercing eyes on her each time her back was turned. He wants me, she thought. This worried her but her stubborn pride stopped her from submitting to his hungry embrace.

This continued for several weeks and Janie wondered when his patience would end. A scouting party made ready to leave in search of the winter supply of buffalo. As the braves brought their horses, the women came to bid them farewell and pray to the Great Spirit for a successful hunt. Little Dove noticed Janie was missing and she hurried to the river to tell Janie to come and join the others. "The men make ready to leave, Wild One."

"Good, tell them to take their time!." she replied.

Little Dove hesitated but she knew how important it would be to her husband to have her there. It would make him proud in front of his people. "It is custom for wives to be present when their men leave. Warbo will be very angry when he returns."

Janie was reading the worn bible she had carried for many years. She read it often as she sat by the river beneath the tall cottonwoods. This was her only communication with the world she once knew. She paused and looked at the anxious face of Little

Dove. Right now she could care less if Warbo was angry or not. Sometimes she relished their angry exchanges."Tell him I'm busy."

Little Dove turned slowly and retreated to camp. She could see her husband's eyes scanning the crowd. He didn't have to ask Little Dove, the question was there on his face. "The Wild One is busy," she told him with eyes downcast."

"When I return, I will drive the evil spirits from the white devil," he said, with clenched lips. He rode out at a furious pace and vowed he would break her stubborn will.

During Warbo's absence, Janie noticed the young warrior; Brave Arrow came to the Lodge frequently. He would pause outside and call to Little Dove and when she was outside, he was at her side immediately. It took little imagination to deduct that he was in love with Warbo's wife.

When the men were sighted returning to camp, Janie made it a point to take a long walk in the woods. It was partly from fear of seeing her husband. For some reason, she couldn't explain she had enjoyed the earlier fights with him. Except for the scaring, she usually managed to outwit him. She was not so sure today, had she pushed him too far? She pictured her husband riding into camp expecting her to be there to welcome him. She could see his grim face and the hatred in his eyes. The only time they softened was when he looked at her and then it was only for a moment. For a minute she felt sorry for the proud man. I wonder if he ever smiles, she thought. The other braves smiled and told funny stories around the campfires. Warbo did not participate in these events but walked away from the camp and Janie wondered where he went.

Perhaps when they spoke of their sons and daughters, he felt the shame of his people. Little Dove blamed herself for not bearing a son for her husband. Since the Wild One was here, he seldom called her to his tepee. Janie wondered about this too. Was he a man with no feelings? Didn't he need to share his lodge with someone?

The day was warm and as she came to her favorite bathing pool, she felt the need for a bath. She felt hot and sticky as she dropped her dress and shoes beside a small cluster of bushes. A movement in the trees stopped her from undressing further. She felt her body stiffen as Warbo stepped from the clearing. She sensed he was looking for her and she moved closer to the bush.

"Go away; I'm going to take a bath." Her hands trembled as she waited for his response.

"Warbo wants to speak to wife, take bath later." He stood in the clearing, his hands folded across his chest, waiting for her to appear.

"I am not dressed, you will have to wait," she said stubbornly.

Warbo's eyebrows raised, his mouth twisted into a cruel grin. This time he would not take any of her sass. He stepped behind the bush and grabbed her to him. "When Warbo says he want to talk, you come." He was breathing hard and if Janie wanted him mad, she had succeeded. "You want bath, I give you bath." He gathered her in his arms and carried her to the deepest part of the river and dropped her, holding her head under for a moment and then retreated to the bank. He smiled as she came up sputtering furiously.

"I just wanted a bath. It wouldn't hurt you to take one now and then." She sputtered at him as she wiped the hair from her face. She lost her balance and went under again. The water chilled her to the bone. When at last she regained her footing and stood there getting her breath and glaring at the angry man on the bank. Then an idea popped into her head and she thought, let's sees if he wants me to drown. She put her hand to her head and swayed dizzily in the water. Then a faint yell and she went under. This time her body didn't move and she let her arms rise lifelessly to the top. She slowly let the air escape from her mouth so the bubbles would rise to the surface.

He stood watching and his heart skipped a beat and his body muscles tightened. He was out of his shirt and into the water. His long arms cut through the water and he was beside her in seconds. He pulled her limp body against his bare chest and hugged her tight. When Janie came to her senses, she realized her ploy had backfired. Now it was her heart's turn to pound. For a brief moment, she clung to him and let the feelings rise. Then she made a quick lunge to him and they both went under. He broke away and swam to the shore. She was afraid to look at him as she followed him out of the water. To her surprise, he grinned and laughed as his eyes took in her figure, with her wet garments clinging to her. She tried to cover herself as she crossed her arms in front of her.

"You are so beautiful, Wild One". He placed his hands on her shoulders as if he were trying to steady himself. Then in halting English he said, "When the sun rises again you will have the evil spirits driven from your body, you will come to me and disgrace me no more."

CHAPTER SEVEN

The camp bustled with activity the next morning. Janie watched as the young braves took twelve willow shoots and set them upright in the ground to form a circle about seven feet across. The door of the lodge faced east. The shoots were bent and secured by bark stripped from the willows. In the center, a pit about fifteen inches in diameter and twelve inches deep was dug.

Janie felt a desperate urge to run and her mind imagined what was to come. She asked Little Dove what was going to happen and she tried not to show the fear that wanted to boil out of her.

The braves were spreading dirt outside the door and placed a painted buffalo skull upon the mound of dirt. Little Dove said, "This is the good road. They prepare for one of the oldest religious ceremonies. This is a Sweatlodge. It is very important part of our religion.

"What does it do for me?" she asked.

"It will drive the evil spirits from your body and then you will be able to accept the Pawnees as your people."

Janie's mind played cruel tricks on her for she had learned not to underestimate the crude rituals of the tribe. She watched as the floor of the lodge was covered with sweet sage. "The lodge must be completely dark inside, so the braves must cover the framework with hides." Little Dove said.

As the braves built a big fire about eight or ten feet from the mound outside, Janie could feel her heart race in quick sickening leaps. Stones were gathered from the hills and placed in the fire until they became white.

Warbo came to the lodge now and behind him were four

braves. All were naked except for the breechcloth. Brave Arrow and another young brave called Broken Lance stood outside the lodge waiting for the signal from their leader. The medicine man called Buffalo Horn, the fourth member of the group.

Warbo looked at Janie, her hair pulled up on her head and, still wearing one of her long dresses. "You wish to remove some of your clothing?"

"I certainly do not," she answered.

"It is as you wish. The sweat lodge will become very hot."

Janie thought for a moment but decided it couldn't be that hot and she certainly wasn't going to strip for these curious savages. Sensing her mind was made up, Warbo entered the lodge on his hands and knees. They motioned for her to follow. The three braves soon followed her into the lodge. Janie was relieved to know they would all go through this together. Anything Warbo can take, I can too, and she told herself. She was seated next to him and the ceremony began.

He took a pinch of Indian tobacco or kinnikinnik and offered it to the sky, the earth and, four quarters, starting to the west. He then put tobacco in the pit. The hot stones from the fire were passed in by one of the braves outside. Buffalo Horn laid sweet grass on the hot coals. The lodge was permeated with a sweet odor.

Warbo then purified himself in the sacred smoke, rubbing it over his arms and body. He then purified his pipe in the smoke. Taking a dipper of water he sprinkled a few drops on the hot coals to clear the air of any smoke resulting from the tobacco or incense. Her eyes already watered from the smoke and she could feel the heat mounting in the small hut. It wasn't high enough to stand in, making it even hotter in the cramped quarters.

Buffalo Horn put water in his mouth and squirted it on the stones. He passed a bowl of water to Brave Arrow. He wet his hair and face and took a drink. Each in turn wet their hair and face and took a drink. The water was a little greasy by the time it reached Janie. Warbo's eyes watched her intently and at this point, Janie was too afraid not to follow suit. She dabbed a little of the water on her face and some on her hair. She refused the drink and passed the water to her husband.

The door was then closed from the outside. Only the glow of the hot stones relieved the darkness. They all sat quietly for a moment and then a loud shot rang out causing Janie to jump. It was only Buffalo Horn adding more water to the stones. The lodge filled with hissing stifling steam. The heat became unbearable, and they all bent forward as far as possible until their heads almost touched their knees. Janie buried her head in her skirt trying to escape the suffocating steam. Then Warbo yelled, "Hi-us, Pilamaya!" which he told her meant thank you for how good the Great Spirit was making them feel.

Janie sat silently refusing to comment on how good she felt. This was no time to arouse his anger and knew they were all taking this very seriously. Four times the water was poured on the stones. The red glow disappeared but the heat became more intense. The sweat formed on every part of their bodies. Janie's dress clung to her and she felt like she was being cooked alive and sincerely wished she had taken Warbo's advice about wearing fewer clothes.

The sweat poured from her forehead and the taste of salt formed on her lips. The noise of the steam, the heat, lack of air and, the bitter taste of sage in her mouth along with the lack of air and the sting of sweat in her eyes in the pitch blackness was frightening. Her urge to escape was almost uncontrollable. The darkness boiled against her eyes and she could barely distinguish their shapes. She prayed it would soon be over. Just when she thought she would collapse the door opened and fresh air came tumbling in. She was glad it was over but then she realized it was only a brief reprieve. More water was passed in and the door shut again. Four more dippers of water were poured on the stones at brief intervals so that the heat increased faster than before. The smell of sweat was rank.

Brave Arrow prayed to the Great Spirit for courage in battle. Buffalo Horn prayed for strong medicine. Warbo prayed for the white evil spirits would be driven from the Wild One. Janie smiled in the darkness. It'll take more than a hot bath, she vowed.

"Lay close to the ground and put your nose near the edge and lift the cover a crack." He told her. She wanted to, she had never wanted anything so badly but she was determined to outlast him. She wished now she had drunk the water even though the others had used the same cup. She found herself unbuttoning her dress in the darkness and slipping it from her shoulders. The white camisole and slip were wet with perspiration. She wiped her forehead with the hem of her dress.

At this moment she would gladly undress in front of any of these savages to cool her tortured body. She couldn't believe the stones could still produce such intense heat after all the water being poured on them. She found it getting harder to breathe and her breath came in short gasps.

Each time the door opened Janie thought it was over, but another dipper was passed in and the ceremony continued. The darkness slapped her in the face and Janie felt her body began to shake. Slowly each bone joined the rhythm and until one by one, bone by bone she shook violently. When the door opened the fresh air steadied her for a moment and then this went on for four sessions. On the third time, seven dippers of water were poured gently on the stones. The stones got colder but the heat of the lodge seemed as intense as before. In the fourth session, Warbo chanted. As Janie watched the half-naked Indian, her first impulse was to laugh but the longer he chanted the more intense were his prayers. She could not recall anyone more earnest or more sincere in his meditation than this savage.

Finally, the soap was passed around and everyone cleaned their bodies. By the time the soap reached Janie, she felt physically and mentally cooked. She could see no sense in washing after sweating like that so she only made a pretense of rubbing the smoke from her face and arms.

When at last the group left the sweat lodge, Janie crawled out barely able to stand. The sky vibrated and spun above her. She had forgotten her dress hung open to her waist until she felt the eyes of Warbo upon her. The sweat ran down her neck and the ringlets of perspiration stood out on her bosom. She quickly pulled the dress around her.

"The Wild One has found favor with the Great Spirit. You are now true Pawnee. The white evil spirits no longer live in your body." Warbo said proudly.

"I think you just finished cooking them all," she said feebly.

He ignored the remark and Janie could see he was proud of her. Why she didn't know. The tribe gathered around the sweat lodge anxiously waiting to see the tolerance of the young white captive. They were surprised she could emerge from the lodge on her own power. Warbo left the circle and for the second time today, she saw him smile.

She dragged herself down the long path to the tepee and then to the creek and collapsed in the tall grass by the cool water. The cool air gradually relieved the feeling of suffocation. She bathed with a cloth, taking care to not chill. She dried herself quickly and for the remainder of the day, she rested in the silence of the aspens. She felt as though she had worked until every ounce of strength in her body had been drained from her.

As she lay in the grass she could hear the water washing gently over the stones as it made its way downstream. The call of the meadowlarks lulled her to sleep. It was not a deep sleep and her mind wandered over the occurrences of the day. Warbos' word came to her now, "You have found favor with the Great Spirit." For some reason, it didn't amuse her and she realized how sincere these people were.

She recalled the smile on Warbos' face as he left the circle. It was a good smile and Janie contemplated how different he looked when he smiled. Gone were the cruel lines in his face and her conscience told her she could be the cause of that. He should smile more often and for some reason, this bothered her and she pushed the memory from her mind.

The sun turned the horizon to a rainbow of orange, purple, and hints of gold and red. It was a peaceful scene with the squaws fixing supper and the young braves sitting around the campfires. Little

Dove brought her a plate and waited on her like a queen. Janie ate and then retired to her pallet of furs.

As she lay there listening to the sounds of the camp, she was conscious of the eyes upon her. When she could stand it no longer she raised herself on her elbow and surveyed the women staring at her.

Running Deer and Little Dove sat at the back of the tepee as though waiting for something to happen. She stared back and then the uneasy silence told her something was not quite right. She could stand the silence no longer.

"Do I look so different? I realize I've been purified and all the meanness cooked out of me, but why are you all staring at me? Why are you not going to bed?"

A frown knotted on Little Dove's brow and the smile was gone. She put some wood on the fire and slipped beneath the blankets. When at last she finally spoke, Janie could not believe her ears.

"The lodge of the great Chief will be happy tonight. We are so happy for you. Go, he waits for you."

A giggle escaped the lips of Running Deer and Janie felt like slapping the fat squaw lying there in her dirty robes. Janie dropped to the pallet and pulled the robes about her. The anger surged through her body. That stupid Indian, that dumb, stupid Indian! Just because he made me sweat like a roast pig, he thinks I'm going to come running to his tepee. I wonder just how many other curious squaws and bucks are peeking from their tepees to watch the big match. I'll be dammed before I'll go willingly to that redskin. Sleep didn't come easy and as she lay there, thinking of her husband, guilt came over her. She had come to realize how much Warbos' pride meant to him. She knew he wouldn't rest until he had taken her and enjoyed the pleasure of his desires. She gritted her teeth and the guilt was gone to be replaced by sheer terror. She knew his anger would be insane if she defied him again. My god, what will he do to me this time? Her hand rubbed the scar and she contemplated what it would be like to give in. She remembered how it felt when he pulled her to his chest in the water. It would probably be less painful than what she would have to go through if she rebelled again. The answer never came as she drifted into a restless sleep. The decision was not left up to her because one mad Indian shattered her dreams. Warbo pulled her from the pallet and his anger in his eyes was enough to send the devil himself running.

"Today you will pay for the dishonor you bring to your husband."

Half asleep Janie stood up and asked, "I suppose you are angry because I didn't come sneaking to your lodge?"

He slapped her hard across the face and sent her to the pallet. "Get dressed. Warbo waits no longer."

CHAPTER EIGHT

Janie dressed quickly her hands shaking. She knew this was coming, but now that it had, she could feel the tension in her nerves, and her muscles felt weak as a child. She started to pull her hair from her face but the big Indian entered the tepee and dragged her out with him. She found herself running to keep up with his long strides. He had a handful of hair and she followed obediently.

They reached the center of the camp in short order and he flung her to the ground. Before she could regain her breath she felt the rawhide thongs being wrapped tightly around her wrists and ankles. He stretched her out where all could see. Water was poured on the thongs and he left her there.

Her hair hung in her eyes and Janie tossed her head to clear her vision. Already the people of the camp began to close in and watch the excitement that was always created by the Wild One. Janie lay there puzzled, wondering what was to come. Throughout the morning he would return and pour water on the rawhide. Each time the ropes grew tighter.

When she looked at him she could see nothing but the stern look in his blue-black eyes. His jaw was set in a hard line and he did not meet her gaze. Her vision blurred as the sun rose high in the sky, the sweat began to gather on her temples and spread to the rest of her body. Although she had a good tan already, she sensed she was in for a better one. Her back ached from lying in one position. This is another test of my endurance, she thought.

How much more could she take she didn't know. Her stubbornness made her bitter and the hatred for this man gave her renewed confidence in herself.

The squaws relished each moment that their captive was put to another test. They waited for her resistance to give.

They were proud that a strong woman was now one of them. They hated her for disgracing their chief but admired her for fighting for her way of life. Each time they came close, Janie would shout. "Take a good look, you rotten savages!" It annoyed her that they couldn't understand. Then one of the squaws came nearer and through her swollen eyelids she recognized the wife of the late Dark Eagle. The memory of the fight between them on that first day was vivid now and she was suddenly afraid of the big, mean squaw standing above her.

The squaw picked up a handful of dirt and let it sift slowly through her fingers and into the face of the Wild One. Janie spit and tossed her head. It caked her lips and filled her eyes.

"Just wait until I get up, I'll pull your stinking hair out." She stopped as another handful of sand rained down on her. A voice in Pawnee sent the squaw scurrying for her lodge and she heard Warbo's voice, and she was grateful for that.

Hunger mounted in her stomach and her thirst was tearing at her insides. She heard the splash of water on the rawhide and felt the cool liquid run down her arms. She spit again. Her eyes focused on the blurred image of his giant figure. "Water, please Warbo."

He gave her water. It poured onto her face in the same manner as the sand. It washed some of the dirt from her face, but when she opened her mouth, she could taste the mud and slimy water. Her head lay in a puddle of dirt and mud. She could feel the dirt matted in her hair.

"Does the Wild One wish to get up?"

She lay quietly knowing if she got up it would mean one thing. Submit to this man. "I would like to get up, but if I do, then I will have to sleep with you?"

Warbo dropped to his knees and bent over her and for the first time his voice was soft and she detected a different sound to it. "Would it be so bad Janie?"

"I'll die first," was all she said and turned her face from him.

He raised his fist to strike her but something stopped him and he stood and disappeared into the trees. He was gone and Janie was left to battle out the afternoon with the sun. She dozed for a time but as the rawhide grew tighter, her arms felt as though they were being torn from their sockets. The sun grew dimmer but she knew the day was not over. Her eyelids were swollen shut and she could no longer open them. Her arms burned and the skin showing on her legs looked like cooked meat. The sun blistered her face and her lips were thick and fat. Her tongue and throat grew dry and she longed to die. Then at last the unconsciousness settled over her and she felt no more pain.

Little Dove stood close by and her heart was heavy as she watched the helpless young girl lying in the dirt. She moved to help her but Warbo appeared and stopped her abruptly. Fear kept her in the darkness waiting for the end to come. She knew Warbo watched and his heart was sad. She understood why her husband had to do this but she prayed to the evening star to give the Wild One another chance. For a moment she wished that she would die. This woman had changed the lives of her family and taken what affection her husband had for her was gone. Her death would not make him forget. If they could only stop hating each other and realized that there is a fine line between love and hate.

At last, Warbo emerged from the shadows. He untied the thongs and held his hand to her brow and then to her breast for a brief moment. Little Dove was beside him and laid a cool cloth on her feverish brow. He did not stop her and he brushed the hair from her face.

Janie struggled to lift her eyelids. It was dark; the dim stars twinkled in the sky. She moaned as Warbo lifted her to her feet. From exhaustion, she dropped her head on his chest as he lifted her gently into his arms. He carried her to the lodge amidst the stares of his fellow tribesmen. The firelight fell on her face as he carefully laid her on the pallet.

"Take care of my woman," he said to Little Dove. He left the lodge and now it was his turn to lie awake searching for an answer. The hatred for this woman melted and he could feel only pride at her show of resistance and strength. The need for this woman mounted and he felt the desire to share his lodge and his life with this woman of fine spirit. He told himself she surely couldn't stand another day so he vowed he would try again.

The vision of her burned and aching body loomed before him and sadness filled his body. He could not understand why it bothered him to hurt this woman and he prayed to the Great Spirit to give him the answer. It a strange and different feeling and one he couldn't explain. It scared him to think that this tiny woman could have such power over him.

When Janie awoke she was so stiff and sore she could hardly move. The blisters on her arms and legs had begun to bubble. Every bone ached from the stretching. She ate because she was starved and something told her that the end was not in sight. She had no sooner dressed and smoothed some of the tangled mass from her hair when her captor stood in the lodge.

He was shocked at her condition. The burned face and parched lips stared at him. She looked as though someone had beaten her. He turned his eyes from the burns on her arms and legs. If Warbo had ever felt compassion for anyone or anything he felt it now. His eyes softened and his hatred melted. He stood staring at her and Janie could see the change in his eyes.

The kindness in his eyes bothered her more than the hatred she had seen there. How could he stand there looking at her like that after causing all of this hurt? She walked slowly to him. Her eyes blazing with defiance she pounded on his chest, "leave me be. I won't submit to you. Not now, not ever."

Her words gave him the courage he needed to continue his torture. "Warbo is proud of your bravery, but you will be my wife and share my bed. Warbo must not lose face again. Come, we will see how long you can last today." He led her from the tepee but this time he took her gently by the arm as though he were taking her for a delightful walk. When they reached the center of the camp, she started to lie down but he told her to stand. He bound her arms and ankles in the same manner but left her standing. Her feet were about a foot apart. Her wrists were secured to long willow rod stakes. She knew this would be worse and she stifled a cry as the thongs bit into the already bruised flesh.

He sat on a log stool in the shade and kept his eyes on her. She determined to stare him down. He didn't blink until she let her eyes wander slowly down his chest and then linger on his buck-skin breeches. She saw the slow flush creep into his face and his eyes quickly left hers. He walked to the post and caught her by the shoulders.

She winched in pain and he said, "Why you look at your husband that way?" His voice had a certain pleading to it.

"Does it bother you?"

He ripped the dress from her body and tossed it aside. The faded cotton camisole covered the bare skin. His anger was renewed and he took his knife from the holder and cut the rest of the dress to shreds and threw it aside. Then the pantaloons until she stood naked except for the drawers and long camisole reaching to her waist. The contours of her body stood out, her breasts heaved and she felt the sting of her pride as the young braves gathered around.

"Can't you let me die with dignity?" She pleaded. "I could never love you; Never!" She choked and the tears flowed from her eyes. Her throat filled with lumps of uncontrolled sobs.

The tears surprised Warbo and he too felt the humiliation she was enduring. He stood beneath a tall pine and prayed she would give up. His eyes only moved in her direction to see if she would fall.

Janie thought of Carl. "Oh, Carl, she moaned. "I tried. I tried so hard. I can't last much longer." She sobbed and her voice was low as she said. "God help me, please somebody help me." She pitched forward and Warbo moved quickly to the pole and stood her up.

"Give up, Janie, give up." His voice was soft again and he spoke so only she could hear.

Janie raised her tear-stained face and she could see the pity in his eyes and she heard the pleading in his voice. Even through her swollen eyelids, she knew he wasn't enjoying this any more than she. It renewed her spirits but she knew she could last no longer.

"Put a knife in my heart Warbo let it be over." She leaned against him to support her body.

Warbo realized he had gone too far in his punishment and he misjudged her. He knew now that she wouldn't give up. He cursed her silently for her stubbornness. As he held her for a moment he thought, the only time that she nearly gave in to him was when he cut the dress from her body. That's all she is fighting for, he thought. He steadied her and whispered in her ear. "I give you one more chance."

His words seemed far away and Janie didn't acknowledge his statement. He took his knife from his pouch and slit the strap of her camisole. Her head came up and her eyes were bright. Her voice was not loud or defying as it had been. Now he felt her shame as she spoke pleadingly. "Please Warbo; I beg you, let me die with dignity? Not like this. Please Warbo." Her eyes sought his.

His decision had come and he knew he must not give in. He slipped the knife under the other strap and looked closely at her. "I will strip your body naked and leave you to die. I ride from camp and not return until you are dead."

Janie suddenly became alert and she knew the decision was upon her now. Did she want to die? What was she fighting for; certainly not her virginity? She had lost that with Carl. Could anything be worse than the pain and torture she had endured the past two days? She felt the knife move against her skin. The braves and squaws gathered around. Janie knew she could not stand naked in front of them and die. She thought of Carl and realized that she wanted to live. "Stop, Warbo, you win. I'll be your woman." The tears ran down her cheek and he could hear the silent sobs.

His shoulders sagged, and relief filled his body as he pulled the knife from her. How he had longed for this moment to hear those words, you win. Now they seemed so small. He untied the thongs and she fell into his arms. Carefully he carried her down the long row of tepees. He didn't take his eyes from her face. He laid her gently on the pallet of furs. He closed the door of the lodge so no one could enter. He leaned over the young woman and his heart went out to her. "Wild One, I didn't want to do this to you. It is the only way I know. I make you promise now. Warbo will never hurt you again or let any harm come to you. Do you understand, Wild One?"

Janie looked up at him and his image was blurred. She didn't know whether there were tears in her eyes or his. The spirit was gone from her body. The fight had been burned out and his words meant nothing to her. She didn't acknowledge him and she felt nothing for him. At this moment she neither hated nor respected her husband. Her mind became blank and complete oblivion settled upon her.

CHAPTER NINE

The next day was one of pure hell for Janie. There wasn't a bone that didn't ache or a piece of skin that wasn't blistered. Little Dove nursed her wounds and she moved as little as possible. She contemplated what was to come that evening. Going to his lodge was a necessity that was for sure.

She cursed the piercing eyes upon her as she made her way in the darkness. Knowing there was no reprieve tonight, her heart pumped wildly as she pulled the shawl closer, as she approached his lodge. She wouldn't give him the satisfaction of asking permission and stepped into the entrance.

Warbo looked up, startled by the intrusion. He sat as he always did on the willow rod backrest, his feet crossed in front. Neither spoke; their eyes met, cold and cautious.

"I'm here, oh mighty chief of the Pawnees." Her voice still carried the insolence she felt.

"Why have you come? Why did you not ask permission?"

"I heard you needed a bed partner," she answered.

He felt the sting of her words and a slow flush entered his face. His eyes covered her body and then he spoke. "Let me see your burns."

She took the tattered shawl from her shoulders. Only her arms were visible.

"All of them," he said.

She raised her arms to reach the back buttons of her dress. Pain tore through her arms and she winced. He was beside her in seconds.

"I will help". She turned slowly and she felt his hands trembling as he undid the long row of buttons. Not being accustomed to the white man's clothes, he lingered over his chore. Janie thought he would never finish. As he worked he said," I did not want you for my wife. I do not want you now."

It angered Janie to hear him say he didn't want her and she whirled to face him. "You lie, Warbo, I can see the lust in your eyes, she said viciously.

"He said, "Then why did you make me fight for you?"

"Because you were the only one that spoke my language. I thought I could make you let me go, not because I wanted you."

He pulled her to him and held her tight, he looked into her eyes and said, "I will make you want me, Wild One!" He let go of her and moved away from her. "Go now and heal your wounds."

"When do I have to come back?"

"When the moon is full." He answered.

"Maybe the moon will fall out of the sky before then and I will be denied the pleasure of your touch", she smiled sweetly at him. "Now if you will button my gown, I will leave your rotten presence."

Warbo face reddened and he said" Great is our hatred." He pushed her towards the door and said," find someone else to button your dress."

She picked up her shawl and retreated. As she left the tepee, she heard him say, in a soft voice, "I'll be waiting for you, Wild One" and Janie was at a loss for a reply.

As she tried to get some sleep, but her mind was in a jumble. She tried to remember how long she had been captured. She knew they were attacked on July seventeen and calculated the days since. This meant that another month was approaching and she knew it was September. Warbo told her she had until the full moon. Winter was upon them and she visualized what it would be like in one of these tepees. I'll probably freeze to death before spring if he doesn't kill me first. If I could just escape before the full moon. Now that he had set a time limit, her brain worked feverishly trying to conceive a plan.

Finally, Janie decided she hadn't cooperated with these people in any way. Maybe this was a mistake and she decided to make them think that she had accepted the way of the Pawnee and earn their trust. I will learn their language so I can communicate with them.

The next morning Janie explained to Little Dove that she wanted to accept the dress of the people. "It is good; I show you what to do." She hurried off to the lodge of Warbo and Janie assumed she had gone to spread the good news. Warbo came from the tepee and she thought she detected a faint smile on his lips. He took several warriors and left the camp.

"Our husband has gone to kill a deer. Then we make dress." Her eyes were full of excitement. The term our husband hit Janie and she realized that she didn't like the idea that her husband had two wives. Oh, what do I care ? she thought. I will be gone soon. As they sat under the shade of a big cottonwood tree, grinding corn, Little Dove talked of the tribe, their customs, and of her childhood. Her father had died two winters ago and their lodge was left with no provider. She was expected to marry as Running Deer had failed to attract any of the young warriors in the camp.

"You love Warbo very much don't you?" she asked.

Little Dove didn't answer and her eyes were sad. "I wish to please my husband."

"How long did Warbo court you before you marry?"

"I don't understand, court? What does it mean?'

Janie said, "a man and woman meet and they spend time together and if they love each other, then they get married."

"Each year, the young maidens desiring husbands come to council. The warriors come to find a wife. Warbo is chief, so he picks his wife first, and he chose me."

"You mean you didn't know him then? What if you wanted to be the wife of one of the other braves? Don't the women have anything to say about who they marry?"

"It is up to the father of the young maiden. If the warrior presents a fine gift, then he accepts."

"What happens if two braves want the same maiden?"

"They both bring gifts to the lodge and then the maiden can choose."

"But your father was dead. Did you want to marry Warbo?"

"Warbo is fine hunter. I was honored." Once again her eyes betrayed her and Janie sensed that there was another warrior that held her heart.

"You told me that the young man provides for the women of his wife's people. You said they live with the bride's people. Why do you not live with your husband?"

"Warbo did not want to live with three women and he chose to live alone."

"Then why did he marry you? She asked. The question bothered Little Dove but she answered quickly. "So I could bear him a son." She walked faster to the lodge and Janie knew she wished to talk of other things.

In the next few days, Janie learned everything there was to know about how things were placed in a tepee. Medicine articles, their shields, and weapons all had their place. The bow and quiver containing the arrows were occasionally slung on the backrest. This enabled the men to sharpen their arrows without getting up. Wood was always put near the door on the south side.

"In Warbo's lodge, he has painted his war records and personal experiences on the lining of his lodge for decoration."

Janie learned that the beds were usually made on the ground because they took up less room and were below the smoke even when it hung low from the dying fire. They were set back further under the tepee to keep them dry and in the winter, skins were placed on the ground for warmth.

The sun slowly sank below the horizon, Warbo and his braves returned to camp, each carrying a deer slung across the pack animals. Warbo dragged the limp form to the door of Little Dove's tepee.

At the sound of his voice, Little Dove hurried to the door. Her face beamed proudly. "Come see, Wild One, he has brought us fine hides."

"So he got a deer. Who cares?" She answered as she sat chewing on a piece of jerky.

Her voice carried to the outside and the proud warrior felt the sting of his pride. He said nothing but walked away. Little Dove saw the hurt for her husband for she had noticed the change in him since the Wild One had come to the camp. He looked at the white woman as he had never looked at her and she knew that her husband cared for the captive.

The following morning the women preserved the meat first and then began the task of making a dress. The meat was divided between different lodges and the hides were given to Little Dove to begin the arduous task of tanning the hide.

Janie coated her skin with the grease that Little Dove gave her. It was made from buffalo fat and it healed the blisters and eased the stinging of the burns. She became accustomed to the smell and gradually the wounds healed. The skin peeled off and new skin began to form.

They soaked the hides in water for a few days and then they stretched them out on a level piece of ground. They staked them out with the flesh side up. After washing the hides, they spent hours scraping off all the fat and excess tissue. The hides were left in the sun for two more days. Janie grew impatient and thought the work would never end. She spent time with Morning Star to help her learn the language but found out that she remembered little of the white man's world. Janie knew she was making an impression so she kept up her show of surrender.

After the sun had thoroughly dried out the hides, they removed the hair with a scraper made from an antler of an elk, called Wahinthe, in Pawnee. Some of the hair refused to come loose and once again they soaked the hides and this time they staked them out with the hair side up. Soon the hair buckled under the hide scraper.

Then Little Dove beat it with the back of an ax. She overlapped the blows so every square inch of the hide was covered. It was now soft and all the hair, fat and, dirt removed. "Now we can sew," she announced.

Janie knew she would truly appreciate this dress once it was made. Little Dove held the hide up to her and marked it with a paintbrush that she said was made from the spongy bone of a buffalo joint. They marked it and then began cutting away the outside edges with a big hunting knife. Tiny strips of the hide were cut and stretched out between two willow rod poles to make the lacing thread. Small holes were punched in the hide and then the thread was woven into the garment in short fine stitches.

Then the dress was finally completed and Janie sewed porcupine quills and beads on it for decoration. A matching headband was made and now they were ready to start the moccasins. One pair for summer and one for winter. These were made from the remainder of the deerskin. One pair was made just to cover around the ankles with long strings of rawhide to tie them on. The second pair came almost to the knee. These were lined with fur from the fox. Colorful beads were sewed around the top for beauty.

When Janie finally slipped into the dress she was surprised at how well it fit. She made a thin belt and tied it around her waist. It showed the contours of her body and made Janie feel more like she was wearing the clothes of her people. It was comfortable and she soon forgot the smell of the hide. The moccasins were just in time as her shoes were almost worn out. She packed her worn dresses in the cloth bag, as she couldn't part with her only possessions from the white world.

When she stepped from the tepee clad in the new dress and moccasins she was aware of the curious glances from the tribe as she made her way slowly to the river. She soon met Warbo standing with his back to her talking to a group of warriors. The men stopped talking to look and Warbo noticed their stares. The braves grinned and he turned slowly. When he caught sight of her, his eyes surveyed her dress and moccasins and, then a smile broke the sternness of his face. It was a good smile and it was the first time Janie had ever seen him look so happy. The smile surprised her and she couldn't help but return it.

I'll just let the old boy think I've changed, she thought as she continued to the river. The talking began again after she left them and she could tell by the boyish giggles that they were definitely talking about Warbo's new wife.

As each day ended Janie watched the moon come out. She studied it but her knowledge of science left something to be desired. It no longer shone with its' magic glow. Now it loomed above her like some hideous monster just waiting to swoop down and take her. She never thought she could hate to see the evening come but she knew each day brought her closer to her fate with her husband.

For the next couple of weeks, she marked a stick with a knife to count the days. It had been fourteen days since she had surrendered to her husband. She could tell she had been accepted by the tribe since that day and she was allowed to come and go as she pleased.

The leaves turned gold, yellow and, brown as the approaching winter crept in. Her time was running out. I must act now she thought and began hiding pieces of dried meat in the cloth bag. Water was another problem. She had nothing to carry it in unless she stole the buffalo water pouch. That was dangerous, she knew.

Her curiosity got the best of her and she finally asked Little Dove when the moon would be full. She answered, "When the sun rises the Pawnees will move to winter camp. Two moons, we make camp, then full moon."

"You mean tomorrow the whole camp is moving?"

Little Dove nodded her head in acknowledgment.

"Why you move?" She found herself talking in the broken language she had listened to for so long.

"Shelter. It is closer to the buffalo grounds, the prairie has no warmth. We need wood for fires and build warmer tepees."

Three days, just three days. She felt the nerves twist in her stomach like a cold knife slicing through her veins. Her mind worked rapidly. I must escape on the trail she told herself. My God, I must escape, I must.

CHAPTER TEN

The sun was barely peeking over the cloudy horizon, its pink rays piercing through the clouds. Janie was awakened by the unusual noise in the camp. The air was sharp and the deerskin dress felt good as she hurried to help Little Dove prepare breakfast. The continuous diet of buffalo with meat and vegetables always tasted strange to her in the morning. Her mouth watered when she thought of hot sizzling bacon frying and the sight of an egg would be a dream come true.

Everything was removed from the lodges. Little Dove rolled the blankets and hides into small bundles and bound them securely with rawhide. The cooking utensils were rolled in a deerskin hide. Warbo brought several horses and the tepees were lowered. The poles from the lodges were tied around their haunches. The huge skins from the tepees were folded flat and covered the poles. He strapped the remaining robes and skins to these and the packing began. The furnishings of the two tepees were then placed on the travois.

Little Dove brought out the large rawhide envelope called a parfleche. These were Indian suitcases and used for clothing and meat. The ones for clothing were much larger and they, like everything else, were made from the buffalo hide. They were identical. She filled the smaller with dried meat and preserved vegetables.

Janie gathered her few belongings and carted the cloth bag and the medicine kit to the waiting horses. Warbo studied her. He let his eyes rest on the healing skin. Janie knew he was checking to see if her burns had healed. He wants to know if I'll be ready at the end of this trip, she thought. She ignored his presence and went to help Little Dove.

Prairie Breeze and Running Deer scurried about like two excited children. They were about as helpless as babies. Janie stood and marveled at the change in the camp. Everywhere she looked, men and women worked side by side to lower the huge tepees. Extra poles were put on a separate travois and tied with rawhide. In a short time, the whole camp moved silently out on the prairie.

The papooses were tied to the mothers' backs in their small wooden cradles. They smiled and Janie was surprised at the good nature of the children. Women, children, and dogs moved out beside the horses. The livestock brought up the rear.

Janie walked beside Little Dove. It aggravated her to watch the women walk and the men ride but she kept still. She didn't want to draw any attention to herself. Now that it was time to try her plan of escape, she was scared. She didn't want to try, but the fear of being caught made her a little reluctant. She knew how fierce her husband could be.

She pulled her hair tightly about her head and covered it with an Indian shawl to make herself as inconspicuous as possible. They walked for miles and Janie could feel herself tiring already. The sun grew hot. The prairie was dusty and the air was dry and hard to breathe. They stopped for lunch which consisted of dried meat and berries. Water was running low and she was thirsty.

The pack horses were burdened down and now each carried a rider. Janie walked along with the horses trying to keep up. She didn't hear the horse but then he was beside her. She could feel his presence even before she saw him.

"You want ride with me, Wild One?" he asked.

She hesitated. I'd rather die, she thought, but her body said otherwise. Her legs ached. I must preserve my strength. She decided to give Warbo the encouragement he had been looking for. She raised her eyes to him and smiled broadly. "I'd love to ride with you."

Surprised by her answer, he returned the smile and pulled her up in front of him. She straddled the pony bringing the deerskin dress up in front of her. Her legs showed long and they looked as brown as his next to the white pony.

"Where are we going?" she asked.

"To the land of the buffalo near the high mountains. Much water and shelter from the heavy snows." His arm encircled her waist and he felt the pulse of her body against him. He put as much room between them as he could and each time he scooted back on the animal, Janie did the same. He knew she was playing with him and he suddenly pulled her tight against him. He held her there and he blew softly on her ear. "It feels good to ride with the Wild One," he whispered.

Her first instinct was to get mad but she didn't want to arouse his suspicions so she put her arm on his and squeezed. "Yes, it does, husband." They rode on in silence, each enjoying the sensations they were feeling.

She knew Little Dove watched them and wondered why she flashed a brief smile in her direction. She wants me to succeed with Warbo, even if she has failed, I wonder if she is ever jealous of me, she thought.

"Warbo, do you love Little Dove?" She turned and looked at him.

He was slow to answer but he knew she would ask again so he said, "Little Dove is a good wife. The Great Spirit has failed to give her powerful medicine."

"You mean because she has not given you a son?

He grunted.

"It could be your fault, you know?"

"Warbo is powerful chief, not my fault."

"Why haven't you been sleeping with her if you want a child so badly?" She could tell she was mixing him up and she chuckled to herself.

"Because I am waiting for you, Janie, the full moon is upon us."

His answer sent tongues of fear lapping at her rib cage and bouncing off her heart. Her face turned a fiery red. It was his turn to make her nervous now and he seemed immensely pleased with himself. She was glad when the time came to stop. Squaws and braves from every lodge spread their blankets on the ground and the campfire burned through the village. Warbo relieved the horses of their heavy burdens and picketed them a short distance from the camp.

Little Dove, Prairie Breeze and, Running Deer spread the hides close together under a large cottonwood tree. The leaves looked like a beautiful carpet beneath the huge tree and made a soft mattress. Janie took her hides and moved them to the other side of the tree but only a short distance from them. She made a big fuss as she piled the leaves into soft heaps of brown, orange and, yellow. She arranged the furs and then went to say goodnight.

She filled the buffalo pouch with water and passed it to the women. Taking it to Warbo, she said, "Would you like a drink of water before you sleep?" she smiled and his face lit up. Too bad it's not poison, she thought. He drank slowly and wiping his chin with his arm he looked up at her. "You make good wife, Wild One."

"I hope so, Warbo. Goodnight." She could hardly keep from smiling as she made her way to her pallet. She kept the water pouch close beside her. When the fires died down and she could hear the heavy breathing of the camp, she rolled quickly off her bed. Putting the clothes from her bag beneath the blankets she made her way silently to the edge of the camp.

The people were silent and Janie prayed the dogs would not detect her movements. It seemed hours as she crept inch by inch through the sleeping Indians. She made her way to the picketed horses. When she finally stood up her heart tumbled through her body. A night guard checked the horses and returned to his campfire a short distance away. This she hadn't expected. They didn't guard them before. She slipped silently behind a big tree and watched the brave. He was an old brave and Janie prayed he was hard of hearing.

Presently she gathered her courage and circled behind the horses, careful to not alarm them. She chose Warbo's spotted pony, as she heard it was the fastest in the camp. She stood patting the animal and he seemed to remember the passenger he had carried just a few short hours ago.

The horses moved and Janie kept her eyes on the brave as she untied the pony and moved slowly from the camp. She spoke quietly to him and he followed obediently. When the lights from the camp were dim in the distance, she led the pony to the nearest rock and climbed on. The pony pranced wildly as he sensed the strangeness of his rider. Janie had a hard time quieting the big, shaggy beast but after petting his mane and talking softly to him he moved out slowly. She nudged him into a fast walk, circling back in the direction they had come that day. She mixed the ponies tracks with those made by the Indians earlier in the day.

The moon came out but it was darker than she had hoped and the going was slow. When she reached the prairie she hung on tight and let the pony run long and fast.

Throughout the night Janie pushed the horse over hill and valley. She had no sense of direction now and her only goal was to put as much distance as possible between her and Warbo. The thought of him now and how mad he was going to be when he realized she had outwitted him again. Renewed terror raced through her. He had been good to her, up to a point but she knew from bitter experience how mean he could be.

"He mustn't catch me," she told herself. For a moment she felt a little sorry for the man knowing he would again lose face when the camp knew she had escaped. He was such a proud man, she pondered, but her sympathy lasted only a minute, "Why should I feel sorry for an Indian when I know he will probably kill me this time if he catches me?" Her legs were rubbed raw from the long day on the pony and she was exhausted from lack of sleep. She drank a little water and forced herself onward. She knew they would soon miss her and there was no doubt in her mind that she would have a very mad man on her trail. The sun was coming up and she headed north, so she changed course and headed west. She tried to cover her tracks in the tall grass as she let the pony catch his breath, then once again she pushed him hard across the open prairie that stretched endlessly ahead. It was hard to hang on without a saddle and only a neck rein to govern the spirited animal.

The sun grew hot and heavy and already Janie knew the horse was tiring. She tried giving him a little water from the pouch but knew she was wasting it. She gave up and walked for a short distance until they reached a long steep hill. They climbed up one side and down the other and then throughout the long hot afternoon they plunged through tall grass up to the horses' stomach. They made little time and finally, Janie knew the beast must have water. She mounted and gave him his rein in hopes he would take them to water.

It was over an hour when the horse entered a dense thicket and moved down a grassy slope to a small stream. Janie half fell from the horse and drank freely. She washed her face and neck letting the water run onto the deerskin dress. She studied the landscape and led the horse downstream to further confuse her followers. When they reached a rocky spot she led him to higher ground and rode into the foothills.

When she found a patch of rocky ground she tied the horse to a tree and then using a tree branch, she covered her tracks. She knew she was using valuable time and prayed that it would be worth the risk. When the night closed in, Janie knew she would have to rest. The horse could go no further and she could barely walk. She tied him securely to a tree and sat nearby.

She took the jerky from the small pouch she had carried all day and sat chewing on it. She couldn't start a fire, even if she wanted to. It would only bring the Pawnees down on her. Sleep came quickly until the cry of a wolf split the darkness causing her to bolt. The spotted pinto pranced nervously and she walked over to quiet the animal.

For the first time in months, Janie had a new fear to gnaw at her insides. The cry filled her with terror and she could see the small eyes gleaming in the darkness. She threw rocks and yelled at them. Slowly the howling stopped and she retreated to her seat, a large rock supporting her back.

Weariness came over her. Warbo loomed in her mind and everywhere she looked she imagined him slipping through the darkness in search of her. I would probably be lucky if those wolves did get me, she thought. If I could just find a homestead or the fort before he catches me. She judged the distance Warbo covered and panic pricked her like a needle. She knew he wasn't far behind. The cool night air chilled her and she moved about to keep warm.

Fear kept her from sleeping and at the crack of dawn; she topped the hill and descended into the valley. She stuck close to the foothills as her eyes swept the countryside. Her heart jerked. Her throat went dry. She stopped the horse. On the far side of the valley, the smoke rose slowly to the sky. A farmhouse, she thought. Then she studied the smoke closely. One, two, three, distinct puffs of smoke and, the blood in her veins turned to ice. She couldn't move. Then on the opposite hill came the reply.

"Damn Indians, think you're smart. Write letters you stupid savages!" she screamed. She cursed them. Her determination mounted and she pushed on. Now that they were so close she knew she could not leave the cover of the trees. She picked her way through the rocky foothills. The sky grew dark and Janie prayed for rain. She knew she could travel by night if she dared rest for a while now. She found a small cove and let the tired animal graze. The water was nearly gone and the animal hadn't drunk since the morning before.

Her body reeked from the two days and now the hours of sleeplessness caught up with her. She slept. When the pony nickered and the crash of thunder split the air, Janie was on her feet in seconds. The lightning was all around her. It stabbed nearer and the pony pranced wildly. She had prayed for rain to hide her tracks, but now the thunder echoed and the lightning lit up the sky. She pulled the pony and finally managed to get back on his slick and wet back. The full moon came out and through the downpour, Janie pushed the nervous animal. Surely the fort can't be too far away. I'll find it tonight. I know I will.

The rain-soaked her body and chilled her until her teeth chattered. The ground was slippery and the pony could not gain much speed. She looked at the full moon and laughed quietly to herself. "That stupid Indian thought he was going to have me tonight."

Maybe tomorrow night but not tonight." The rain came in torrents and Janie knew her tracks would be hard to follow.

This ought to slow that cunning Indian down. The crack of thunder followed by a fierce bolt of lightning sent the frightened pony down the slope and he raced madly for the prairie. She pulled on the reins. He was out of control and all she could do was hang on. The tall grass was slippery and she felt the big horse sway in the mud.

Another crash of thunder and the ground seemed to tremble. A ditch and Janie felt herself flying through the air. Then the taste of mud in her mouth and the darkness closed in. She lay still and quiet in the tall grass.

CHAPTER ELEVEN

The rain did indeed slow Warbo down but it only made his desire to find her more intense. He rode with a sense of urgency. His eyes scanning the hills in every direction. His horse was not as fast and he cursed her for taking his best pony. She had surprised him by the clever way of hiding her tracks. It had taken many hours to find where she had left the trail of the previous day. He covered the ground between them, riding with confidence.

Night made the scouting impossible and they camped, waiting for daybreak. He had sent Brave Arrow on with the camp to the hunting grounds to speak for the Pawnees. The camp was quiet, Broken Lance and Twisted Hair sat warming themselves by the fire, while Warbo worried about his captive. They knew what the recapture of the Wild One meant to their leader. It was a matter of pride and each relished the thought of what Warbo would do next to punish his new wife.

Warbo walked away from them and sat alone under a tree and thought back to his trial with this white woman. She had fought him from the minute she was captured and suddenly the thought of her getting away and finding her people overcame him. What if she did find help? He considered the effect it would have on the tribe and suddenly he knew it no longer mattered. Only his own emotions plagued him, and he clenched his fists in frustration. No one could take her from him and for the first time, he realized how much he would miss this fiery-haired woman. He knew that his feelings were not like that he felt for Little Dove. He cared for this pale-skinned woman in a way that he couldn't explain, even to himself. The feeling excited him and he felt as though an unknown force was pushing him towards her and he was powerless to stop himself. I know she cares for me. I saw it in her eyes when she forced me to kill Dark Eagle. She wanted to be my woman, he told himself. He knew by the memory of her body next to his as she had ridden beside him on the day before and the way she looked at him. He thought of how it would be to have her share his tepee, his life, and his plans for his people. Fear tore at him as he felt his dreams fading into the darkness of the night.

Her violent temper and the way she had fought so bravely to outdo him brought a sense of pride to Warbo. He remembered her defiance of him and the cunning way she had sneaked from the camp. Now he cursed her for being so nice to him and he realized it had been a part of her plan of deception. Maybe she does hate me, he pondered. I will find her, he vowed and the lines in his face hardened, I will make her care.

He didn't sleep from the time he learned of her escape and now he kept pushing his braves and himself until the weariness filled his body and they stopped for a short time. They moved into the hills and found the trail leading to the stream. They scouted the hills and came upon her tracks into the mountains. Warbo smiled. She was going in the wrong direction of the white man's fort. He was closing the gap between them, stopping only to water the thirsty animals.

As dusk settled upon them they entered the canyon where Janie had waited for darkness. They hovered under the trees seeking shelter from the torrent of rain. The lightning lit up the sky and Warbo knelt and prayed to the Great Tiwara for the safety of the Wild One. He feared for her safety and the anger he felt for her melted. All he wanted was to find her and hold her close to him.

As the moon showed through the clouds his anxiety built. When the sun rises, three days had passed. He knew her food would be gone and he hoped she would have the strength to control the spirited pony in the fierce autumn storm he could see approaching them. It struck and the rain-soaked the weary searchers and they stood in puddles. There was no fire to warm their bodies and they shivered in the darkness. They moved among the animals, quieting them. Warbo thought the sun would never show its face and when the first rays streaked the sky, he mounted and moved out in from of his companions.Broken Lance and Twisted Hair, followed close behind and they too were weary of the search. Only respect for their leader kept them on the trail. The horses picked their way down the wet grassy slope to the prairie that stretched below. The whinny of a horse stopped the mare and her ears stood tall and straight, listening. Warbo too had heard the whinny and his eyes scanned the country. He saw his spotted pony grazing in the tall grass.

His spirits lifted and he sent the dun down the slope at break-neck speed. When he seized the reins a cold chill swept through him. The Wild One was afoot. The spirited pony had been too much for her in the storm. The three men lead their horses through the tall grass and he knew she could be anywhere.

The Pinto limped and Warbo stopped to examine his foot. There was a nasty cut above the ankle, the blood had crusted and the bleeding stopped. Warbo knew the horse had fallen and the concern for Janie grew in him like a fire waiting to be quenched. Janie needed him now; she was fair game for any wild animal that could be prowling around looking for dinner. Warbo patted the pony reassuring him that he would take care of him. He handed the reins to Broken Lance and instructed him to take the horse to the nearest stream and clean the wound.

Warbo followed the tracks, still fresh in the damp ground. He walked for miles, hoping he would reach her in time. He tried to convince himself that she was not hurt and had escaped unhurt. The sun rose high and the sweat poured from his temple. At last, he came upon the still form lying in the wet grass.

He had pictured the fight between them and the whipping he would give her when he found her but his fury melted as he saw her still form lying in the wet grass. She did not move and his heart leaped, he was beside her in seconds. Only the joy of finding her, as one would a lost child, was in him now as he pressed his ear to her chest. She is alive but certainly not conscious. He checked to see if she had any broken bones. Lifting her into his arms, he asked Twisted Hair to bring a blanket. He poured water on her face and wiped the mud from her eyes. As the dirt slid away the bright red cut on her forehead was swollen and ugly. It was deep and Warbo spotted the rock covered in blood that had knocked her out.

Swollen red lines covered her legs and arms. The bruise on her forehead was not broken but swelling from within. This worried him and he laid her gently on a bed of leaves. He made a compress of wet grass and mud and placed it on the bruise, hoping to bring the swelling down. She did not regain consciousness and she began to tremble violently.

Twisted Hair built a fire and Warbo moved her closer. Her skin was cold and he lay down beside her and pulled the blanket over them, hoping to warm her and stop the trembling. He wrapped his arms around her and held her close. He listened to her heartbeat. It was slow and steady and he breathed a sigh of relief. They slept for several hours and then she moved in his arms. He sat up and said, "Are you alright?" She hugged him to her and whispered, "Oh Carl, I knew you would come. Hold me please. I've missed you so much."

Warbo did not know what to think. Who is Carl? Why is she clinging to me? He just laid there and enjoyed the feel of her next to him. Her manner did not change when she woke in the morning. This was not the Wild One; this is a completely different woman. They built a travois and he tied her to it to keep her from falling off and they moved out ever so slowly. She slept most of the time and he stopped to give her drink, but she didn't want anything to eat. He encouraged her to eat, telling her she needed to regain her strength. She was in a different world and she called out to this man called Carl. "Help me, Carl! Hold me, Carl! She called as she thrashed around on the travois. They traveled slow and made camp early in the evening. He got her up and tried to get her to walk. She was like a limp doll and he made another soft bed and laid her down. She said," Carl, come to bed". She reached out her hand and he took it and sat down beside her. She acted strange, so different than the wild one, he worried that she did not know him.

"Who is Carl?" he asked.

She looked at him and smiled and said, "what do you mean? You are my finance, come and love me."She patted the spot beside her and he didn't know what to think. Has she lost her mind?" he wondered. That night they lay together like contented lovers. Sometime during the night, he could feel her hands on his chest, exploring his body. She moved up to his face and pulled him down to her and placed her lips on his. "Kiss me, Carl, she whispered.

"What is kiss?'

She wrapped her arms around him and said, "Place your lips to mine."

He hesitated only a moment and then he took her in his arms and pressed his lips to hers. A fire burned in his body as she clung to him. A feeling like nothing he had ever felt came over him and he moved his hand down to her breasts. She arched her back and let him have his way. "Make love to me, Carl"

It was like a slap in the face and he pulled away from her. He could have her now but he did not want to take advantage of her when she was not in her right mind. When he made love to her, he wanted her to ask him to make love to her and remove the other man from her mind. "Go to sleep, little one. You need your sleep."

He left her side and moved away. She didn't seem to mind and shortly she was asleep again. He crawled in beside her and covered her up, but sleep did not come easy.

They traveled for two more days and Janie seemed to be getting stronger. She still wanted him to sleep beside her but she never seemed to recognize him as Warbo. She still thought her white lover was there. He did not stop letting his hands roam her body. He untied the strings on her dress and pulled her breast from the strange clothing. He teased her nipple and she pressed against him trying to halt the cravings that she was feeling in her troubled mind.

They continued using the travois and travel was slow. He knew he was needed at the council soon, but he was enjoying the nights that she slept in his arms. The need for this woman made him put the needs of his people aside. Twisted Hair and Broken Lance shook their heads and spoke quietly expressing their fears for their people. This white woman was causing much trouble for their people.

They moved out slowly over the rough terrain and Janie stirred, the dust swirled above her and her throat was dry. It had been over four days since she was found, but time meant nothing to her. She felt the life had been zapped out of her and she lived in a strange unreal world. The horses moved slowly and she could tell that the man in charge was taking every precaution for her safety. There were times when everything was in focus for her and then the world would spin around her. The trees seemed to hover above her and she felt they would crash down on her at any moment. Janie had been a nurse long enough to know she had suffered a concussion, but what to do about it escaped her mind.

Sometimes she knew the man treating her was Warbo and other times, she knew it was Carl. Her mind reeled from the confusion. She was surprised at how well this Indian was treating her. His concern was evident and she wondered how she got here. Who was this strange man that held her so gently at night? He bathed her body and helped her stand. His strong brown arm encircled her as he made her walk to renew her strength.

Janie could see the weariness in his face as looked at her. Damn this stinking Indian, she thought, as dreams of his past torture came back to her. For some reason, his kindness nibbled at her mind, and total confusion filled her head. She pushed his hand away when he tried to help her up from the travois. He let go of her and she staggered to her feet. She gave him a haughty glance and then the ground stared her in the face and the sky spun above her. She was terrified of her lack of self-control. She reached for him and he caught her before she fell. She clung to him, realizing that she needed him and that she was totally out of control. The tears came and she sobbed. "I need you, Warbo, take care of me, don't let me die."

Twisted Hair moved a distance away and rested. It had been a long trip and the Wild One needed rest. The terrible temper had waned and he watched as she clung to Warbo like a child.

Warbo smoothed her hair and spoke softly to her," I will not let anything happen to you, Wild One." As he spoke reassuringly to her she quieted. "I made Wild One a promise that day in my lodge."

"Promise? She asked. "I don't remember."

"When Wild One says she be my woman, I believed you. I promised you that I would not hurt you again."

"Why are we here?" she asked.

"You escaped and I found you. I will return you to my camp and my lodge. From now on, you will sleep with me and you will not escape again."

Janie shuttered and he felt her tremble in his arms. He tried to tell himself she was beginning to care for him but he knew it was only because of the sickness that raged in her head. He helped her to the fire where Twisted Hair and Broken Lance had roasted a rabbit.

CHAPTER TWELVE

The Pawnee tribe moved slowly across the plains. The braves helped the women of Warbo's lodge. When they stopped to rest or to eat, the talk was always about the return of their Chief. Prairie Breeze was silent but listened as Running Deer spoke to Little Dove of the Wild One. She was getting old and the wrinkles in her face nearly hid the small pinched mouth. As she sat by the small campfire in the middle of the desolate country, suddenly she was very tired and weary. She knew she was drawing near to death and all hope of having a grandson left her. She had lived to hold him and watch her daughter have reason to be proud.

Her eyes rested on Running Deer. She too was showing her age and she knew her chance of marriage had died many years ago. She sat in amazement at the two girls chewing on the dried meat. The Great Spirit had been good to Little Dove; her beauty was a sense of great pride. She felt only sorrow for her other daughter, who was destined to die alone and sad.

She recalled how proud she had been when Warbo had chosen her daughter to be his bride. Until then her family had no social position in the tribe. She wished Two Hands; her husband could have lived to enjoy the pride she shared. Two Hands died gloriously in battle as he would have wanted. He would long be remembered for the many coups he had taken, not only from the white men but from their enemy tribes as well.

Yes, the Morning Star, the God of the Pawnees, had been good to Little Dove. Nearly two winters had passed and still, Prairie Breeze waited for her grandson. She prayed to the Great Spirit to grant her this one last wish before she died. The voices of the young girls brought her back to the present.

"I hope the Delaware's capture her and cut out her heart." It was Running Deer speaking. She spoke in bitterness and her jealousy was apparent. Inwardly she admired the beauty of the Wild One but never let her admiration show.

"Running Deer speaks with evil tongue. Warbo will not rest until he has recaptured her. I hope she is alive and well." Little Dove scolded Running Deer for her meanness.

"The Wild One does not deserve to be wife of our leader. She has taken the love of your husband from you. How can you wish her to come back?"

Little Dove was stunned at the words of her older sister. She started to speak but she realized she had nothing to say. It was true. She had known this for a long time but didn't think it was obvious to everyone else. The Wild One had taken her husbands' love but she had not returned it. For a moment she hated Warbo and the Wild One. She felt the sting of her sister's words but she said nothing and said, "Come it is time to go.".

"Do not listen to Running Deer, Prairie Breeze said. "Warbo has love for you too".

Little Dove mounted and rode beside her Mother. She let the bitter words of Running Deer run through her mind and now she felt ashamed that she too had wished the white woman dead. She knew that no matter whether the Wild One returned or not, his heart belonged to the white captive. My chances of bearing Warbo a son is gone, she thought, because she knew her husband's heart belonged to the Wild One as hers belonged to Brave Arrow.

She thought of him now and her spirits rose just thinking of him. Why could she not speak of her love for him? She could see the love returned to her each time they passed in the camp. They both knew that they must keep their feelings to themselves because if they ever told one another of their feelings, their passion would rule their minds. What if the Wild One did escape? Would Warbo ever feel anything for her again? Her shoulders sagged and for the first time, she let the tears slowly trickle down her face. Inwardly, Little Dove knew that the Wild One couldn't help what had happened to her and she knew that she could never hate or resent her. Her love hadn't been stolen as she had kept it reserved for Brave Arrow. She had married for honor and to please her mother. Now she sent a prayer to the heavens to protect Warbo and send him back to his tribe soon.

It was getting late in the evening when they stopped and made camp for the night. She knelt in the tall colorful aspens praying for the return of her husband and his captive. She felt a soft hand on her shoulder. She jumped, startled. It was Brave Arrow coming to check on the love of his life. "I didn't mean to frighten you." He had been riding in the front of the caravan to guide them to the Grand Valley.

She embraced him before she realized what she was doing. He had been on her mind so much that day and now he was here. His arms pulled her close and he held her to him. For a brief moment, she stood there letting the thrill of his touch fill her body. Never had she been this close to him and suddenly she was frightened. She pulled away, her cheeks flushed and she felt the awkwardness of the moment.

He too had felt the wonder of being close to the woman he loved and stood taking in the beauty of her body. He said Warbo loves the Wild One as I have loved you. He was surprised at his boldness but now that he had spoken of his love, he felt a sense of freedom sweep through him.

"We must not speak of love. I have no right to love you."

He turned to her to him and said, "But you do love me, Little Dove. I could see it in your eyes the night of the council. I know you accepted Warbo for honor but your love was for me. Say it is true." His voice was demanding and he wanted to hear those words.

"Yes, my love, it is true. I have dreamed many nights of giving you a son, but I have not given my husband a son and it is better to fail someone that you do not love rather than you. I could not bring that shame on you."

He hugged her tight and his hands stroked her hair. "You could not fail me, but I have failed you by not bringing many fine horses to offer to Warbo, so he will make trade. Then you will be mine."

Fear was in her voice and her body trembled. "No, Brave Arrow, he might kill you. You dare not ask for wife of Chief."

"I will take my chances with Warbo. I would rather die than spend my life without you."

"We must go now or someone might see us." She pulled away and stepped into the darkness.

"I will wait for you each night until Warbo returns."

She hurried from the thicket, her feet flying over the rocks. She could think of nothing but Brave Arrow and that night and she hoped that if Warbo had someone he loved, he might understand if she chose to go with Brave Arrow. That night she made a decision. If Warbo killed Brave Arrow for asking for her hand she would join him in the land of the Great Spirit.

Brave Arrow was constantly by her side during the next few days as the tribe entered the Grand Valley, the central meeting place for all the Bison Indians. Little Dove kept her distance from Brave Arrow. She had respect for her husband and now she had real hope to live on. As the days went by, she too worried and wondered, what is taking Warbo so long?

Warbo was worried too. He knew he was needed at the council and he was torn between his woman and his obligations. Janie lay in the travois and pulled the blanket about her. She knew that for once in her life she did need someone and an Indian at that.

They made camp on the prairie and the horses were watered and settled for the night. Warbo gathered buffalo chips for the fire as the prairie was desolate and bare. Only a few scattered rocks and sand dotted the landscape. She watched him take his hatchet and poke through the sand. He took the blanket from the travois and fixed it in the mound of soft sand. He smiled as he came to her.

"Come, Janie, the sand is soft and you must sleep." He helped her to the blanket and brushed the sand from her deerskin dress.

When he used her white name, the color mounted in her cheeks and she avoided looking at him.

Warbo handed her some freshly roasted rabbit that Twisted Hair had caught. He sat close by and chewed on another piece. His eyes were upon her but the lines of worry still played in the wrinkles of his brow. "Wild One getting better?" he asked.

Some of her old bitterness crept into her words and she retorted. "I'm fine, just fine, sitting out here on this stinking desert as your captive, what more could I ask for? "

Warbo smiled and he thought, Wild One is getting better. Temper returning.

"I don't remember coming this way, it is so desolate"

"Easier by desert. Mountains too high. Travois not cross mountains. We go around. Better for Wild One."

The meat stuck in her throat or was it a lump. She started to speak but now she was at a loss for words. This big mean savage, first he tortures me, leaves me to rot in the sun and now he is doing everything possible to make it easier for me. How do I cope with this man? She remained silent. She wanted to thank him but something held her back and she shivered. "How long before we reach camp?"

"Brave Arrow and the other braves have escorted the tribe to the Grand Valley. He can sit in council if we don't get there in time."

"Where is the Grand Valley?" she asked.

"Many moons travel. Many tribes meet in the Valley to divide up the hunting lands."

"How many tribes?" she asked.

"The Crow, Blackfoot, Kiowa, Sioux and the Assiniboin Indians will be there. Each tribe hunts in their territory. Keep peace."

I guess these people aren't as dumb as I thought, she told herself as she washed the meat down with some water. She wanted to walk for a few minutes before she slept. Unsteadily she got to her feet and once again she looked to Warbo. He was watching her and now the look in her eyes told him she was in trouble.

His arm encircled her waist and only their eyes spoke of their feelings. They walked a short distance from the camp and watched the sun go down, taking its warmth with it. She clung to Warbo for support. As Janie stood watching the sky turn purple and gold, she thought the sun would bring her new hope for the future. I must live for the sunrise, she thought. I hope one day it will be a good one. "I'm tired, let's go back."

He led her back to the camp where Twisted Hair was already sleeping. He lay in the sand with only a small blanket covering him. Warbo tucked his blanket around her and moved a few feet away and lay closer to the fire in the sand. Janie was cold but she looked at Warbo, she could feel only compassion. He must be cold and he gave me his blanket, so I should share it with him. She started to call to him but the words wouldn't come out.

He's an Indian, a savage, pay him no mind. Save yourself for Carl. She tried to think of Carl but now his face was faint and the features were replaced by the sandy-haired Indian. She felt something move against her leg and sat up. In the moonlight, she could see the lizard. She screamed.

The scream echoed in the desert and brought Warbo hurrying to her aid. When he saw the lizard he promptly used his hatchet and flung it some distance from her. As he turned to Janie, he suddenly laughed. The brave Wild One, unafraid of him or his people but afraid of a lizard. It amused him and he laughed loud and clear. Her scream had awakened Twisted Hair and he sat up his knife ready.

Warbo spoke to him in Pawnee and he looked at the Wild One and back to Warbo and a smile broke his wrinkled face. He returned to his sleep and Warbo moved to cover her up again. The laughter had left Janie puzzled and now she trembled. He was laughing at her. Her fist lashed out and connected with his chest. It stunned him but he only laughed louder. As quickly as it started it was over.

She regretted hitting him and she thought, he'll leave me or beat me. I'll die out here. She reached for the big man and clung to him. "I'm sorry, Warbo, I was scared."

"Wild One not be scared. You know I will take care of you."

As he moved away, she suddenly couldn't bear to be alone. "Don't leave me, Warbo. I need you, I'm cold."

She moved over and made room for him. He lay beside her, cold and unmoving. She pulled the blanket over them. Her body felt cold and numb. Suddenly she was a child. The days of her youth came back to her. The time spent with Aunt Agatha, the many long days in the orphanage. No one cared. Maybe Carl, but he wasn't here. Even Carl had never proved his love. Her mind played cruel tricks on her. She wanted to cry, to scream, to escape. Why was she always locked in her room at the orphanage for punishment? Locked in the bedroom of Aunt Agatha's. Now as her hand touched the sand she was lying in the Pawnee camp, the sun shining in her face. It seemed she had always been in some form of prison. She longed for freedom, freedom of a young child playing in the winter snow. She pictured the snow, so soft and cold. This brought the chills and her body shook violently. Tonight I'm not alone, I have Warbo. She turned to him and rested her head on his chest.

As he touched her skin his heart pounded. She was indeed cold, so cold that she shook. As her body shook with uncontrollable spasm, he moved closer and covered her body with his. She made no move to resist him as his weight rested on the blanket. She nestled closer and he doubled the blanket and covered the other side. It was a long time before the trembling subsided and she lay quiet and peaceful. He was not cold as her body warmed him. As he lay watching her sleep he looked for the Evening Star.

"Give her good medicine. Make the Wild One well. When she awakes, make her need me as she does now. Make her my woman." He prayed silently and at last sleep came. They lay together in peaceful tranquility.

CHAPTER THIRTEEN

Tension was running high in Grand Valley. The council had gathered. Yellow Snake, Chief of the Crow, sat smoking on his calumet pipe. He in turn passed it to Crazy Horse of the Sioux. Black Hawk, Chief of the Kiowas, puffed long and hard. As he did his dark black eyes watched as Sharitarish(White Wolf) of the Blackfoot stood and paced back and forth in front of the council fire. Sharitarish was mad. The veins in his neck stood out in the firelight and his face was contorted. He watched and when the peace pipe was passed to Brave Arrow, he grabbed it from his hand.

"Brave Arrow, not Chief of Pawnees, you do not vote. Where is the great Warbo?"

Brave Arrow stood up and looked straight up into the big man's eyes. Sharitarish was a big muscular savage and several inches taller and he tried to make the younger brave insecure in his role.

Brave Arrow knew he was no match for this man but his tribe depended on him and he said, "Warbo will return, captive not able to travel. I speak for the Pawnees."

Sharitarish hears Warbo is looking for his squaw. Is this white squaw more important than his people? Warbo grows foolish." His voice was loud as he pranced around like a wild stallion. "I say, we exclude the Pawnees from the council."

It was now Brave Arrows turn to raise his voice. "Warbo not foolish, he has given me and Buffalo Horn the power to speak in his place." Without our lands, our people will suffer. Warbo is wise Chief; he has taken many coups against his enemies. He has high respect among all tribes. Your words will anger him."

Black Hawk stood up and moved towards Sharitarish. "Brave

Arrow speaks truth. Warbo is fine leader, let the council vote if Brave Arrow shall speak for his people."

Sharitarish's eyes searched the faces of the Chiefs and only Crazy Horse of the Sioux, felt as he did towards Warbo. Jealousy over Warbo's war record had always brought dispute between the two warriors. He said, "Is Warbo not man enough to keep white squaw from running away? Does he not satisfy this paleface? He laughed and his half decayed teeth added to his mean and ugly face. The sound died quickly as the remaining Chiefs refused to join his cause.

Black Hawk told the Chiefs to stand with Brave Arrow. Sharitarish quickly sat down. Slowly Yellow Snake lifted his frail body from the ground and stood with Brave Arrow. Black Hawk remained standing beside of Brave Arrow. The count was two to two. Only one chief remained undecided. This was Big Bull, Chief of the Assiniboins. He was a short fat man and his face showed the hard years of his life. Sharitarish carried a lot of weight with the tribes, only because they were afraid of him, Big Bull knew this would make him an enemy. The Blackfoot outnumbered the Assiniboin, and he was hesitant to go against him. He was not quick to make a decision.

He studied the faces. He could see the hope in Brave Arrows eyes, the hatred in the face of Sharitarish. What if Warbo failed to return? He spoke to Brave Arrow. "Warbo will return to his people and he is still Chief of the Pawnees?"

"I speak the truth. The Wild One escaped and it was a matter of pride to recapture her. She has had a bad fall and could not travel. Warbo brings her, he will return soon." Brave Arrow felt sick. Never had he carried such a loan on his shoulders. He looked to the Evening Star and uttered a prayer for their chief to return quickly.

Big Bull slowly rose to his feet. Brave Arrow breathed a sigh of relief. "The council shall begin," he said as he took his place in the circle.

Sharitarish knew he was beaten but he would still bargain for the best lands. He took a long stick and drew a circle in the dirt. He divided the circle into six parts. Each tribe in turn thrusts their knife into the territory they wanted. Yellow snake and Black Hawk placed their knives into the area they had hunted for many years. Big Bull did the same.

Crazy Horse debated for a moment and then set his blade. Sharitarish waited for Brave Arrow to claim their lands. Brave Arrow knew he must claim the land in the northern plain, as it was close to their winter camp and his people were familiar with the terrain. He had no sooner marked his territory and the knife of Sharitarish embedded itself beside it.

Brave Arrow had expected this and he looked to Buffalo Horn. He shook his head slowly. They could not accept this and he knew that Sharitarish waited only to claim the same lands. It would be a hardship for his people to travel in that direction but he only thought of himself. He wanted to outsmart the chief of the Pawnees.

The Pawnees have hunted this land for many years. We cannot travel that far to hunt and return to our winter camp. I will not accept this. Brave Arrows' voice was calm and steady.

The other Chiefs watched Sharitarish. He would not give up easily. The Calumet pipe or Peace pipe was passed among the Chiefs. They all smoked and waited for Sharitarish to retrieve his knife from the circle.

"We shall fight for the land."

Brave Arrow said nothing. He smoked the pipe and passed it to Buffalo Horn. "Brave Arrow is no match for you, he said, looking at Sharitarish. Warbo will return and you can argue with him. Our answer is no."

He rose from the circle, returned the knife to his belt and, left the council fire. Buffalo Horn followed and the two men stood in the shadows discussing the predicament that the Chief of the Blackfoot had put them in. Brave Arrow suddenly felt a deep admiration for the man he had hated for so long. For the first time, he realized the great strength of Warbo. His hatred for the man melted and he felt proud to stand in his place if only for a while. His young mind debated what he should do. He wanted to impress Little Dove but even more, he wanted to help his people and not let Warbo down.

"I shall sneak into his tepee tonight and take his scalp. The Blackfoot will be sorry."

"You speak like a child." It was Buffalo Horn, a wise man and not one to act without deliberation. "Even if you succeeded in taking his scalp, his people would not rest until they had their revenge. Many of our people would die. We must stall him until Warbo returns. He will handle Sharitarish."

"Sharitarish make Brave Arrow lose face. He will pay." The words were defiant but he knew he was only soothing his wounded pride.

"If you want to help your people, you will remain silent and pray that the Great Tiwara brings our Chief back to his people soon." He left Brave Arrow beneath the tall cottonwood tree and disappeared into the night.

The music of the drums filled the cool night air and the sound of the young laughter reached his ears. In the center of the large camp, a great celebration was taking place. The young, braves and, maidens gathered to dance and play games. The older women cooked and the men stuffed their bellies.

He stood in the pile of yellow, brown and, orange leaves listening. Every tribe always claims the same lands, why must the contract only last a winter? He thought. Then he remembered Warbo had made that rule so that with the migration of the buffalo so went the lands.

Suddenly Brave Arrow didn't want to be alone. He wanted to join the carefree youths, forget the burden he carried, and push the responsibility from his mind. He went in search of Little Dove, walking slowly around the big circle scanning the crowd. His eyes found her sitting on her knees beside of Running Deer and Prairie Breeze.

He made his way up behind her and stood looking at the enjoyment on her face as she watched the young men and women dancing. The girls formed a large circle and the men right behind them in another circle. They stood facing each other and as the drums beat slowly they swayed in time to the music. The pace increased as they moved in the circle. The braves yelled and shrieked and stepped high to impress their partners.

As the tempo increased so did the frenzy of the dancers. They twirled and moved so fast that the night was a blur of moving figures. Brave Arrow kept his eyes on Little Dove until the dance ended. The girls collapsed in exhaustion on the hard ground. The braves sat close by, catching their breaths.

Suddenly Little Dove could feel his eyes upon her. She glanced slowly from side to side. When her eyes met his, a warm feeling stirred in her veins and she smiled. The drums rolled again and the dancers slowly moved back into the circle. She trained her eyes on the dance and tried to forget he was so near.

His hand was on her shoulder and he pulled her up. "We dance," he said as he took her into the circle.

"I can't dance, Brave Arrow. It isn't right." She tried to move away but soon she was into the circle of the fast-moving dancers. In a moment they were part of the group, laughing and clapping their hands in time to the music.

Prairie Breeze watched carefully and she worried about what would happen if Warbo found out. Surely he was bound to. Then a smile touched her tired and wrinkled face. It gave her pleasure to see the sparkle in her daughter's eyes. Never had she seen her so happy. She felt the uneasiness within herself and she pushed the possibility from her mind. This was no more than two young people enjoying being together.

She found herself clapping and sharing the joy that Little Dove had found. Her face beamed as the dance ended. She showed no scorn when Little Dove fell to her knees laughing. The sound was music to the old woman's ears and the carefree laughter of her childhood came back to her. For the rest of the evening, Little Dove and Brave Arrow danced and their faces lit the night with the sparkle of happiness. Running Deer did not attempt to join the happy group. She sat sulking and shaking her head every time Little Dove or Prairie Breeze caught her eye.

Her unapproved looks failed to spoil the evening for Little Dove and she continued to dance until her feet ached from the rough ground and her body could go no longer. When at last they made their way to the lodge, Little Dove could only feel pity for her sister. She knew that running deer only longed to be loved by someone. She thanked the Evening Star for the wonderful evening and Warbo was far from her mind.

CHAPTER FOURTEEN

At this moment Little Dove was far from Warbo's mind as he prepared a temporary dwelling for the Wild One. They were secluded in a dense grove of trees at the base of the high mountains. Time was of no importance to Warbo. His concern lay with Janie. All he cared about was her recovery. Now as he braced the side of the logs his eyes darted to the sleeping girl on the ground. He worked fast and formed a small tepee of logs and branches. He laid sticks across the top and then covered the sticks with leaves.

The room was big enough for only a bed which he made of soft leaves. He carried his wife to her new home and laid her gently on the mattress. She stirred lightly and returned to her sleep. A fire was built close to the door for warmth. The horses were tied a short distance away. The travois was too much for Janie and Warbo knew she could go no more. Twisted Hair returned with a couple of squirrels and impaled them on the makeshift fire. The smell of the cooking meat drifted into the hut and Janie woke. She was relieved to feel she was no longer strapped to the moving travois. The bed beneath her felt good, and the food smelled wonderful. After the nights in the desert, anything would taste good.

She moved to the doorway, her eyes searching for Warbo. Only Twisted Hair sat by the fire. Fear nibbled at her security. Warbo had left her; he had gone to the council and left her with this Indian. She moved unsteadily from the hut, yelling his name, Warbo! Warbo!"

Twisted Hair felt the hair on his arms rise slowly as he screams pierced the air. He was on his feet in a flash and moved toward her. The thought of him advancing toward her brought terror to her feeble mind. She screamed again as she clutched the big oak tree for support.

The old Indian stood rooted to the spot. He knew this woman was not right in her mind and he wouldn't have wanted to touch her before, much less now. He had gained high respect for her temper tantrums and was surprised at her serenity whenever Warbo was near.

A loud crashing noise in the trees behind her sent Janie quivering to her knees at the foot of the tree. It sounded like a huge buffalo running through the timber as Warbo came running to her aid. As he lifted her into his arms she was like a wild animal. In her mind, all she could see was Twisted Hair and she lashed out at him. She screamed and kicked and Warbo found himself yelling as loud as she.

"It's me, Wild One, it's me!"

His shouts went unheard and Warbo knew she was not in control. He slapped her hard across her face and the screaming stopped and she focused her eyes on him.

"It's all right, Janie, I'm here." His voice quieted her.

At the sound of his voice, the relief swept over her and the tears came in uncontrolled sobs. "I thought you had left me. I couldn't find you," she sobbed.

He held her close and comforted her. He could feel her body trembling in the cool night air. He spoke to Twisted Hair and he returned from the hut with a blanket. He wrapped it about her and sat her close by the fire. He took his knife and cut a little piece of the animal on the fire. He did not tell her what it was and she took it and ate slowly. All was good, Warbo was here, and he would take care of her.

Janie felt as though a thick cloud had settled in her head. Nothing was clear. Her mind was a jumble of mixed-up emotions. She couldn't explain the sudden need for this man. Nor could she bear to have him leave her sight. Even at night, she wanted to feel the warmth of his body.

The two men talked in Pawnee.

"What are you talking about?"

"Wild One needs much rest. We stay here until you are strong enough to travel. Twisted Hair will return to our people and tell them the council will meet without me."

Janie was so confused. What did it matter what they were talking about? Why did everything seem so fuzzy? Why did she need this man? The questions mounted and she stumbled to the hut. She buried herself in the blanket and sobbed.

Twisted Hair killed a small doe and brought it to the camp before he left to join the Pawnees. Water was close so Warbo didn't leave her side for the next three days. She slept most of the time and when she awoke she took short walks with Warbo supporting her. Gradually she grew stronger.

Warbo was nearly as confused as his wife. This wasn't the woman his tribe had captured. Certainly not the one who mocked him and fought him. As he looked at her sleeping so peacefully it seemed only a dream that a few moons past she had stood in the center of the Pawnee camp and endured the sun and torture and defied him.

Each night he waited for her invitation to share her blanket. He expected her to unleash her temper at any moment. He enjoyed each minute he lay close to her. He knew the time to prove his manhood was not now so he waited and bided his time.

During the day Warbo talked of the Pawnee Nation. They talked of the Great Spirit and Janie realized that their God was no different from the white man's God. The Pawnees believed in a male being who was supreme and who was hidden from the human eyes. They believed he caused the world to be. Their God was expressed in the sky or the arch of the heavens, a being so remote that he never revealed himself to man. They said he transmitted his power to lesser gods. Warbo sang and spoke to his God in song. He told Janie that he prayed to Mother Earth, because she was the bosom of all life and that Mother Earth would give Janie strength as it was given to the flowers and trees.

Janie sat and listened to him speak and she tried to make sense of all that he told her. Her mind marveled at his reasoning. She had heard Little Dove speak of the Morning star or the Evening Star but in her fuzzy mind, she could not comprehend all that she heard.

As the sun went down and the stars began to light the sky, Warbo moved closer to her and pointed out the stars. They thought of them as Gods and his people had great faith in them. They determined the time for planting corn, for hunting the buffalo, and, for certain religious observations. The stars were their calendars, and their gods and guiding light.

That night Janie found consolation in Warbo's words and found herself uttering a prayer to the Morning star. "Make me understand what is happening to me. Make me strong." She felt better as she snuggled close to the big Indian that night and she looked to a new sunrise.

Twisted Hair pushed the brown, mangy mare at breakneck speed across the rough terrain. The brisk autumn breeze moved the tall grass gently back and forth until the whole prairie seemed to move. This short fat man on the pony rode with certain urgency about him. As he entered the foothills he knew that winter was almost upon them. The trees were nearly bare and the ground was covered in a beautiful array of colors.

As he rode through the carpet of leaves, the old Indian's face wrinkled in worry. The hunting grounds were of great importance and he knew they must hunt soon to prepare for winter. He ate on the move and stopped only to water and rest the tired animal. When at last the camp of Great Valley came into view and he could see all the tepees of the other tribes mixing with his people, he breathed a sigh of relief.

The camp was quiet and only the laughter of the children at play came to his ears. He was puzzled. This was a time of great feasting, dancing and, playing games. He approached cautiously and rode slowly through the long row of tepees. The people from the lodges cried their welcome as Twisted Hair returned.

Brave Arrow ran from the tepee and embraced the weary man as he dismounted. His face was filled with anticipation. "You have brought news of Warbo, he asked.

Buffalo Horn joined the two men and they spoke in earnest conversation. The trio left shortly for the tepee of Sharitarish. He let the three men wait outside his lodge just long enough to make them wonder if he would parley with them. At last, he emerged and invited them to enter. Sharitarish grinned and relished each moment of torment he knew they were enduring. It angered him that he could not push Brave arrow into a fight and take the hunting grounds in his rightful glory.

He listened intently as Brave Arrow spoke. When he had finished he sat unblinking at the faces before him. When at last he spoke his voice was clear and concise.

"Sharitarish will parley with Warbo when the sun rises three times. If he does not return my people will leave for the hunting ground. We will kill anyone who enters our territory." He dismissed them with a wave of his hand.

"How long did it take you to get here from Warbo's camp?" he asked Twisted Hair.

"It is at least a two-day ride to get there and two days back. We need four days." Brave Arrow stated and that's a hard ride."

Warbo must return before midnight on the fourth day or I will leave", Sharitarish said. He only bartered with him because he was interested in seeing this white captive that had caused so much trouble for Warbo and he couldn't understand how a captive could sway the chief of the Pawnees to miss the council of the tribes.

Brave Arrow took only a moment to tell Little Dove that he was riding to speak with Warbo. He took a water pouch and some jerky and waited for Twisted Hair to recover enough to ride. It was still early in the day and he figured that they could cover a lot of ground before dark. Twisted Hair told Brave Arrow to bring two horses so Warbo could ride back by himself and the Wild One could ride when she recovered.

He walked slowly to his lodge and explained to his wife that he was the only one who knew where Warbo was camped. If he didn't bring Warbo back in time, they would lose their hunting grounds.

"White squaw causes much trouble. Why does Warbo keep her?"

Twisted Hair shook his head and said, "You are right, she is much trouble."

The two braves rode out in the early afternoon. His every bone felt the pressure of the last few days. Now the fear for his people pushed him onward. Twisted Hair thought of the Wild One and the question of her health plagued him. Was she well enough to travel? Would Warbo leave her with Brave Arrow if she wasn't? He could not understand his Chief and his concern for the white woman who was putting his people in danger. Could they find him in time? With this fear, they pushed through the evening twilight.

CHAPTER FIFTEEN

I f Warbo had any doubts about Janie's recovery, he pushed them aside one morning when he was awakened by one mad, raving white woman. The thick veil of fog lifted from Janie's head and she was amazed to find herself sleeping in the arms of this big, stinking Indian. She pounced on him like a mountain lion springs on his prey. Her fists beat his chest and her fingernails clawed at his face. He grabbed her to him and rolled over on top of her so she couldn't escape. "Many nights you have begged me to sleep with you and hold you in my arms. You enjoyed being my wife," he said grinning at her.

"I must have been out of my mind!" she said, as she struggled to get up.

It didn't take long for him to clear the small hut, knocking the post down as he rolled away from the enraged woman. The roof swayed and the frail support tumbled to the ground as he exited the enclosure. As he stood a short distance from the hut, he could hear the high pitched tones of her madness as the branches and leaves descended on her. He made no move to help her and he smiled. It was music to his ears to hear the mad temper returning. He breathed a sigh of relief and sent a prayer of thanksgiving to the Morning Star and then stopped to touch his lips to Mother Earth.

When at last she found her way out of the tangled mass of grass, leaves, and branches, her temper was indeed back in full force. Her eyes held their old challenge for a good fight. "Why were you sleeping beside me, you filthy redskin?"

The words stung Warbo, but he was so happy to see that her fever was gone and she was well. He grinned as she pranced around like a tiger set free from his chains. "You asked if you could come to my bed, and I was more than happy to hold you in my arms, Janie."

"You're out of your mind. I wouldn't ask you to sleep beside me if I never slept with anyone. Did you ravish me when you had the opportunity?"

"Warbo will not forget the many nights we lay together. It was a good time. It brought much happiness to my life. I did not prove my manhood to a sick woman. We shall lie together again soon and you will remember." It was his turn to add some defiance to his voice.

He walked to the deer hanging in the tree and cut some small pieces and impaled them on a stick over the fire. She went and arranged her clothing and packed what little she had and was ready to ride once more.

Warbo brought her some meat and she sat on a rock and chewed on the meat. It was probably the best food she had eaten since her capture. Definitely not buffalo," she said.

"Twisted Hair got a little deer before he left for the Grand Valley."

"I am grateful for you taking care of me when I was sick."

"Other braves say Warbo should kill white squaw. Much trouble. Maybe I should have," he said as he tossed the bones in the fire.

"But the great Chief of the Pawnees doesn't give up easily. Does he? He must win all battles even those of the heart." She laughed cuttingly.

Warbo grunted and kicked the fire until the life was snuffed out. He left and brought the horses. "You will have to ride today, no more travois. We have much ground to cover. I have wasted too much time away from my people. He lifted her onto the pony and secured her bag behind her. They rode slowly and stopped frequently to rest, not knowing how strong she was. The ride was tiring but Janie felt she should try hard to make up for the time they lost with her being sick. She thought I must try to ride as far as possible to repay this savage for the kindness he had given to her those many nights. She thought, I probably did ask that savage to sleep beside me.

They made camp early and as she stood by the fire she felt goose-bumps on her arms as two men emerged from the shadows. She yelled for Warbo. Just the thought of any other Indians capturing her made her stomach twist in sickening turns. It was not until they reached the fire that she recognized Brave Arrow. Relief flooded her face and her tense muscles relaxed as she extended her hand to him and said, welcome to our fire." Twisted Hair sat down by a tree and slept immediately.

Brave Arrow was surprised but gripped her hand tightly. He could only speak the name of Warbo in English. She pointed to the trees just as the big man stepped cautiously from the shadows.

Warbo embraced his fellow brave and they began talking fast. She could tell by the tone of Brave Arrows' voice that the news was not good. He pointed to Janie and Warbo looked at her from time to time as they talked. She could contain herself no longer.

"What's the matter, what are you mumbling about?"

The conversation stopped and they both stood staring at her. To be interrupted during an important discussion was surprising to them. A squaw would have known better.

"Squaws do not take part in men's discussions." Warbo's voice was no longer soft like it had been for so long. He now spoke as Chief of the Pawnees. He paid her no mind and continued his conversation as though she were not present.

Presently Warbo came and sat by Janie. He didn't speak. He looked into the flames as they licked at the sky. For the first time in his life, he had put his people in danger. Never had he put anyone or anything in the way of his duties. He looked at Janie and wondered if she were worth all the trouble she had caused. How he needed to hold her at this moment.

He stood up and pulled her from the log. She stood obediently before him because she was dying of curiosity. "I must return to my people at once. Sharitarish, Chief of the Blackfoot, has claimed the hunting lands of our people. I must return before the sun sets two times or we will have to fight for our lands. Many braves will die. I must go."

"I can ride, let's go." She didn't want him to leave her with Twisted Hair and Brave arrow.

"Warbo ride fast, not stop. Too long and too far. Wild One must ride slow. You will return with Brave Arrow and Twisted Hair and do not try to escape." He pulled her to his chest and tried to hold her for a moment but she pushed him away.

"Then go to your people, they need you more than I do. I don't care if I never see you, Warbo"

He gathered his gear and some meat and packed his horse. He took only the water pouch with his weapons. As he turned to leave he pointed to Brave Arrow and said, "Don't let her escape, let nothing happen to the Wild one. I will not lose face again."

"What did you tell them?" she asked.

"I tell them if you try to escape, just kill her." He spurred his horse and Janie shook her fist at the departing horse. Janie felt the loneliness surround her when the hoof beats faded in the distance.

In the many weeks since her capture, she had never felt completely alone. Even when she fled from the camp she knew they were close behind. Now Warbo rode away from her. She told herself she didn't care. She should be glad to get away from him. Escape crept into her mind but she remembered his last warning to Brave Arrow and Twisted Hair. Just kill her. She had neither the strength nor the desire to run again.

She spread the blanket on the cold, hard ground and pulled the cover about her. She was cold and miserable. She couldn't explain her feelings and she asked herself if she was beginning to care for this savage. Why didn't she want him to leave her? She answered her own question when she looked at her two guards and thought; they probably would kill her to please Warbo. She remembered the words he had spoken when he found her, "You will share my tepee and be my wife in every way." She shivered in the darkness and panic built within her. I know he'll take me. What will I do? Oh God, what will I do! From the time of her capture, she'd had time on her side. The fight to decide who she belonged to; the wedding ceremony; her long recovery; the choice of going to his tepee; then the escape. Now in a few days, they would reach Grand Valley and Warbo would be waiting. She prayed for a good sunrise and for strength to endure the coming months until she would be rescued and returned to Carl. She wondered how Carl had reacted when she failed to reach Sacramento. Had he come in search of her? Would he find her? Russ Fentley, their scout. What happened to him? She checked the horses and his was not amount them. She had never seen his scalp. Maybe he did get away. If only she had a little hope to live on maybe she could endure what was to come. There were no answers to her questions and they lurked in her mind like an evil monster. She missed the soft bed of leaves that Warbo had fixed for her each night. At least he could speak English and thought, as she listened to Brave arrow and Twisted Hair ramble on in Pawnee.

Twisted Hair had gotten up long enough to eat and then he slept soundly after the long night he had ridden. Brave Arrow sat by the fire and kept watch. Janie was in his view and he checked often to make sure she had not moved. He too was weary but he knew she must not escape again. She was the key to Warbo's happiness. If he had the Wild One, he might release Little Dove.

Although Warbo rode in the opposite direction of the Wild One, she was still with him. The concern for his people was important to him now and he wondered how he would deal with his enemy, Sharitarish. If he had been with his people at the council this would not have happened. This was the Wild Ones fault. He should have felt anger but he sensed the change that he felt within and he only remembered the last weeks had been full of precious moments.

He smiled to himself as he thought of her coming from the water that first day and the hut this morning, covered with leaves and mad as a wounded buffalo. He also remembered the stinging words she had spoken. I'll make her care for me, I'll make her care, and he told himself as he rode to meet the challenge of Sharitarish.

CHAPTER SIXTEEN

Warbo entered the Pawnee camp a few hours before the sun rose. He moved slowly down the long row of tepees. He encountered many scouts on guard but he quieted them in his reassuring voice. He didn't have to awaken Buffalo Horn as the old Indian sat in his lodge warming himself and offering kinnikinnik to the sky, earth, and the Evening Star. He knew the time was upon them and Sharitarish would leave at the break of day.

At the sound of his voice, Buffalo Horn jumped to his feet. He embraced the big tall man as though he too had doubted that he still existed. He discussed his plan and throughout the morning hours, he moved his braves into position. The Blackfoot horses were surrounded and braves lined the outskirts of their camp. When the warriors were in position, Warbo took his finest headdress and put on his best buckskins. The good-luck piece, the buffalo teeth, hung from his neck.

He did not wait for an invitation into the Blackfoot camp. Women and young braves stopped their chores and stared after the big Indian. He had taken them unawares and no one moved to stop him. He moved towards the tepee that housed his enemy. His loud voice could be heard long before he reached it.

"Come out, Sharitarish, The Chief of the Pawnees demands his hunting grounds." He waited for an invitation to parley.

As Sharitarish heard the voice he moved quickly to the opening of the tepee. He hadn't expected to meet Warbo and his confidence faded. He gathered his courage and stepped through the opening.

The sudden arrival and so early in the morning confused Sharitarish. For a moment he only stood and stared at the big mad

Indian facing him. "Why you enter the camp of the Blackfoot without invitation?"

"Sharitarish has stolen the hunting lands of the Pawnees from young brave. You not take from Warbo." He thrust the lance into the ground in front of the still dazed Indian.

Sharitrarish was nervous; he had not expected to be dealing with Warbo. "Why were you not at council? I was told that chasing a white woman prisoner was more important than your people. You let boy sit in council and you lose hunting grounds. Sharitarish thinks Pawnees try and trick him. I thought you were dead." His confidence returned a little as he spoke of the white woman.

"White woman is my wife. My duty to bring her back to Pawnees. Brave Arrow is fine Warrior and he spoke for my people and me."

By now the crowd gathered to listen to the angry Chiefs. Sharitarish's braves moved in behind him and he pushed the issue of the white woman. "Is the Chief of the Pawnees not man enough to teach white woman not try to escape? Perhaps you want me to teach her respect for Indian." He grinned and his large teeth were brown with tobacco stains.

Warbo spoke calmly, his eyes focused on the face of his enemy. "Wild One is brave woman. She killed two of my braves and stood much pain. Wild One is cunning and hid her tracks well. Many days to find her. She will not escape again. I now claim the hunting grounds or do you wish to fight me for our lands?

Sharitarish mind was taking in everything Warbo said about the white woman. He would like to see her. He had listened with interest to the stories told about her from the Pawnees visiting his camp. Perhaps he could trade the hunting lands for his captive.

"Where is this woman you speak of? Maybe Warbo lies. I want to see this white woman."

"I left her with Brave Arrow and Twisted Hair so I could ride faster and get here before you left. She will be here tomorrow."

"We will wait for the white prisoner and then we will know if Warbo speaks truth. We parley then, he said and turned to his lodge. The meeting was over.

As he returned to his lodge, the people waved and shouted their happiness at seeing their leader back. Why was Sharitarish so interested in his woman? His woman, he thought. It felt good to know she was his woman and he smiled thinking about her and her challenges. Am I going to have to fight him for the hunting lands? Warbo didn't relish the thought of fighting the big man.

Warbo thought of the Blackfeet tribe and he frowned, he had heard stories of how they treated the white captives. They were well known for the hideous torture and few survived long in their camp. Captives were passed from lodge to lodge and when they were no longer of any use they would kill them as sport.

He laid down on the pallet of furs and the loss of sleep and the long ride was now upon him. Weariness overcame him and he slept with a troubled mind for several hours. He awoke when he saw Sharitarish take his woman and he felt a chill sweep through him. He got up and spent several hours preparing his lodge for her return. He went and collected all of Janie's things from the lodge of Little Dove. As he touched the soft dresses, once more the image of her coming naked from the water, her fingernails clawing at him, fighting him at every turn. Her bravery and then how sweet she was after her escape and letting him lay by her side on the trail when her mind was troubled.

He knew that he had changed since this wild person had entered his life. The white man is my enemy, why had he accepted a white squaw for his wife? He thought of the many fights they had and he longed for the peace he had known before she came into his life. He tried to convince himself that he didn't want her anymore than she wanted him. He vowed that he would not let any of his feelings show again.

He stuck close to camp and kept a watchful eye on the Blackfeet to make sure they didn't try a sneak attack. Extra guards were posted and the horses were brought to the center of camp for the evening. He spent a restless night and was up early patrolling the camp. He rode down the back row of the Blackfoot camp to see what Sharitarish was doing today. He decided he would ride out and meet Brave Arrow and bring his wife safely to his lodge.

Janie had other ideas. She had recovered sufficiently enough to stage a grand entrance. She had been so obedient to Brave Arrow and Twisted Hair that they had decided she had indeed lost her desire to escape. She rode slowly between them. As they topped the rise she gasped in amazement at the tepees in the valley below. Her two companions stopped and they too scanned the camps.

Janie could pick out the familiar lodges as they rode toward the camp. Suddenly Janie kicked the pony into a gallop and took off unexpectedly down the hill and across the valley. It stunned Brave Arrow and he yelled in Pawnee for her to stop. She was gone in the dust and all he could do was follow.

"Might as well let these stupid savages know I'm back." She yelled and her high pitched tones could be heard in the distance. She kept it up as she neared the village and by now she was acquiring an audience. The Pawnees had learned to expect anything from her so they clapped and returned her shouts as she went flying by.

The Blackfeet people scurried from the trail with their children and watched the red-haired woman on the horse go racing by. Janie's hair blew gently in the autumn breeze. She raced along the outlines of the camp taking a good look at the neighboring tribes. Her war whoops could be heard in the distance as she rode the length of the camp. As she turned the pony and started back to the Pawnee camp she was suddenly confronted by three braves. Their faces were not familiar and she realized she was now in dangerous territory. Her little game had gone too far. She rode slowly toward them, her eyes scanning the crowd for a familiar face.

Warbo heard her and saw her flash by the tepees. He ran toward the sound and he could see Sharitarish and his braves standing in her way.

She stopped in front of them, her heart beating hard in her chest. She called out, Warbo help me!" Then Sharitarish closed in on her but before his hands took the reins, Warbo came out from behind the tepee and grabbed the reins and in a moment he mounted the pony and pulled her close to him.

"This time, Wild One, you make big mistake."

Sharitarish didn't take his eyes from her. She could feel those eyes piercing her like a knife. His face beamed as he looked at the beautiful white woman. "This white woman Warbo searched for?"

"This is wife of Warbo, called Wild One."

"It is good name for one so wild. Now we parley. I trade you lands for white woman." he said grinning.

When Warbo answered Sharitarish, Janie sensed the anger in his voice. He turned and was very angry as he rode towards his camp. Suddenly Janie felt very lucky to be protected by her husband. There are worse Indians she decided as he held her and rode to his lodge. She was surprised at the reception she received as they rode through the Pawnee camp. The squaws waved and yelled and the bucks whistled and cheered loudly. They lined the camp on both sides.

"My people are happy to have the Wild One return. They welcome you." He rode tall and proud among his people and at this moment he knew he had won. She was back with the Pawnees. When Janie realized they were cheering for her instead of Warbo, she felt a tight lump in her throat. She looked at their faces and they were indeed jubilant at her return. When Little Dove extended her hand to her and said, "It is good, you have come home," Janie could only see her blurred image through the tears forming in her eyes.

Warbo dismounted quickly and lifted her from the pony. Broken Lance took the pony and put it with the horses tethered close by. Warbo and Janie stood before the lodge. Janie hesitated not knowing which direction to move.

Warbo entered his lodge, his heart beating rapidly. Would she follow or must he be disgraced again?

Janie was uncertain of what she should do. She could see the tepee of Little Dove close by. It had been her home. She could feel the eyes of the Pawnees upon her. I must do the right thing this time. It is important to Warbo. I owe him that much. He had saved her from those evil-looking Indians. Then she remembered the words he had spoken that night on the trail. "I will return you to my people and to my lodge. You will sleep in my bed and you will be my woman." The words were clear and the meaning was plain. For a moment the defiance was there but it died quickly. He had helped her when she needed him. I must go in, she told herself. I must go in.

She stepped slowly to the opening. Her heart felt like it was lodged in her throat as she entered her new home. He stood with his back to her. It had seemed like an eternity before he heard the movement behind him. She stood quietly trying to calm herself and was getting the courage to ask if she had done the right thing. Her answer came when he turned to face her. A pleased smile erased his stern face. He had to admit he was a little surprised, for once she had done him proud without arguing. As his eyes met hers, he could see the defiance was not gone and his confidence faded. Suddenly he was embarrassed. Never had a woman's presence bothered him. He moved to the small fire and poked at it.

Janie thought she saw a look of triumph on his face, and all the happy Pawnees standing out there grinning like a bunch of nit-wits. They weren't happy to have her back. "They were happy because they had won and she had lost. "Must I stay in this stinking tepee with you?" she asked.

No, you can walk down to the tepee of Sharitarish if you want. Some of his hatred for the white man grew in him, and he thought, why should the great chief of the Pawnees be insulted by a white woman? This time it was the Indian that answered her question. "Since you have come to my village, you cause much trouble. You anger your husband, you not make good wife. I should have let Dark Eagle have you. You would be dead by now and my life, be much better."

"Perhaps, we would both be better off. You know I'll never be happy with you. Why didn't you let me return to my people if you hate me so much?

The sound of approaching horses outside stopped his answer. He pushed her aside and opened the flap of his tepee. He could see the chief of the Blackfoot advancing towards his lodge. "It is Sharitarish."

She felt the threat of impending danger at the mere mention of his name. "What does he want?"

Warbo met the man squarely. His eyes were counting the horses that were paired off in twos behind Sharitarish. Eight horses, a few mangy looking duns but several fine-looking mares. "Does Sharitarish wish to council with his brothers?"

The big, mean savage nodded and left the horses to the safety of one of his braves. He followed Warbo into the tepee. The surprise showed on his face at the sight of the Wild One. He had heard that no woman shared the tepee of Warbo. His eyes lit up as they roamed her body. His half decayed teeth showed as he smiled.

When Janie saw them coming into the tepee, she retreated to the far corner. She sat on the edge of the pile of furs. Fear of this man, made her cringe at his sight.

Warbo moved to the back of the lodge and motioned for the man to sit. He took the peace pipe from the wall and began filling it with kinnikinnk. When he finished, he lit it and took long puffs from it. He offered it to his visitor. As he smoked he kept his eyes on Janie.

She kept her eyes fastened to Warbo. When Sharitarish pointed to her and smiled, she realized they were talking about her. Although she had been warned never to interrupt a discussion, she could contain herself no longer. "What does he want?" she demanded.

Sharitarish was speaking and he stopped and stared at her. Warbo didn't even turn to answer. "He trades the Chief of the Pawnees many fine horses for white squaw."

He didn't have to see the look on her face. He could visualize her horror as he heard her gasp. He rose and stepped from the tepee. Janie was afraid he was going to trade and she was on his heels. He walked among the horses and examined them carefully. He was enjoying the terror he was putting her through. At this moment he realized he would have no more problems. The white woman would be gone from his life and he could return to the way life was before.

"Why are you looking at these horses? You can't be thinking of actually trading me to that savage?" Her nerves pulled together in hard twisting knots.

He lifted the hoofs of each pony and then checked the teeth. He seemed pleased and stepped back to survey them. He smiled at Janie. "You not want to share my stinking lodge and you say you not ever be happy with Warbo. You be happy with Sharitarish. He has many wives."

Janie's mind worked quickly. She had to think of a way to stop him. She stepped toward him but he pushed her aside and called to Sharitarish.

The big, ugly Indian stepped from the tepee and Warbo spoke to him and he smiled. He had a very happy look on his face as he took his ponies and left the camp.

"He will return for his woman when the sun rises." He pushed her into the tepee and left the camp.

CHAPTER SEVENTEEN

J anie slumped to the pile of furs. At this moment she knew there was no fear like that she was feeling now. How could he do this to me? A thought whisked through her head. He is not like you Janie. Maybe he is incapable of feeling anything but lust. It seemed incredible to her. Can Indians love? Could he sell her for a few horses? Did they mean that much to him? She knew she had fought him so much, but never did she think about him just trading her to another tribe. The face of Sharitarish looked like an evil monster in the fire. She wanted to run, to hide, anything to get away.

She peeked from the lodge only to see Broken Lance standing nearby. She paced the floor. Escape is impossible this time. Since the camp was moving, only a few articles were left in the lodge. She spied her travel case in the corner with Warbo's things. She opened the case and took out her worn and tattered Bible. The words seemed foreign, it had been so long. Soon her nerves quieted and she suddenly became calm.

I must get a hold of myself. Her mind studied the problem. How I can get Warbo to change his mind, she wondered. He is too cunning for words. She came to the conclusion. I must surrender to him and be his woman or go with Saritarish. Nothing could be worse than lying with that man.

I have until morning to change his mind. I must show him that I can be a good wife. She took the furs and one by one, she shook them until they looked fresh. Warbo had brought clean leaves and the bed had been prepared carefully. Leave it to a man to make sure his bed is arranged to his liking. She mused to herself as she replaced the furs onto the leaves.

She took a small piece of wood from the pile by the door and using it as a broom she cleaned the loose dirt and leaves and put them outside the door. She coughed from the dust she was accumulating and finally threw open the flaps of the tepee. Broken Lance watched from a short distance. Not taking any chances, she smiled to herself.

By now she had acquired a small audience. "Go ahead and watch you stupid savages! They probably thought she was incapable of working. She had seen the more industrious women cleaning their lodges so why should they be shocked to see her doing the same. She spread fresh leaves on the floor of the lodge. She brought one of the backrests from the travois lying beside the tepee and placed it near the fire. His buffalo robe was hung over the back.

She could taste the sweat of her body on her lips as she finished her chores. The sun was sinking slowly and she thought of how long since she had bathed. The long sweaty journey and not once had she bathed. She took the remaining clothes from the bag and there was one dress she had not worn since her capture. It was velvet and dark emerald green. It will be perfect she decided.

She could feel the cool September air as she came from the warm lodge and she knew that winter was upon them. As she started for the river, Broken Lance stopped her. He motioned for her to return to the lodge.

Knowing she would never get by him, she called for Little Dove. When she came from her lodge, Janie explained that she wanted to go to the river and bathe. "Warbo say you not to leave his lodge until he returns. I bring you water. River is very cold."

She is probably right and I just might run into that stinking Blackfoot. She agreed and shivered as she moved about the big tepee she felt the safety it offered. Warbo had become her protector instead of her enemy. She knew now that she must convince Warbo to keep her any cost. What a grim thought.

Little Dove brought the water. She set it in front of the lodge and called to Janie.

Janie took the water and asked her to come in and talk with her.

"Little Dove not allowed in Chief's tepee."

If I could be so lucky, she thought. "Not allowed, you're his wife, same as me? I permit you to enter." She placed the water over the fire and Little Dove came in timidly.

"Wild One is honored to share the tepee of the Chief."

"Pleasures all mine, she mocked. "Only for tonight, I'm afraid."

What do you mean? She asked?" Warbo take your clothes to his lodge."

"He told me he is trading me to Sharitarish for many fine horses and the hunting lands. Do you think he will?"

Little Dove was silent for a moment. She did not want this to happen. With the Wild One gone she would have no chance with Brave Arrow.

"Well, do you? Janie interrupted her train of thought.

"I saw the horses he brought. Warbo has great love for fine horses. You cause husband much trouble."

"I know all that, but do you think he will trade me?" Her voice grew impatient, waiting for an answer.

"If Warbo say he trades you, he trade. He speaks only truth."

Janie's heart hit bottom, she dropped wearily to the pallet. She sat in silence.

Little Dove's voice was soft and she replied, "I do not want you to go. I will speak for you to my husband."

Janie looked at the young girl. She was sincere. "You would do that for me? Why? I have caused you to suffer, too?"

She crossed the tepee and knelt in front of Janie. "You have made much trouble but have also brought great love to my husband. A love he does not feel for me. I can see it in his eyes. I wish for him to be happy. I pray to the Evening star to give you the same love for him."

The tears formed in her eyes and Janie knew she had truly found a friend in the middle of all these savages. Before she realized what she was doing, Janie pulled the Little Dove to her feet and embraced her. "Oh, Little Dove, what I can do. I don't want to be the wife of the Blackfoot monster."

"You must give Warbo the love he needs. It is the only way." She returned the squeeze and then turned away in awkward embarrassment. "I must go now before Warbo returns. You must try, my sister."

She was gone and Janie watched her walk proudly to her lodge. She is a real friend, she thought. She undressed and dipped the worn cloth into the water and wiped the dirt from her body. She found a small bottle of lavender tucked in her bag and put a little dab behind her ears. As she bathed she contemplated the words of Little Dove."You must give him the love he needs. It is the only way." She knew there was no alternative. I will make him want me so bad, he will not trade me. Her body quivered at the thought.

She dressed carefully as she didn't want him to catch her unclothed. He'll come to that soon enough, she mused. The bath refreshed her and gave her renewed energy. She put on the green velvet gown and brushed her hair, letting it hang softly over her shoulder. She no longer looked like a red-haired squaw with her hair braided and deerskin dress. She kept the moccasins as her shoes had long worn out. The dress felt uncomfortable and cold after so long. She wrapped her shawl about her shoulders and sat by the fire, keeping the bible in front of her to stop the trembling hands. Her plan must work if it wasn't too late. She lay on the pallet thinking, I'll try to outsmart that cunning savage with words. They were her only weapon. If that didn't work then she would use her body. Long before she heard him, she knew he was there. He moved quietly into the lodge and stood surveying his lodge.

His eyes took in the neatly arranged room and came to rest on the lovely woman on the pallet. His heart leaped and the blood rushed in his veins. She had changed back to her white people's clothes. It was as though this were the first day she had entered his life. Never had he seen a woman so beautiful. "Why you change tepee?" he said angrily.

Too scared to face him she answered, "I cleaned some of the dirt out and made your lodge more comfortable."

He moved to the fire and rubbed his hands over the flames and then moved to the willow rod backrest. It angered him that she had changed clothes but she took his breath away when he looked at her and a warm glow went through the man. He smiled. Maybe she could change. "Why you not wear the clothes of your people?"

Janie gave him the sweetest smile. "I do not belong to you anymore. I am to be wife of your enemy. I think he will like this better than the deerskin dress. Don't you?"

Jealously already formed in his mind as he pictured them together. "Sharitarish think you beautiful woman. You like him too?"

"I hate him more than I could ever hate anyone. You know he will kill me."

"If you do not make good wife he will kill you." he answered with no remorse.

"If you want me dead, then why don't you kill me yourself" I would rather die here and now then be traded to that savage. Warbo, listen to me. I have suffered much for you and proved I am a brave woman. This I will not do for that monster. I will die when I leave your lodge."

He looked at her for a long moment and he moved his eyes quickly to the fire. She had spoken the truth but his soul longed for peace and tranquility. He thought of the horses and his hunting grounds. She has messed with my mind. I do not know what to think anymore.

"Warbo, I cleaned your lodge, I can be a good wife. Give me another chance."

"It is time for Warbo to eat. Bring supper," he ordered.

Any other time she would have resisted his order, but not tonight. She got up quickly and took the wooden bowls from the parafleche case and left the lodge. Returning shortly, she handed the steaming meat and corn to him. They ate in silence. After a long pause, he finally said. "You like Warbo better than Sharitarish?" His eyes held a sparkle of devilment and he relished his power over her.

"I don't like either one of you," it slipped out. "I mean, you know I like you much more than he." She smiled so sweetly at him and the color rose in his cheeks.

When he finished eating he locked his feet in front of him and pulled the buffalo robe tightly about him to keep him from swaying. This left his arms free and he lit the long pipe and puffed on it for a few minutes. He took a few pieces of fat and threw them on the fire. It sizzled and lit the tepee like a huge lantern.

It made her hair sparkle and her face was radiant in the darkness. Warbo marveled at her beauty.

"Why did you do that?" she asked.

"Makes more light." he said, "Is Wild One ready to make good wife?"

"Oh, yes Warbo, I promise."

"You sleep with your husband tonight and make him very happy man. I not trade you to Blackfoot. If you do not please me then I trade you," he said softly and directly at her as he spoke.

"That's not fair, Warbo. You leave me no choice. If I sleep with you it will be only because I am forced. Not because I want to."

"How you know you won't like to share my bed. Maybe Warbo please white woman. He grinned at her. You not sleep with man before? You change your mind when sun rises."

Janie could feel the redness in her face and she avoided looking at him. "I never said I hadn't slept with a man."

Warbo thought about that for a minute and they sat in silence and Janie could feel her heart thumping. She could tell by the look in his eyes it wouldn't be long now. They had never spoken so deeply of love before and she pushed the excitement feeling aside, thinking it was fear. Maybe he won't have the guts to take me, she prayed.

"You have husband before we capture you?"

"No."

"You sleep with white man and you not married?" He seemed surprised and waited for her answer.

"I was engaged or promised as you say to a man. His name was Carl Downer. A very handsome man and I loved him very much. She paused now as she spoke his name.

"Why he not be with you on wagon?" he interrupted her thought.

"He left for California and I was going to meet him when you savages murdered my friends and drug me to this miserable camp." She spoke with bitterness.

He ignored her remarks and asked, "What is California?' he stuttered trying to say the long word.

"it's a place far from here. A big country with lots of warm weather. He bought a small piece of land and we were going to raise cattle. We were going to get married."

"You sleep with this man and not married. You like to sleep with him, then why not with Warbo?" We married.

Why? Because you are a dirty, stinking Indian." She regretted the words as she spoke them. She waited for his anger to show.

He did not wish to fight. He had other things on his mind. "Warbo is not dirty stinking Indian. He thumped his chest proudly, me clean Indian."

"Well, maybe you're not dirty but you're still an Indian. I don't want to belong to any Indian."

"Better me than Sharitarish." He watched her face and he saw the fear at the mention of his name.

Janie knew by the tone of his voice as he spoke of his enemies' name that she could stir some jealousy. She attacked his manhood. "If you give me to Sharitarish, it will mean that you are a coward.

He dumped the pipe on the ground and pulled her up close to his chest. "I am not coward. I have proved I am strong warrior." Did I not kill Dark Eagle, my own people, for you?" he was mad now and her words stung.

"Strong warrior but not a strong lover. You know you can't make me love you so you are quitting and giving me up. You don't want to admit that you can't force me to care for you. You're not man enough to try and win my love." She was in his face and their lips nearly touched as she yelled at him.

"Because of you, my people have lost their hunting grounds. You must get them back for the good of our people. You go to Sharitarish." His arms grew tighter about her.

"If you are trading me to that monster, then why bother sleeping with me? You can't win, Warbo.

He let go of her and pushed her to the pallet. Prepare yourself Wild One, your husband will be back to claim what is mine. Tomorrow you go to Sharitarish. With that, he left the lodge.

Janie took off the fine garments and pulled on her old flannel gown and crawled under the furs. "Oh Lord, help me to survive this horrible night."

He returned shortly and as the fire dimmed, he added some more wood and slipped out of his long breeches and his fringed shirt, only his loincloth remained. He looked at her on the pallet of furs; his heart was in his throat. He debated a moment. The time he had waited for was here. There could be no more waiting. I must have her and now.

He pulled the furs from her and lay beside her. His hand hovered above her. He trembled. Why was he afraid to touch her? He felt his manhood rise as he felt the warmth of her body and his hand moved on her leg.

She jumped. "Leave me alone, Warbo. Give me the time and I'll give you my body willingly. But not now, please!"

His hand tore at her gown and he pulled her to him. Nothing would stop this passion he felt within him.

Her fingernails lashed out and she could see the faint traces of blood on his cheeks as he caught her hand in his. He held them tightly above her head and pulled the gown up until he could see the soft naked bosom below him. His eyes took in the loveliness of her body. He caressed her nipples and ran his fingers down her smooth soft skin. His manhood was ready and he heard her muffled cry of pain as he forced his body upon her.

She fought and cursed him. "I hate you. I hate you Warbo." She bit her lip to ease the pain as her body trembled beneath him. She prayed it would soon be over. Her throat was dry and she gasped for air between the sharp thrusts that pierced her.

He released all the pent up hatred for this woman and lay panting beside her. His passion was temporarily satisfied, he lay enjoying the ecstasy he felt within him.

She turned her back to him. Nothing she could say would stop the hurt. The tears ran slowly down her cheeks and her throat ached from the lump that wouldn't melt. I'm sorry ,Carl, I've tried so hard she whispered."

Long after the fire died out, he could hear and feel the silent sobs that racked her body. It bothered him, for never in the many long months except when the fever raged in her head had she submitted to tears. He had only slept with Little Dove and his body didn't respond to her as it did with the Wild One. She had never fought his body and he couldn't explain the feeling of loneliness. Even though he had never felt such joy, something wasn't right and he was at a loss to know what he had done wrong.

Her words came back. "Strong warrior, but not a strong lover." Was she right? Could he make her care? Should he give her to his hated enemy? The answer came fast. I want her to respond to me and feel the pleasure he had felt, if only for a moment.

CHAPTER EIGHTEEN

Warbo was gone when Janie stirred from her troubled sleep. The lodge was quiet. The fire had long died. The coals smoldered in the bed of dirt. She sat up and pulled the robe closely about her. He's gone, she thought, as she searched the tepee. Then the chill racked her body and she knew he was not gone. His presence was with her still. She imagined she saw his face in every corner, a triumphant smile of victory engulfing him.

She fell to the pallet sobbing. She covered her face with the robes to block out the heinous monster that loomed above her. His eyes pierced the blackness. The robes reeked his smell and she threw them from her.

She focused on the morning and where Warbo was. The realization came to her that he had gone to trade her to that monster. I must wash his stench from my body she thought as she grabbed a small bar of soap made from the yucca roots and hurried to the river. Twisted Hair watched her from a short distance and then followed her slowly to the edge of the camp. She knew he was behind her but she plunged through the tall grass, oblivious to anything about her.

She unbuttoned the nightdress as she ran. She slipped the moccasins off and the dress fell around them. The cool autumn air stung her small body as she ran from the bush and plunged into the icy water.

"Oh, my God, she realized the water was far too cold for bathing. Should have listened to Little Dove, she thought and she quickly took the soap and scrubbed her body fast.

Twisted Hair stopped short in his tracks when he heard the

splash. He was far enough behind her that he was quite unprepared for what he saw when he entered the clearing. He stood dumbfounded at the lovely young creature bathing before him.

"Get the hell out of here, you ignorant brute," she screamed.

As though he understood, he retreated red-faced to the nearest tree. As he stood there making sure she didn't go the other way, he thought to himself. Now I know why Chief is so determined to keep this white captive and he chuckled to himself.

The water chilled her to the bone and her teeth chattered as she lathered her skin with the soap. She washed her hair quickly because she needed to get out of this water fast. She ducked under the water and rinsed the soap off. She scanned the woods for a glimpse of Twisted Hair and then darted for the seclusion of the bushes. She dressed quickly and then moved into the sun to warm herself.

As she combed the tangles from her hair the silence of the woods surrounded her. Only the trickle of the swirling water broke the stillness of the morning. Hatred mingled with the silence and came to rest in her tortured mind. I hate that big, stupid Indian. I hate him with all my heart. You think you have won, but I'll show you Warbo. I'll make you hate me as I hate you.

Her thoughts came abruptly to an end as Little Dove ran toward her calling, "Come, Wild One. I have been looking for you." She was out of breath from running and she spoke in short gasps.

"I had to wash the stink from my body. What's the matter."

"It is Sharitarish," she panted.

The very mention of his name sent renewed fear through her nerves. Her mind raced. I fought him last night. He told me--Did he trade me, she asked. She was shaking so badly she could hardly get the words out.

"Sharitarish has challenged Warbo to a fight for you and the hunting lands. Our husband has accepted. We must give him strength." She caught her by the hand and pulled her toward the camp, and she found herself running with the young Indian girl.

"Then he didn't trade me to that monster?" she yelled as she ran. Little Dove did not answer. When they reached the edge of the camp, Janie stopped short. The sudden stop jerked Little Dove backward, and she nearly lost her balance. "Where are we going?"

"Warbo prepares for fight. It is wife's duty to tell him how brave he is and give him strength in battle."

"I don't care if he dies or not. I hate him, she said through gritted teeth. Don't you understand?"

Little Dove looked at her as though she couldn't believe her. "You came to this camp and took his love for me away. You cause tribe to lose their hunting lands and now this brave man is fighting for you, for our lands and you don't care?" she yelled back at her.

Janie had never heard her get excited and she felt the seriousness of the moment.

"You go give Warbo the courage he needs or you will belong to Sharitarish? Put your hatred aside and think of someone else besides you. He must not fail in this battle. Do you understand?" She pleaded with her.

Janie followed her to the center of the camp where already the squaws and braves were forming. They encircled Warbo's tepee and sat in silence waiting for him to emerge. Little Dove pushed her towards the lodge. "Go to him and give him strong medicine."

"Why don't you go? You are his wife too." Janie hesitated.

"Wild One has great medicine. You help our Chief."

Janie could see the anxiety in her face. She moved toward the lodge. Never in her life had she felt so inadequate? What should I say or do? She hadn't faced him since he took her in such an unfeeling way. The hatred flared for a moment but died quickly as she scanned the sober faces surrounding the lodge. She felt their need and suddenly knew that their need was also hers. As bad as she hated this Indian, she knew she would be far worse off if he didn't win this fight.

He stood at the back of the lodge when she entered. He smeared the war paint upon his chest and face. As he turned to her she gasped at the fierceness of this man. The day of her capture flashed rapidly before her. She had not seen his face in war paint since that day and she covered her mouth with her hands to muffle the scream within her.

His face colored and he averted his eyes. The sound of the drums broke the stillness of the day. He pulled the shirt from him and dipped his fingers into the paint. He used red, green, and white to form jagged lines on his torso. A white buffalo he drew on one arm. Finally, he spoke. "What you want?"

"I have come to give you strength but I don't know what to do. How do I give you strength?"

He looked up at her. "Do you want Warbo to win fight with enemy?"

"Of course I do, she said as she moved toward him. I told you I hate him."

"Wild One say you hate your husband." He spoke softly and she could see his need of her. She sensed the seriousness of the moment and it hit full force. She went close to him and spoke directly to him. "I will not lie to you, there is no time. I do not love you and I wish to be free but I do need you."

His eyes met hers, as she spoke. "You say you need me? Why? You don't want me in your bed or your arms."

"I could not live with Saritarish. I want to live with you and maybe someday we will come to understand each other. But more important is your people. They are depending on you and you will not let them down. I am very sorry that I have caused this battle. But I have seen you battle Dark Eagle and I have faith in your ability as a brave warrior. You will win, Warbo", she said with as much conviction that she could muster.

"And if I don't win?"

"Then you will die and I would wish to die."

"You fought my body, you do not care and you do not love me. Why you wish to die if I die? I do not understand.

Janie was silent for a moment and then she remembered his kindness. "You have been good to me many times. You saved my life when I was captured and again when I escaped. You have been mean but only to save face, Sharitarish would not be so kind. He is not like you. I would rather die than be his woman."

"You mean that, Janie?"

"Yes, I truly do, husband."

He turned and went to the flap of the lodge and called for Brave Arrow. He entered and when he spoke to Warbo, his eyes jumped to Janie in surprise and disbelief.

"If Warbo lose fight to Sharitarish, you will have your wish. You will die too. Brave Arrow will stand with you at the fight. If I fall to the Blackfoot, he will put his knife in your heart before Sharitarish can claim you."

He looked at Warbo and said, "She is brave woman. I do not want to kill her."

"Is it the wish of the Wild One?' Warbo asked.

"Yes, it is my wish", she said in a whisper. She took Brave Arrows hand and shook it and nodded that it was what she wanted. She turned to Warbo and pulled him close and embraced him. "You must win Warbo, for us."

Warbo spoke to Brave Arrow and then to Janie. "If you change your mind and wish to be bride of Sharitarish, hold your hands over your heart. If you wish to die with me, put your hands behind your back. Do you understand?"

Janie nodded and the tears formed in her eyes. The agreement was sealed between them. Brave Arrow left the lodge and the drums told Warbo it was time to go. He stood tall. "You have given me strength, Wild One."

She reached up and pulled his head down to hers and placed a wet kiss on his lips and said, "You will fight for your life and mine and the lands of your people and you will win she said with tears running down her cheeks."

He stepped out of the lodge and entered the circle of braves as the warriors chanted and began their spiritual songs to the Great Tiwara. Buffalo Horn brought his bundle filled with his sacred articles. He spread a white buffalo robe in the center of the circle and upon it he placed the small bundle. From it, he took a necklace of white teeth from an eagle. In a sing-song voice he began a chant to the Great Spirit.

Janie sat next to Warbo, with Little Dove on the other side. She didn't speak but prayed with the other Pawnee people as they bowed their heads in reverence. The teeth of the Eagle were given to their Chief so he would have the power to scratch out the eyes of his enemy. Next Buffalo Horn took a rabbits' foot and held it high above Warbos' head to give him the swiftness of the hare.

Braves with many coups to their name entered the circle and chanted their special rituals. Each in turn wished their Chief much success in his battle. A Foxes' tail appeared next. This to give the cunningness to outwit his foe. A hoof from a small deer was to ensure his footing. The sun was now overhead and the time had come. Buffalo Horn brought the white buffalo robe and wrapped it about his shoulders. He was now prepared for battle.

The tribe moved out slowly behind their chief to watch the great match. As Janie walked beside Warbo, she felt a sense of pride she could not explain. Brave arrow followed close behind, his knife close at his side. Janie felt a deadly cold creeping up her back as the knife caught the rays of the sun. The chills turned to fear as she heard the distinct sound of the Blackfeet drums mingling with those Pawnee.

Warbo felt her eyes upon him. He could see the worry in her face. She held out her hand and he took it proudly. A bond was sealed between them. If he was to meet his death he could ask for no greater honor than to go to the great land in the sky with the Wild One. They would ride the beautiful valleys together.

CHAPTER NINETEEN

The tall autumn grass had been trampled in the circle and rotten limbs from fallen trees formed the boundary. The Blackfoot slowly gathered on one side, the Pawnees on the other. Sharitarish entered the circle. His face was confident and his rotted teeth added to his ugliness. He was painted in the tribes' war paint. Janie had thought Warbo looked fierce but decided nothing could surpass the hideousness of the half-bald Blackfoot. His head was shaved. Only a small amount of hair across the top of his head held the long braid hanging down his back with a white feather tied at the bottom. In his hand, he carried a tomahawk with a long keen blade. Attached to his belt hung a heavy war club or skull cracker. With the shield in his other hand, made from the hide of the buffalo, and the figure of a white buffalo painted on the shield, he looked to be a formidable opponent.

Warbo removed the heavy robe and entered the circle only wearing a knife at his belt. Sharitarish was not as tall as Warbo but he carried a lot more weight and his arms were long and stout. The drums stopped and the two men spoke. Sharitarish grinned and feasted his eyes on Janie. He removed the knife and war club from his belt. He entered the circle with only his shield and lance.

Twisted Hair brought Warbos' shield and his long thin lance. It looked smaller than that of his opponent. Tension invaded her stomach and spread like fire throughout her.

"Why are they just using shields and lances?" she asked Little Dove.

"Sharitarish challenged Warbo, so he picks the weapons. They must depend on the strength of their shield and how fast they can move.

The two Indians stood with their backs to each other and paced twenty to thirty feet apart. They turned and faced each other. Janie's heart leaped as Sharitarish sent his lance flying through the air at Warbo. He side-stepped quickly and the lance plunged into the dirt less than a foot away. Now it was Warbos' turn and with all his strength he sent the lance hurdling toward his deadly foe. But Sharitarish, too, was quick on his feet. He smiled and waited for the brave to retrieve his lance.

Warbo looked at Janie and she gave him a big smile of encouragement. He motioned to Brave Arrow to knell beside her. The lance came again and Warbos' eyes were upon it. He took a few running steps backward and it imbedded itself between his feet a few steps away. Janie breathed a sigh of relief.

The chief of the Blackfeet was not being outdone. He tried the same maneuver when the lance was cast upon him. He was not quick enough as the thinner lance was much swifter than his. His shield bore the brunt of the impact and he lost his balance and fell to the ground. The Pawnees yelled their support and their faces were laced with excitement.

The lances were staked into the ground and the next weapon was chosen. The war club came next and the two marked their paces. The Pawnee War club was made like a gun-stock. It carried a sizeable stone held tightly with rawhide tongs. The Blackfoot club had a long handle and a slightly larger stone.

The two Indians with the war clubs lashed out at each other. The shields taking the blows. This would depend on strength as well as speed. Each sent the club toward the midriff of the other as hard as he could. The loud crashing of the skull-crackers shattered the stillness of the day. It sounded like two buffalo fighting in the forest. The men grew weary and the blows came slower. Sharitarish made a deep cut as though he were aiming for the legs of his opponent, then with the swiftness of a deer; he brought the club up and under the shield of Warbo. The shield jerked upwards and out of Warbo's hand.

"What a barbaric fight Janie thought as she closed her eyes, unable to look. The cheers of the Blackfoot now rang through the meadow. The War Club match was over and the two fighters moved to their side and sat down. Twisted Hair brought water and poured in on Warbo. It ran down his face and smeared the paint until it looked like a blur of red, green, and white. He drank from the water pouch. He rinsed his mouth and spit, and then took long gulps of water.

"How long does this insane match go on?" Janie cried out.

"We will use the tomahawk next and whoever wins declares the last weapon to the death." Before he returned to the circle, he placed his hand upon her shoulder. "You will not belong to Sharitarish. Brave Arrow is ready if I fail. Are you ready? Janie."

"It is good, Warbo. My husband will not fail."

The word husband renewed his strength as she had never referred to him as her husband but only her captor. Once again the battle was renewed in all its fierceness. Sharitarishs confidence was with him again and he fought well. There were no shields and nothing to protect their bodies. They swung and ducked and each time, Janie saw the blade swing close to Warbo, she closed her eyes and waited for the final blow.

The tomahawks locked in the air. Sharitarish brought his down hard and Janie heard the muffled groan of Warbo as it tore at his flesh. She saw the blood splatter and she felt sick. He stepped back swiftly and changed the tomahawk to his other hand. This pleased his opponent as he knew Warbo had less strength in his left hand.

He closed in as Warbo guarded his head. The tomahawks met head-on and Sharitarish used both hands to push against the strong Indian. It was a test of strength and the blood came profusely now from the wound of Warbo's hand. Even with the blood flowing, Warbo managed to take the big Indian to the ground. It was a tie. One round Warbo, one round Sharitarish.

Janie rushed to him and led him from the circle. She poured water over the wound. She tore a strip of cloth from her petticoat and wrapped it tightly around his wrist. The bleeding showed through the cloth but it slowed steadily as she applied pressure to his upper arm. She put a tourniquet around his arm just above the elbow.

"Not cut there, why you do that?" he asked and his face contorted with the pain.

"Trust me, Warbo. It is the white man's medicine. Good medicine. It will stop the flow of blood."

For some reason, he felt assured and his eyes widened at the slow trickle of blood. It had stopped for the moment. He spoke to Twisted Hair and then took the long shiny knife from its holder. He touched her hair and moved it slowly down her dress. She shivered. He reassured her. "To give me strength."

Janie did not think that she possessed any miracle powers, but if he believed, so be it. She thought she could stand no more. It seemed like hours since the two angry men and begun their battle. She knew this would be the last round and she trembled. This round decides if we live or die. She added another prayer, just let it be over.

Clouds formed heavy and foreboding in the blackened sky. A cold wind settled across the meadow but Janie didn't feel its bitterness. In the excitement, she could feel only the heat of the fight. Sweat poured from Warbo's body. His muscles stood out taut and drawn. The children were cold but no one moved. They focused their attention on the two braves who stood so proudly waiting for death. Janie looked at the earnest young faces. The young boys soon to become warriors watched eagerly and admiration was written upon their smooth and inexperienced countenances. For the first time, Janie felt the guilt of what she had done. She was now sharing their problems, and ones caused by her acts of selfishness. She found herself praying for the tribe and for her life and her husband.

Warbo watched her for a moment and then he met his adversary to begin the next bout. It was time to put his plan in action. He looked at his enemy and he could tell that he too was tired and losing much strength.

Sharitarish said, barely able to talk, "I will take your woman this night."

"You win one match, and I won one match. It is tied. There will be no more fighting. It is done." Warbo told him, If you kill me then Brave Arrow kill Wild One, you will never have my woman, he said.

"Look around at your people. They need you as mine need me. Fighting is not good. When your warriors were watching us fight, my braves stand behind yours, ready to strike the moment I fall. My best trained brave on bow will take you down. We both die. Your people will have no chief as will mine."

"See the Wild One. If she puts her hands behind her back she chooses to die with me. Brave Arrow will plunge his knife into her heart."

As Sharitarish looked at Janie, she put her hands behind her back and nodded to Brave Arrow. He took his knife from the sheath and held it to her heart. He was concentrating on Warbo waiting for the signal. He sent a prayer to the Great Spirit to stop this now. I don't want to hurt Warbo's woman.

Sharitarish surveyed the crowd and he saw behind his warriors were the Pawnee Warriors ready to strike. This was not going as he planned. The realization that he was outsmarted by his enemy brought great pain to his head. He stood there for a moment thinking about what Warbo had said.

"What do I tell my people? The fight is equal and now we stop. We will never know who best warrior is."

"Tell them, Wild One is not worth fighting for. Many will die. Let us go in peace with our neighbors."

To Warbo's surprise, Sharitarish did exactly that. His people as well as the Pawnees raised their voices cheering the decision. Sharitarish turned to Warbo, extended his hand, and said, "You are wise leader" and walked slowly from the circle. Sharitarish mind was stunned, as he took the fine buffalo robe he had worn and took it to Warbo. He accepted it and accepted it and the fight was over.

Janie could see the pain burning in his eyes as she ran to him. The blood spurted from the deep cut on his wrist as they made their way back across the meadow. She could hear the low chanting of thanksgiving to the Great Spirit spreading across the valley.

When they came into their camp, the people cheered and the loud guttural yell of victory was heard from the warriors as he passed. The cry sent chills up her spine.

When they entered his lodge, Janie immediately took charge. "Little Dove, heat water and, bring it to me. Warbo sat down on the pallet and his body relaxed for the first time that day. She took the bloody tourniquet off and cleaned the wound. It was still bleeding as the cut was deep. She replaced the tourniquet and the bleeding was slowed. It still needed stitches she thought. She went in search of her medical bag and cleaned the needle that she was going to use. Buffalo Horn was moving about the tepee, chanting softly to the Great Spirit for strength of healing. When he saw the Wild One hold the needle up to thread it, he only stopped for a moment. He remembered the first time his chief was hurt with much larger wound and she had sewed him up then. We must trust this strange white woman he thought.

She threaded the needle and held it up to Warbo. "Do you remember when I sewed your body after fight with Dark Eagle? It saved your life then and it will save you now." She couldn't remember if he was awake at that time so she tried to reassure him once more. "Warbo, this is white man's medicine. It is good. I need to close the wound on your arm. It is deep and you are losing a lot of blood."

She took some water and bathed his brow. Warbo's eyes fluttered. He smiled faintly. It was good medicine just having her here. "Warbo can trust you now Wild One?"

"You know you can trust me, I was ready to die with you, now just be quiet and let me fix your body," she spoke sternly to him. She held the needle over the fire until it glowed in the dim light of the tepee. She cooled it and cleaned the wound again to see where to start. "This will hurt, Warbo. Are you ready?" He nodded.

Janie gritted her teeth and dipped the needle carefully into his skin. His body jerked, but no sound came from his lips. She pulled the thread through and tied it securely. With each stab of the needle Warbo winced and the sweat dripped from his brow. She could tell that he was in deep pain.

Little Dove patted the blood and rinsed the rag and sponged his brow. He smiled a small grin and said, "Don't enjoy this too much, Wild One."

She finished her grizzly task and looked at him and said, "It is finished. We need to keep the wound clean and free from dirt so you don't get an infection."

"What is infection" he asked.

"If your wound gets dirty, then your body will get sick. A high fever will set in. The cut is not that deep and you should be a little sore but not bad like the last wound. I am afraid that you will live, Warbo." she said.

He did not catch the humor in that last statement and he frowned at her. "You don't want husband to live?" he asked.

She realized he didn't understand her and she gave him a big smile, leaned over him, and pressed her lips to his cheek. "I was teasing you. You understand?"

He looked up at Little Dove and his eyes were wondering if she understood the actions of this wife. She looked as confused as Warbo. "If Wild One is finished, I will go to my lodge." She slipped quickly from the lodge.

Warbo caught her to him with his good arm and groaned as the pain shot through his other. Lay with me for a while. It is good to feel your body next to me. We rest.

Janie was so tired and relieved that the ordeal of the day was gone and Warbo had saved her life as well. I can't believe that I have saved this miserable man twice. He is a great warrior and leader. He had formed a good plan, carried it through, and saved their lives. She lay beside him and soon she could feel his deep breathing and she drifted to sleep thinking that if not for his brilliant plan she would be the slave of that horrible Blackfoot. Looking at Warbo, she thought, this is no dumb Indian.

CHAPTER TWENTY

When Janie awoke her concern was evident. Warbo was not moving and he lay stiff and still beside her. She panicked and put her hand to his brow. It was cold and her heart pounded as she grabbed his wrist and then as a last resort she laid her ear to his bare chest. His good arm pressed against her back. "Your husband lives" he grinned as she looked up at his face.

She jumped at his words and anger replaced the concern in her eyes. "You're a devil, Warbo. You scared me half out of my wits." She tried to hide the happiness she felt but he could see she was glad to see him.

"I was just enjoying you sleeping so close," he said.

Janie practically jumped out of bed as she heard those words and hurried around getting dressed. "Are you hungry?" she asked. She couldn't recall when last she had eaten and her stomach was letting her know.

"I am hungry too," he said as he started to get up. He put pressure on his bad arm and groaned and fell back to the pallet.

Janie offered her hand to help him up. "Use only your good arm for now. The other is weak from combat," she said showing concern.

Using his good arm, he rolled over and pushed himself up-on his knees and stood before her. He looked down at his arm and could see the many bandages going up and down his arm. "Is the injury very bad?"

"The cut was long and deep. The loss of blood was worse than the cut. You must keep it level and not let it hang by your side."

"Why?"

"When you leave your arm hanging down, the blood runs down

your arm and makes it worse. I will make you a sling to keep it level so you won't have to hold it up."

"Wild One is wise woman. You make good wife someday." He said, smiling.

"What do you mean, someday, I am good wife now, she said in defense.

"Good wife, bring food" he pushed her gently to the door.

"I'll get you some food and I might drop a little poison in it while I'm at it, she said, laughing as she exited the tepee. When she stepped from the lodge, she was surprised at gifts lying beside the entry. Food, beads, and blankets some arrows for their leader.

Days before she would have thrown the gifts in their faces. But today nothing could explain her feeling. Janie smiled for the first time in days and for the life of her, she couldn't understand why she was so happy.

Little Dove had the food ready and inquired about the health of their chief. Janie assured her that Warbo was fine and told her she was welcome to visit him anytime.

They ate meager portions while traveling and she filled up on some of the dried jerky the people had dropped off. Warbo finished his meal and started to put on a shirt. Janie stopped him.

I must check the wound before you dress. He put the shirt down and put his arm up for her inspection. She removed the bandage carefully and surveyed the wound for any red marks going up to his arm. She could tell he was having a hard time holding up the arm and she raised it to her shoulder. As she worked on his arm, he studied her intensely. He made her nervous and her face turned as red as her hair as she looked into his face. She kept her eyes on the wound and satisfied that he was healing, she bandaged his arm again. He picked up his shirt and tried to wrestle himself into it. Janie could see her was struggling to get it on.

"Kneel and I will help you put on your shirt."

He dropped to his knees as she took the shirt and held it above his head. "Hold both arms up." He obeyed and she slipped the shirt down with little difficulty. She picked out another of his shirts and placed the wounded arm into the end of the sleeve and wrapping the other arm around his head; she tied the two sleeves together forming a sling. "How does that feel?" she asked.

"Better, arm not so heavy. You good nurse, I keep you," he said and Janie thought for a moment she saw him wink.

"I could be so lucky," she answered.

He ignored her and left the lodge. The morning air felt good and he decided that he was able to travel. He went to Little Dove's lodge and called her name. She came quickly and stepped out. She was surprised to see him up and about so soon after his injury and said,

"How are you feeling?"

"Will you tell the tribe that we are ready to travel? Much delay and we must get on to our hunting lands."

"I am glad that you are doing so well. Wild One makes good medicine," She added. "I will have the horses brought to load the tepees."

"Bring horse for Wild One. She rides with me." Knowing Janie had helped him to live didn't lessen the memory of her escape. He had learned in the last few weeks that white women could not be trusted and the Wild One was certainly proof of that. He knew that he would never know what she was thinking or planning and this new challenge added a zest to his life that he met with the keenness and cunning of his race.

Janie knew she was no longer dealing with a stupid savage and inwardly she cursed him for his ability to outsmart her. After the camp was once more loaded on the travois, the tribe moved out.

They rode ahead and with each hill fading into the distance, Janie felt her contact with her people becoming more remote. She found the trip a welcome change after the long hot summer months of tending the crops. Janie pushed the memory of Warbo and his lovemaking to the back of her mind and prayed it wouldn't happen again for a long time.

As she watched the squaws making their way up the dusty trail with their babies on their backs, she shuttered. The fear that she might be pregnant shook her. It hasn't happened to Little Dove so maybe it was his fault. Little Dove would be ecstatic if she were pregnant but the heartaches it would bring to herself was more than she cared to think about.

She stopped the horse abruptly. Warbo was on guard for any possible trick she might try. I would like to let Little Dove ride for a while beside her husband."

He thought for a moment and then rode down the long row of moving Indians until he spotted Little Dove. Janie dismounted and motioned for Little Dove to ride.

"I do not need to ride," she said.

"I want you to ride. I would like to walk for a while. She handed the short rope to her and smiled.

Little Dove mounted quickly and moved to the edge of the group. Warbo didn't ride beside her as he had with Janie. He moved farther out and kept in range of his errant wife. After a lunch of Pemmican and a short rest they moved out again. Janie watched as Warbo kept pace with her. He never glanced her way but Janie knew he was watching. The mischief played on her lips and she decided to shake him up a bit. She moved beside the horse and travois and then quickly stepped ahead to the next pony. Soon she was several ponies in front of him. She darted in and out among the moving caravan and covered the fiery red hair so he couldn't find her.

Warbo only glanced her way every few minutes and now he found himself scanning the squaws. His pace quickened as he moved nearer the group. He didn't want to draw attention to himself so he rode searching the group.

Janie had graciously offered to carry a squaw's papoose. She walked with a stoop, the infant on her back. The squaw grinned, relieved of her burden for awhile. She felt it was a great honor for this brave woman to carry her baby.

Warbo rode right past her and Janie chuckled to herself. The baby grew heavy but Janie wouldn't have given him up for anything. She enjoyed every moment of anxiety she was putting him through. For some reason I feel my best when I'm tormenting that cunning savage, she thought.

Warbo moved his spotted pony from side to side and kept his composure. No one guessed what was going on until Little Dove decided it was Janie's turn to ride. She looked for her also and then to Warbo. Something told her Janie wasn't where she was supposed to be. She found herself studying the women. It didn't take long to spot the moccasins she had helped make for the Wild One. She laughed to herself at Janie carrying a child.

Since she was doing no harm, Little Dove wouldn't betray her for anything. She rode a little way ahead of her and smiled at the bent figure of the mischievous white woman.

When Janie felt the aching in her back and legs grew tired, she waited for Warbo to pass her way again. He had ridden the length of the tribe on both sides and now he came toward Little Dove. As he neared, Janie gave the baby back to his mother and then called to Little Dove.

"Hey, Little Dove, how about a ride?"

She pulled up and dismounted. As she handed the pony to Janie she smiled. "The clothes of the Pawnee might not be good idea for the Wild One."

"Thanks for not giving me away," she said.

Warbo stopped in his tracks. He watched her take the papoose from her shoulder. I do believe that she has outwitted me again and he chuckled to himself.

She tried to mount but hadn't yet mastered the technique of getting on by herself. She turned to Little Dove for a boost but she had already joined her Mother and sister. She led the pony to Warbo and smiled sweetly.

"Hi, Chief, where you been? I've been looking all over for you." she giggled.

Warbo failed to see the humor of her actions. He had spent hours riding up and down looking for her.

As she looked at Warbo, she saw his arm in the sling and realized he couldn't help her mount. "I was going to ask for a boost but not with one hand. Or are you mad?" She pursed her lips into a pout.

She looked so lovely standing there pouting and laughing at the same time that he couldn't help but smile. "I see you have done it again, Wild One." He dismounted and with his good arm he swung her up on the pony. As he did he swatted her firmly on the butt. It stung through the deerskin and she jumped. She glared at him then he laughed. "Now is the Wild One mad?"

Janie giggled, "You rode past me so many times, I thought you would hear me laughing."

"I wasn't looking for a squaw with a papoose and I couldn't see the hair of fire." He mounted his pony and positioning his arm he said, "Come Wild One, we go." He pushed his pony and Janie followed in close pursuit.

They moved away from the Indians and climbed a small hill. He was well in front but this time he made sure she followed. It was a beautiful scene. The Indians were moving toward the water hole in the late evening. The sky was aflame with its different hues of pink and lavender and deep purple hiding the golden rays of the sinking sun.

"There lies the hunting lands of my people, where we shall hunt and prepare our winter food.

"And where may I ask are the hunting land of my people? She asked.

She wasn't joking now and Warbo studied her question. Finally. he spoke. "Many moons ride, Wild One."

"Will, I ever see them again?"

"If it is on my power, you shall not look upon a white man's face ever again." He spoke bitterly and with hatred for the whites in his voice.

"When I escaped, why didn't I get to the fort? Is it so many miles away?"

Warbo picked up a few rocks and sent them whizzing through the air until he felt the pain in his injured arm and stopped. You could hear them drop to the valley below. His good humor was returning and he chuckled softly.

"Why are you laughing?" She grabbed his good arm and shouted at him. "Why didn't I get to the fort? Tell me?

He held her at arm' length and said, "Because my little wild one, you were going in the wrong direction," He laughed and the hills echoed his amusement.

She stood there looking at him and listening to him laugh. When he realized she wasn't laughing he stopped. She spoke softly. "It isn't funny, Warbo. I tried so hard."

He let go of her and could find no words to comfort her.

"If the white man captured you, you would have done the same thing, wouldn't you?"

He couldn't stand the pleading in her voice. She grabbed his arm again and shook it. He turned to face her and tried to lift both hands but the one stayed locked in the sleeve. With the other hand he pinched her shoulder. "I will never let you go, Wild One."

Janie pulled away from him and retorted. "And I will never come to you willingly." He pushed her away and went to bring the ponies.

CHAPTER TWENTY-ONE

Warbo led his Pawnees into the buffalo country. It lay lush with tall grass now turning brown with the approaching winter. The air was crisp and sharp as they assembled their lodges for a temporary camp. Janie watched in amazement as the little village sprang up in a few short hours. When the lodges were made ready, Warbo came and told her that she was to join him in his search for buffalo.

She agreed willingly as life in the camp became boring to her and it would give her a chance to study the country. The braves were surprised to see her ride out with them. Squaws weren't allowed on scouting parties. Janie could see Warbos' face color at the grinning faces. He spoke gruffly to them in Pawnee. Their faces sobered for a moment and then they took out at a high gallop with a loud war-whoop piercing the air.

Janie smiled to herself. There isn't one of those stupid savages who wouldn't give his best buffalo robe to ride with me, she thought. They moved out behind the others through the morning dew. Frost covered the tall grass that swayed in silvery waves with the brisk autumn wind.

Janie found the pace that Warbo set a most exhausting one but she refused to show any weakness. She was fast learning to be a good horsewoman. After three days on a pony, her legs were becoming accustomed to straddling the big brown mangy dun.

"Buffalo can smell for many miles. They can hear the smallest noise." Warbo cautioned.

"Thank you for bringing me with you," she said.

"I bring you so you not escape," was all he said.

Fury raged in her and she stuck her tongue out at him with a dirty face.

He said nothing as he kept his eyes on the herd below. He motioned for her to follow him and he took the horses and went down-range of the buffalo. During the next several days she watched as they brought logs from fallen trees and covered them with mounds of dirt. They packed the earth around the logs until they were camouflaged so well that it looked like a true wonder of nature.

Janie found herself thinking about Carl and wondered if he were building a corral for his cattle. It made her sad to think of Carl and his sweet love. I wonder if he has given up hope for me. If he could just see me now, helping a bunch of savages build a corral for buffalo.

It came to her. What if he could see me now? What would he think? Would he think I was a willing victim? Would he ever believe how hard I fought to save myself for him? Can he accept me after all I've been through? Fear built in her mind and the determination to survive in this Indian camp and resist the advances of her husband became her priority.

Morning came and the squaws were placed in the trees far from the corral. Warbo left her with Little Dove and said, "there are no horses around so do not try and escape. You not ride with me today. I ride with my braves to get much meat for winter."

"Don't worry, Warbo, your little prisoner will be here when you return, if the buffalo don't run over you first." She glared at him. One day I work with the brute and the next day I hate him.

There was a long period of silence in the hills. Only the chirping of the birds in the timber broke the stillness. Janie felt the coming of the buffalo long before she saw them. Hugh animals with shaggy manes thundered down the valley toward the enclosure. The earth trembled and it felt like an earthquake was splitting the country apart. The braves yelled and frightened the already terrified beasts into a frenzy of confusion. They were trapped in the enclosure and many fell to the arrows and long lances of the braves. Warbo and Buffalo Horn donned their buffalo robes and concealed themselves among the herd. Their lances found their mark and one by one the buffalo fell to their death.

Janie found herself yelling with the rest of the squaws and her heart raced each time Warbo moved among the herd. The women moved down the hill and started working on the huge carcasses on the ground. She helped Little Dove until she saw the squaws eating the raw meat and the warm blood running from their lips. Her stomach did a flip flop and she was sick. She sought the seclusion of the trees. They cut the meat into quarters to be loaded onto the travois along with the skins and taken back to camp.

During the next few days, the camp was a beehive of women working to preserve the meat for winter. Little Dove showed Janie how to pound the meat and fat along with berries they had picked, into a pulp. This was known as pemmican and stored in the rawhide bags called parfleches.

When at last the meat was ready the tribe was once again on the move. They traveled several days and Warbo selected the land for the winter camp. A beautiful spot set in the timber at the foot of the mountains. A mountain stream ran close by.

While Warbo was helping the braves set up the lodges for Little Dove and Running Deer Janie decided if this was to be her home for the winter she might as well make it as comfortable as possible. She took a large scraper they had used to work the buffalo hides and scraped the tough grass and rock from the ground. She used a rawhide rag to wipe the ground clean of the slightest pebble. She brought dried leaves so no moisture would be in the lodge and spread a soft carpet. Next, she placed the skins on the floor overlapping for warmth. The skins were those of rabbit, beaver, badgers and a few foxes added color to the gray skins. She arranged the woodpile on the south wall near the door. The willow rod backrests were placed on each side of the fire. Warbo's bow and weapons were stored on the north wall, so they would always be ready at his slightest need. The quiver and arrows she hung from the backrest so he could sharpen them at his leisure. The beautifully decorated pillows, she put near the fire to be used as backrests. The worn medicine bag containing her bible and her small bag still holding the faded and worn dresses that linked her with her people were placed on the south side. She made two separate beds, knowing she might regret it. She was strong again today and ready for a new confrontation with him.

Warbo's shield and his sacred religious objects held the place of honor at the rear of the lodge. She put the buffalo robes across the nose of the tripod and let it cover the back-rest. His riding gear was stored north of the door. As Janie reached for the last bundle she felt chills racing up her back, as the coups, Warbo had collected fell to the floor. She hesitated for a moment and despised him and his people for their savage ways. Slowly she kicked them back into the bundle and put them with his special ceremonial regalia.

She built the fire and sat for a moment resting after her long hours of work. The lodge looked quite comfortable and she was proud of the work she had accomplished.

As she studied the lining of the lodge she decided Warbo was a good artist. There was no mistaking the spotted pony or the elaborate headdress he wore. His brave deeds in battle were depicted clearly for all to see. Lively figures in thin delicate lines were painted in a colorful array on the animal skins bleached white from the sun. The cultivated areas were done in rich colors. Brown and green and blue separated the sky, earth, and trees. One wall was left untouched and it suddenly came to mind that it probably wouldn't be too long before he thought of some wonderful thing he had done to brag about.

Throughout the day the braves built a wall of brush packed with mud about ten to twelve feet around the lodges. Warbo braced the lodge with forked branches of Aspen. Great precaution was taken in preparing the lodges for winter. As many as twenty skins were used to cover the entire lodge for warmth as well as protection for the Pawnees. The lining prevented drafts and dampness and kept rain from dripping off the poles. It increased ventilation.

It was late when he finally summoned his courage to enter the lodge. He was amazed at her knowledge and assumed Little Dove had arranged the furnishings. Yet something was different. Never had his lodge felt so warm and inviting. The floor was of soft skins and he could feel nothing of the cold hard ground that lay beneath.

He sat in the willow rod backrest and looked around. He said nothing. When his eyes rested on the two separate pallets his pulse raced madly but he said nothing. The courage didn't-come.

"Do you like your lodge? Did I not do a wonderful job?"

Surprise filled his face. "Wild One do this?"

"Who do you think done it?'

"How you know where to put weapons?" he asked

"I'm not dumb. I've been living in your lodge for a long time."

Warbo made sure every part of the lodge was lined. He checked the work and then nodded his approval. "Quondam not sneak up on Warbo. My lodge is warm and safe."

"Quondam, what is that?"Janie asked.

"Quondam means enemy in Pawnee," her replied.

"You mean like Sharitarish? He is the enemy."

"Sharitarish would not sneak into Pawnee camp. He brave warrior. He fight face to face. Delaware tribe our enemy. They are mean quondam. If they sneak into our village at night and our lodge is not lined, they could see my shadow and know at what part of tepee I am sitting. Lining keeps from casting shadows from fire to outer wall."

"Do they try to kill the Pawnees very often?" she asked.

"Not kill women and children. They want to steal our horses and gather coups."

"Coups, you mean scalps?"

He grunted.

"Scalps," she said, "it is a barbaric tradition. I saw Dr. Crowders and Maria's but I never saw Russ's." The bitterness came quickly to her voice when she spoke of them.

He looked at her strangely. "Who is Russ?" he asked.

"Russ was our scout. You mean you don't even remember killing him, her voice trailed off. She looked at Warbo waiting for an answer. He deliberately turned his eyes from her. She grabbed him and looked up at him. "You didn't kill him, did you? He got away! I've wondered but I never knew for sure and I checked the horses to make sure his was not there. Hope grew in her heart. She dropped to her knees and for a moment her illusions told her that he would not forget her.

As though he read her thoughts he spoke, "It makes no difference, Wild One. If he not stay and try to save you then. He will not try now."

Janie jumped up, full of hope, but he'll tell the officers at the fort. And if Carl came looking for me, he'll know. I'm Carl's woman, not yours, he won't let me down." She poured out her hopes and thinking he would understand.

Warbo shook her roughly. Anger was in his eyes as he spoke. "You are no longer white man's woman, you are Warbo's woman. No white man or any officers from the fort can take you from me." He walked to the backrest and seating himself, he pulled the robe about him. Bring supper, he ordered.

Janie moved to the small campfire and brought out the beans and pemmican that she had cooked for her unwanted husband and handed it to him. They ate in silence and Janie was thankful for their days of travel as well as the many nights on the trail with no privacy. He had been preoccupied with getting the winter hunting done and finding the new camp for winter and with no shelter he had not bothered her. Now the time had come when he would once again force himself upon her.

As Warbo ate his supper he glanced her way and he thought about how hopeful she was when she found out the scout lived. Surely the white men knew she was taken alive as her body had not been left with the others. Would they try and rescue her? He knew if it had been his woman like Janie, nothing would keep him from trying to find her and take her from any man who held her. He thought of the young white man losing her and he felt some of his hatred for the man melt.

Warbo thought of the first time he saw her coming from the river. Her naked body, a firm reminder of why he fought for her and protected her from the start. He remembered how he tried so hard to hate her. Where had his strength gone? I vowed I would not fight for her, but I did. I vowed again I would not touch her but I did. Should I force myself on her tonight? Sweat built on his forehead and he knew it wasn't from his labor. Why was it harder to make love to this woman than to ride into battle against the enemy? It is an even bigger battle with her and a losing one, he thought. And what of her hatred? It hadn't changed. He could tell by the look of hope in her eyes when she found out that they had missed the guide and he had lived to tell of her capture.

Janie took the bowl from him and went to clean up the evening meal. She left the lodge to seek the shelter of the pines and relieve her body for the night. "It was so very cold out tonight," she said as she entered the lodge.

Warbo smiled and said, "Come let me warm you, Wild One."

"I would like to get ready for bed. Would you mind leaving while I change?"

"This is Warbo's lodge. I will not leave."

"It's too damn cold to undress outside," she said angrily.

He smiled. "Then undress. I watch. Warbo see your body many times." He grew bolder as they argued.

"You miserable, disagreeable savage!" she shouted.

He was on his feet and covered her mouth with his hand. He was grateful that so few of his tribe spoke English as her voice could be heard for quite away. "Wild One not disgrace her husband. Now undress."

She undressed with her back to him and left on her under-clothes. She slipped beneath her furs without a word.

Warbo took off his leggings and shirt. With only the breechcloth about him, he came to her pallet. He did not touch her but looked at her lovely face. He stroked her hair and prayed that she would not resist him.

"This is my bed. Go get in your own," she said.

He pulled the robes from her. "My bed is your bed Wild One. Are you going to fight me?"

"I will fight you as long as there is breath left in my body." She reached for the robes.

He threw the robes off the pallet pulled the other pallet next to hers. He unleashed all the ferocity and hatred within him with each stroke of his body, showing her he was the one in charge. When he was totally spent, he rolled onto his pallet and cursed the Wild One for her stubbornness.

Janie sobbed quietly thinking, they will come for me, I know they will.

CHAPTER TWENTY-TWO

Winter came to Pawnee country. The soft white snow carpeted the hills and valleys and frostbit the remaining leaves. The heart of the Wild One froze with the flowers and her capacity for love died. Her hatred and bitterness were in full bloom. Until now she had tolerated her plight, but now she lived on the hope of spring and her rescue by Carl and the soldiers.

Tears came no more to the Wild One. Bitter laughter replaced her feelings. She cursed him and attacked his manhood. She told him the white man was a better lover and lay stiff and cold each time he was beside her. Her pallet lay beside his but only to show that he was indeed the ruler of the lodge.

She laughed and ridiculed him until he knew he could no longer touch her. His pride could take no more. His love became withdrawn and sometimes he felt her hatred slip into his heart and he knew he had lost his fight.

Warbo left the lodge early in the mornings and didn't return until he could withstand the cold no longer. Janie was silent and brooding now and he could see the hatred in her eyes each time she looked at him.

She thought of Morning Star and how she had adapted to the life of the Indian. She must get to know her better, so she went to her lodge and asked to enter. Morning Star was busy sewing beads on a shirt and she welcomed her to the lodge.

Janie said, "I have come to seek your advice. How did you learn to live with the Indians? I am so lonesome for my people and Warbo and I do not speak much anymore. She looked to the old lady for guidance.

Morning Star looked up from her sewing and smiled at her. "It is good for you to come to see me. I can see much sorrow in your eyes as well as my son's. When I was captured I had a small child, a little girl. She was a sickly child and I could not possibly escape with her. It was late in the fall and the tribe moved to this winter place soon after I was taken. Not long after I was married to Warbo's father, and my little girl passed away from breathing problems. I became pregnant and I knew I could never leave my child or enter the white world again. I stopped resisting the ways of the Pawnees and lived for my child. He was the joy of my life. He has become a strong warrior and because I taught him English, he could speak the white man's tongue. He was chosen for chief because of his many abilities and a keen mind. Why do you hate my son so very much? "Is he mean to you?" she asked.

"You know how bad he treated me, how can you ask that?"

"Did you not use your womanly powers to entice him to fight for you? Her eyes held a small twinkle and she smiled at her new daughter.

"Yes, I did only because I thought I could reason with a man that spoke my language."

"Why is he mean to you? What do you do to make him mad?"

Janie thought about that and she was silent for a moment. "I just don't want to sleep with him. I feel nothing but gratitude for him saving me from Dark Eagle and Sharitarish.

"Are you sure it is only gratitude that you feel? Do not deny your feelings, Wild One. You are only fooling yourself."

"I can stand his meanness, I just can't stand his kindness, and she got up quickly and left the lodge.

Soon after she left, Morning Star asked Little Dove to send her son to her lodge. Warbo was surprised at the request because his Mother didn't ask for much. He sat by her fire warming himself and looked at her inquiringly. "What do you need my Mother," he asked.

"Are you happy in your marriage?" she asked.

Warbo was so surprised by her question; he just looked at her saying nothing.

"Wild One came and visited with me this morning. She is a very unhappy woman. Do you visit the lodge of Little Dove? She asked.

"No."

"Perhaps you should."

Warbo was stunned by her question. His Mother had never interfered in his life or asked such personal questions. "Why would you ask that?"

"I am thinking in the white man's world right now and as I remember, women never shared their man with any other woman. It would make us very mad and jealous. Maybe if the Wild One thinks that you no longer want her and you are going to Little Dove, she would be jealous and maybe try harder in your lodge."

Warbo thought about this for a time. Then looking up to his mother, he saw her smile, and he felt his face turning hot. Finally, he spoke.

"Will you talk to Little Dove?"

"I will ask the Wild One to come to my lodge for a meal. While she is here, you need to summon Little Dove to your lodge."

"Do you think it will work? He asked.

"There is an old saying in the white man's world. "Killing with kindness." She said Wild One said before she left my lodge. "She can stand your meanness but she can't stand your kindness."

He sat there and thought about her words. It would be worth a try, I guess. He got up and as he exited the lodge, he turned to his mother and said, "You very wise mother, we do it tomorrow."

The plan was set in action and the next afternoon he told Janie that she was invited to have dinner with his mother that night.

"What are you going to eat?"

"My other wife will bring my dinner, "he grinned.

Janie thought this to be a little strange but anytime away from him was okay with her.

"That will be just fine," she answered a little loudly.

When the time came to leave for the evening meal she was watching Warbo. He was changing into different clothes and he wore his tribal buckskin shirt. Janie thought he looked like he was going on a date.

Little Dove must have been watching for Janie to leave because she stepped from her lodge as soon as she saw Janie leave Warbo's.

Janie was surprised when Little Dove stepped out of the lodge carrying a large pot of stewed meat and vegetables. She was dressed in a buckskin dress that Janie did not remember her wearing before.

"You are looking special, Little Dove tonight," she said.

"Long time since Little Dove go to her husband," she said blushing.

As Janie walked to Morning Star's lodge, she stopped and looked back at Little Dove, Well if that don't beat all. Maybe he will give me a reprieve she thought. Good Lord, I think Warbo is having a date night. She tried to put it out of her mind as she walked to the lodge to visit her Mother in Law.

Morning Star studied Janie as they ate their meal. She could see why her son was so infatuated with the young white woman. She was a beautiful young woman, no doubt, but she knew her son was going to have a hard time melting the bitterness in this young lady.

They talked of the white man's world and Janie enjoyed speaking about her people to someone that understood what she was going through.

"You know that the white man may be your people, but they will never accept you back."

"Carl loves me and he will forget as soon as we are married. I just know he will," she said.

Little Dove entered the lodge of her husband and sat the food down to be served. She was so timid; she didn't know what to say. "I bring dinner," she said quietly.

Warbo went to her and put his hand on her shoulder. "Thank you for coming, Little Dove. I believe that I owe you an apology for not sharing my lodge with you."

Her face turned red and she turned to dish up his dinner. He sat down and accepted it. She ate with her eyes downcast to the floor.

Warbo looked at her and suddenly he realized the great hurt he must have brought to her. He was doing the same thing to her that Janie was doing to him. "Little Dove, I asked you to come over here tonight to make Wild One jealous. I am sorry for that, but do you understand how hard it is to love someone, who doesn't return that love?"

This was the first time that they had ever had a discussion of love and it surprised her. She looked up and she could see the hurt in his eyes. My husband, I cannot take away your feelings for Wild One. But I too have seen other men that cannot have the woman they love. It is our prayer that someday she will learn to care. I will help you make her jealous and she giggled and Warbo was amazed at her understanding.

Warbo made no advances to her and they talked of the weather and buffalo hunts and anything else he could think of to pass the time. At last, it was getting late and he said, "It is time to go, I thank you for helping me and for understanding. You are good woman."

"We will try hard to make Wild One look at you the way she should," she said laughing as he walked her to the lodge.

He took a few minutes and surveyed the camp. Everything looked as it should and he smiled as he walked to his mother's lodge and opened the flap and said, "Come Wild One, it is time for rest."

"Yes, your highness, and she rose from the pallet. Thank you, Morning Star for the meal and good conversation."

"You are always welcome, my child, she said. She looked at her son and winked and he could tell this was a good day.

She was burning with curiosity when they returned to the lodge. She looked at the pallet to see if it had been disturbed. Seeing the pallets spread here and there, she felt a lump in her throat. "Did you and your wife have a great time, Warbo?"

He grinned at her and said, "It was a fine evening."

She didn't argue with him, she went to the pallet and undressed quickly and rearranged the covers and turned to the wall. She was mad but didn't know exactly why.

Warbo sat by the fire for a long time and thought about the evening. He concluded that his mother was very smart in her old age.

CHAPTER TWENTY-THREE

O ne day when she sat mending one of her dresses he came in cold from the heavy snow. As he warmed his hands on the fire, her leg showed beneath the deerskin dress. He reached out and put his cold hands on her warm legs.

Always on guard, Janie jumped. She started to say something but the sly grin spreading across his face melted the hatred for a moment. She smiled back and then she laughed. It was like medicine to her veins, and it felt good to her soul.

Warbo had not seen her smile like this since the day she had hidden from him on the trail. The memory flashed back to him now. "Remember when Warbo not see you on trail? You carried the papoose."

"Yes, I remember."

"You liked Warbo then." There was sadness in his eyes as he spoke.

"That was when you treated me like a woman and not like a toy or plaything."

He came and sat on the backrest beside her. His voice was soft and he said, "Why do you fight me, Wild One? Is it so different from the white man's love?"

It was the first time he had spoken of love. "Love is when two people give themselves freely to one another, Warbo. Unless they both feel the same you can find no satisfaction."

He was quiet for a moment and then he answered, "When we captured you, I hated you. I promised I would never care for a white woman. I tried to hate you Wild One because of my hatred for the white man, I could not love you." When you escaped and I searched so long for you and when I found you, Warbo know he was wrong."

Janie was at a loss for words so she held her breath and waited for him to speak. She was afraid to hear his words.

"My heart is with the Wild One, I wait each day for you to return my love."

"Oh, Warbo, if you love me then let me go back to my people! Don't keep me here."

"I cannot do that, Wild One."

"You're afraid you will lose face with your people. If you want me to be happy you will let me go."

"If Warbo wants to save face, he would have killed you long ago, as any other Pawnee brave would have done. How can Warbo teach you to care? How did your white man lover teach you to love him?"

Janie could feel her face color. "Well, he didn't capture me and force his body on me," she said bitterly.

"How you meet this white man?"

"You see, in white man's world a man and woman don't just get married and have babies. The man takes the girl to parties and dances and they have fun learning to know about each other. Then if they both love one another they will get married. They just don't go to bed and make love before they have feelings for each other."

"Not like Warbo."

He was embarrassing her but she could see she was making a point so she said, "You don't even know how to kiss a woman," She was sorry the moment she uttered that word.

"What is kiss?"

"When a man puts his lips on a women's lips, her voice trailed off. It was useless to explain and she was not about to give him a lesson on the subject.

He was quick with his answer. "You teach Warbo to kiss?" He grinned at her. His eyes roamed her body and a chill ran through her body.

"In time, Warbo." she answered. Each time you take my body, I hate you more. I try not to, but I need time.

Warbo studied the matter to himself and wondered when he

was eating if this was another trick to outsmart him. He remembered the time when he was wounded by Sharitarish. Had she touched his lips then?

"You kiss your husband when he was wounded. It gave me strength to get well. Why did you save my life?"

"I pledged my life to die with you that afternoon because if you were dead, I would die a horrible death with Sharitarish."

"Warbo told Brave Arrow to kill Sharitarish if I died and set you free."

His words shocked her like an intruding wave washing over the sand. If I let him die, I would be free. She looked at the man sitting there beside her and suddenly the hate for him was gone. If I had known, Warbo, I would not have let you die. You are a great leader and your people need you. I do not wish you dead. I only wish to be free.

He sat quietly thinking over what she had said. "If Warbo not touch you, you learn to care? I do not understand white man's ways. I give you time, Wild One."

That night as she lay beneath the robes she felt a burden lift from her shoulders. Maybe there will be a good sunrise for me, she thought.

Warbo built the fire and pulled the robes over her like one covers a child. He was happy that they had reached an agreement and he hoped time would erase the bad times. Throughout the winter, Warbo lived on the hope Janie would change. He longed for the time when she could forget her people and accept him as a man. They talked of the way of his people and hers. Warbo thought of the white man taking her to parties. He decided he would take her anywhere he possibly could. One day he asked her to go with him to check his trap lines. He waited for her laughter but instead, she jumped up and smiled.

"I'd love to go. Anything is better than staying in hibernation all winter." She grabbed her heavy robe and the mittens Little Dove had made her from a raccoon and hurried to catch up with his long strides.

She followed the big man into the timber. He said nothing and she watched him take the helpless animals from the traps. He kills everything, she thought. She was cold and now she felt the numbness enter her body. She turned from him and walked slowly out into a clearing. She looked to the sky and the sun for warmth.

The sun threw apricot lining into the soft white clouds. For a moment its beauty penetrated her body and she smiled. "It's beautiful," she said aloud.

Warbo was behind her now and his eyes followed her gaze. "It is like you, Wild One, white and lovely with hair of fire."

She stood watching the apricot streak through the clouds but in a moment a dark purple cloud engulfed the white cloud with the savage coming of a winter storm. The apricot cloud disappeared and now it too was black and ugly. Her face twisted into a frown and she said. "If I am the white cloud, then you must be the ugly purple cloud, devouring all the beauty around you."

He turned from her and his heartfelt the burden of her words. His first try had failed to melt the ice in her heart. He felt the fury build and then remembered his Mothers words.

"Kill her with kindness." Each day he debated about taking her with him but he was determined to win this woman the white man's way.

One day the sun shone bright and warm and Janie seemed to be in a cheerful mood. He heard her humming as she fussed about his lodge. She dressed quickly and stood waiting for him as he gathered his hunting gear. She enjoyed the fresh air and found herself singing as they walked through the heavy snow. Janie made a snowball and threw it at him. She missed and Warbo whirled. She laughed and threw another. It only took him a few minutes to catch on to her little game. He dropped his gear and sent a snowball flying her way.

She ducked behind a tree to ward off the avalanche of snowballs coming her way.

"I give up," she hollered as she peeked from her hiding place. He was no longer there. She looked for him but he had vanished.

Then she felt the strong arms about her waist as he pulled her to the snow. She was laughing and he landed on top of her. He brought his lips tenderly to hers and felt her body respond to his cool lips.

It caught her off guard and she responded without thinking. Her body trembled as his lips touched her. She pulled him to her and they kissed one another until they both lay into the snow breathless.

Finally, Warbo stood up and gave her a hand. She stood up facing him and not knowing what to say. Warbo said, "Wild One is right about one thing."

"And what would that be?"

"Kiss is good. Very good." He left her standing there and walked down the trail.

The color in her cheeks already red from the cold grew redder and she yelled. "Wait for me." He stopped and took her hand and they walked from one trap to another.

Janie came to know Warbo, not as an Indian, but as a person, one with a feeling for his people and her. She began to understand their resentment for the white people stealing their land acre by acre. Slowly she began to admire the contentment of these people.

When the snow was deep and the sun was shining, Janie would go walking with Warbo. She taught him how to make a circle and play fox and geese, a game she played as a child. He always caught her and they rolled and laughed in the snow. The other young braves watched from a distance and finally after much persuading they were convinced to join in the fun. Soon it became a tribal game even the children learned to play.

Warbo taught Janie to use the bow and arrow. Each time he put his arm around her to steady the bow; Janie could feel her blood rushing a little faster. "Aren't you afraid to teach me to shoot? I might kill you."

"The Wild One would not kill husband. You have learned to care for me. You will not admit it, but I can see it in your eyes and the bitterness is gone from your heart."

"Warbo, I do care for you more than I did. I believe these last few months were not so bad at all. It has helped a lot since you haven't---you know.

"I can't wait forever, Janie."

"I know Warbo. I know."

Janie worried about this and each time he used her white name she felt all shaky inside, and she didn't know why.

He moved closer each night and she found herself moving his way to feel the warmth of his body.

CHAPTER TWENTY-FOUR

One cold winter evening as they finished the evening meal as she was looking around the lodge she noticed the one wall of the lodge that he had not painted. Curious, she asked, "What great feat have you accomplished to paint on the last wall?"

"I save that wall for important battle. It is place of honor," he answered. She paid no attention until a few nights later he got out his paints and started working on the lining of the tepee. She watched him for a long time, uncertain of what he was drawing.

"Where do you get your paints?"

"From the earth, make colors from clay, flowers, grass, and berries for color."

"And just what great thing have you done to use on your special wall. Killed anyone special?"

"This will be special painting. I think you will like it."

The bottom of the painting was done first in rich colors of green. The unmistakable figure of a woman came into view. When he drew the long hair to the shoulders and colored it fiery red, she knew there was no mistake. He painted her dress white and the black ribbon down the front in a V. He remembered each detail of the dress she had worn the first night she had entered the Pawnee village and she had forced him to fight for her. Tears welled up in her eyes and a hidden feeling nibbled at her complacency as she saw herself painted so beautiful on the wall of his lodge.

During the next two days, two Indians appeared beside her. She knew it was Warbo as his hair was light and Dark Eagle's black and long. When he had finished he waited for her approval.

"It is beautiful. It means that you killed one of your own for me.

You even remembered the dress I wore." The tears dropped slowly and Warbo was puzzled.

"Why you unhappy?" he asked.

She went to him and wrapped her arms about his waist. She hugged him and for the first time, she wanted to feel his arms about her. He stood still, not knowing what to do. "White women cry when they are happy and when they are sad. Tonight I am happy."

Warbo stood with his arms limp at his side. How he longed to hold her but he didn't want anything to spoil this moment.

"Hold me, Warbo," she said.

He put his arms clumsily about her. She looked up into his face. She waited for the kiss, and Warbo took advantage of the night. He gently laid his lips on hers and felt the excitement in his lower body. She answered his kiss as she clung to him. He pulled her tighter and whispered, "Come to me little one. I need you so."

Frustration built in her. She couldn't explain the feeling that had come over her. Why had she wanted him to hold her? What was this sudden feeling that was gnawing at her insides? She didn't resist when he pulled her to the pallet and pulled the deerskin dress up and released his pent-up passion upon her and for once she did not turn her face to the wall.

The next morning Janie visited the tepee of Morning Star. She talked to her about the painting and explained that she wanted to do something for Warbo. She asked her to teach her the Pawnee language. It was to be a surprise for Warbo and no one must know. His mother smiled and said it would be a great present for her husband.

Warbo questioned her when she told him that she was helping his Mother sew, so she would not be going every day with him for a while. He missed her on their morning walks but decided she needed to learn the ways of his people.

Janie went every morning and she was a fast learner but the language did not come easy. Morning Star was a good teacher and showed her how to cope with the language barrier. She shared her secret with Little Dove and the young girl beamed her approval.

"You have made our husband very happy. He will be pleased."

Since she had given in to her husband without fighting, he ceased having Little Dove come to him. She was not invited to go to his Mother so often and for some reason, she decided that was okay. Wild One maybe jealous, she thought and then pushed that possibility to the back of her mind.

The relationship between Little Dove and Warbo had grown cool. She accepted this in a quiet and humiliating manner. Even though his one night of love with Janie, he could find no satisfaction with his first wife. Janie knew she had caused this and she couldn't help but feel sorry for her.

One day she watched Brave Arrow bring the wood to Little Dove's lodge. The love in their eyes could not be hidden. She spoke of this to Little Dove one day as she sat in her lodge stringing beads. Little Dove's face flushed and the color mounted in her cheeks.

"Brave Arrow spoke for my hand but Warbo had his choice of the Indian maidens first so Little Dove was honored to be his wife."

"Honored? You mean you don't love Warbo?"

"Little Dove try to be good wife to husband but I failed to give him a son. Since Wild One comes, Warbo has no interest in me." She stopped short knowing that she had given away the secret she shared with her husband.

"No interest in you? What about all those nights he calls you to his lodge?"

"My husband not touch me since he fought for you. He calls me to his lodge to make you care for him. I'm sorry; I was not supposed to tell you."

Janie laughed and she suddenly was jealous of all his visits with her. It made her heart feel good just knowing that her husband was not sharing his bed with two women. No wonder he is so amorous.

"Would you like to be the wife of Brave Arrow?"

The quick smile gave her away and Janie knew the answer. She looked at Janie and her expression turned to fear. "You tell Warbo, there be much trouble."

"I suppose our great leader would lose face again she joked. "You are my friend; I will keep your secret."

"Little Dove hopes Wild One will soon bear Warbo a find son."

Janie smiled and changed the subject. A child was the last thing she wanted now. Understanding of this man and herself, perhaps compassion, but love was impossible.

As the snow slowly died away and the spring grass began shooting through the frozen ground, the tribe moved back to the fertile lands of the valley. It had been nearly a year since her capture and Janie watched for signs of cavalry or someone coming to her aid.

Janie and Warbo rode out slowly side by side and Janie decided to race him. "Bet I can beat you to that tree on the other side of the meadow," she called as she pushed her pony into a fast gallop. She stayed quite a distance ahead of him but as they neared the tree he let the spotted pony run free and he stood waiting for her, a smile of triumph written on his face. "No woman can ride faster than Warbo. Spotted pony best horse." He grinned.

He helped her from the horse and they sat under the shade of the big cottonwood tree catching their breaths. She spotted some spring sweet peas that had always been her favorite and she ran to pick them. She gathered a large bouquet and stood smelling their fragrance. He watched her and contentment was his. Each time she smiled he told himself she was slowly beginning to care for her husband.

Each time they rode out she would return with a bouquet and put them in an old pottery jar and the aroma filled the lodge.

Warbo was returning to camp after a three-day hunting trip and as they rode down the hillside, he saw a patch of beautiful spring violets and white daisies covering the hillside. Before he realized what he was doing, he was standing in the field picking a bouquet. The braves sat on their ponies looking at him in amazement. As he mounted his horse he could sense their laughter in their eyes but for some reason, it failed to bother him.

He smiled at them and rode proudly into camp displaying the flowers. Janie was nowhere in sight. When Little Dove saw the flowers, she knew they were for the Wild One and she said, "Wild One is at the creek."

He stepped from the thicket and handed her the flowers. He said nothing but waited for her reaction.

Oh, Warbo, they are beautiful, where did you get them?" she exclaimed as she buried her nose in the soft petals.

"On top of great mountain Warbo know you like flowers."

The tears came to her eyes and then without thinking she stepped forward and pulled his head down to hers and kissed him softly on his cheek. "Thank you," she said.

He stood there not moving. He cursed himself for not answering her caress, the sweet sensation of kissing her once before rushed over him. The color on his face was now a deep red.

Janie felt the flush in her cheeks too. "I better put them in water before they die," she said as she retreated to the camp. Damn him, she thought, as she left him. Why does he have to be so darn nice? She found coping with his kindness was harder than fighting his brutality. It was harder physically to endure his torture and his body but her mind was suffering now in a way she couldn't explain. She began to think of him and her plans to escape became second to trying to reason with her heart and her mind.

Soon after when they were riding, they topped a small hill on their daily outing. Warbo suddenly pulled his horse to a standstill and motioned for her to be quiet. He jumped from his pony and moved cautiously up the hill. She did the same and there below was a herd of twenty or more wild mustangs. A beautiful white horse tossed his head and took charge of the mares.

"Isn't he beautiful?" she whispered.

"He is white, like my beautiful wild one."

He watched the white horse prancing wildly about and decided this was the gift he had to give to Janie. With this horse, he could win her love. He took her back to camp and rode out alone. It took him many hours to track the stallion. With much skill, he roped the wild creature and took him to a secure area away from camp. Many hours later he had built a large enclosure in the small canyon. No way to get out on three sides and he secured the front entrance.

It was late when he returned to camp but Janie thought little of it. She was hurt the next day when he told her he must do some scouting and could not go. Little did she dream of the danger he was in while taming the wild stallion. Each day he rode out alone and Janie could feel the resentment building within her. She told herself she didn't care how he felt. She refused to talk with him when he entered the lodge and he knew she was reverting to her old ways.

"Why you mad at Warbo?" he asked.

"I'm not mad. if you no longer want me to ride with you. I'll leave you alone and you leave me alone. It suits me fine."

He smiled to himself. She had missed their rides together. He didn't answer her. He just left her to fume.

Her temper was at its height the next day as she sat on the creek bottom dangling her feet in the water. It was almost meal time so she slipped her feet into the soft-soled moccasins and turned toward camp. The slimy moss between her and the bank caused her to lose her balance. She fell into the cool water and caught herself on her hands. As she pulled her hands from the water the moss clinging to her, she waved her arms in the air to rid herself of the dark green slimy moss. It hit her across the face and she shrieked as she pulled it from her. She heard someone laugh and turned to see where it was coming from. There on the bank under the big gnarled cottonwood stood Warbo. The smile on his face was the last straw. The angry young woman stomped out of the water splashing herself all the more with her pronounced footsteps. He laughed again and the sound filled the woods, as she sputtered he laughed louder.

When at last she cleared some of the mud and moss from her hands and face, she stood glaring at him. "Stinking, rotten river, just like everything else in this miserable country."

"I see Wild One has found her temper. I was afraid you lost it."

"What were you doing watching me anyway? I suppose you thought I was going to take a bath."

Instead of getting angry he leaned against the big tree and grinned. "Wild One need bath. You look like you play in mud."

"And just how long has it been since you washed that dirty body of yours."

"Warbo not take bath near camp. Squaws always come for water."

"I just bet you have a secret spring to wash in." The anger still raged at him for ignoring her for so many weeks. For some reason Janie couldn't stand the thought that he no longer cared. She enjoyed fighting with him.

"There is special place in the mountains, the water runs blue and clear. I go there many times."

"Special, ha! Too special for me." She started for the camp yelling at him as she left. 'Go to your special place and stay there. I wouldn't go riding with you even if you begged."

Warbo watched her from the tree until she was out of sight. I think she likes me. She misses riding with me. If she didn't care for me it would make no difference. I think I am beginning to understand white woman better. He shook his head and followed her through the woods and back to their lodge.

That night she retired without a word. Warbo lay in the darkness thinking. He could smell the wild sweet peas he had brought her each day when he returned from training Brave Warrior. He was now ready to meet his master. He wondered if Janie would kiss him as she had when he first brought her the wildflowers. How he had wanted to kiss her again.

"Janie."

"What do you want?"she asked crossly.

"Why you mad at your husband."

"Who said I was mad?"

"The Wild One misses her rides with Warbo."

Oh, how I've missed them, she thought, but I won't let you know I have. "It makes no difference," she said.

"If Wild One not care for her husband, she would not want to be with him. You do care for me. I have seen it in your eyes."

Janie tried to shut her mind to his words. Fear ripped through her mind. She knew he was telling the truth but she thought, Dear God, I can't fall in love with an Indian.

"Janie."

Each time he used her white name, she felt weak inside. "What?"

"When I brought you the flowers, that was kiss?" Why you kiss me?"

"I guess I wanted to show you how much I liked the flowers. I kissed you but you never kissed me back. You don't even know how to kiss" she said angrily.

"Will you teach me to kiss you like white man?"

She turned to him and saw the seriousness in his eyes and her eyes rested on his lips. I could bribe him she thought, and the idea didn't seem distasteful to her. "Will you take me to the special place in the mountains?"

"You teach me to kiss, I take you to special place." he answered.

Janie could not resist the pleading in his eyes and she said. "It's a deal, husband."

"We go tomorrow." he said.

That night she dreamed of a cool spring running in the tall timber and of a young white girl wrapped in the arms of a tall dark Indian.

CHAPTER TWENTY-FIVE

Janie was up early preparing a small picnic lunch to take into the mountains. The sun rose high and she grew impatient waiting for Warbo to bring the horses. When at last arrived his eyes sparkled like a child with a new toy. There seemed to be a certain mystery about him as he gaily took the bundles and tied them together with rawhide and slung them across his pony's back.

She bubbled with enthusiasm as they rode through the green meadows and far into the hills. Several hours later they entered into the timber. Warbo picketed the horses and broke a trail through the tall evergreens until they came to a small clearing. Janie sucked in her breath at the beautiful waterfall in its entire splendor gushing over the small canyon. They stood below and marveled at the beauty of this place. Water so blue, it was almost green, trickled and, gurgled as it made its way down to the valley. Cattails and willows lined the creek bank and the smell of pitch was in the air.

She spread the blanket on the bank and prepared the small lunch. Warbo sat cross-legged and watched her every move. He could hardly eat thinking of his surprise. He ate a few berries and a small piece of pemmican. He brought fresh water from the stream. His moment was here. Brave Warrior must meet his new master.

"Warbo has surprise for you, come with me." They made their way through the timber. He held the long branches apart so she could pass through. She wondered what he could possibly have for her. She thought of the flowers and smiled. He left her standing by the horses and said, "Wait here, I bring it to you. Trusting old soul, I must say, she thought.

Shortly thereafter she heard him coming through the trees.

When he appeared, she couldn't believe her eyes. Warbo moved into the clearing on a beautiful white horse. He slid from the animal and waited for her reaction.

She looked from the horse to her husband and her face registered her excitement. "Oh, Warbo, he is beautiful!"

"This is Brave Warrior, he is yours. I caught him and trained him for the Wild One."

"However did you catch him," she said in disbelief.

"Much trouble, Wild One. Long time to catch and train. Each day I come to mountains to work with him."

Janie's eyes filled with hot steaming tears. She couldn't speak for the lump in her throat. She stepped closer and caressed the horse as though she didn't believe he was real. The horse pranced as she approached. Warbo spoke softly to him to quiet him and he calmed down. She stroked the smooth white neck and pressed her head to him. She searched for the right words but she couldn't force the words over the ache in her throat.

"You like?"

She looked at him with the tears blanketing her eyes. Then she remembered the surprise that she had planned for him. She thought carefully and said in Pawnee. "Thank you, Warbo. It is an honor to be your wife,"

Now it was his turn to be surprised. He just looked at her and his eyes lit up with joy. He tied Brave Warrior to a tree and came nearer. He tested her as he spoke in the language of his people. "Warbo called him Brave Warrior because he came to me as you, Wild One, and hard to tame."

"It is still hard to understand each word. For now, tell me in English. I am learning the language to make you happy."

"Warbo say, horse called Brave Warrior because he came to me as you. Dressed in fine white clothes and Wild and Brave. He fought me for many moons, even as you." reverting to English.

She went to him and her arms encircled his waist. "I love Brave Warrior and if he has stopped fighting, so will the Wild One." She hugged him tighly.

"My mother teach you to speak the language of my people. Warbo is happy." He put his hands beneath her chin and moved her face to his. His lips brushed her cheeks and Janie felt long-held defenses crumble. He could go no further. He let her go but she quickly pulled him back to her. She guided his head to hers and placed her lips firmly on his.

He didn't move and she could feel her pent up emotions that had so long been locked behind closed doors trying desperately to escape. "If you want to learn to kiss, just do as I do." She didn't give him a chance to reply. She kissed him again and her arms went about his neck. Trying to release the passion she felt, she touched his lips with her tongue and moved her lips slightly on his. Still, he did nothing.

She pulled away from him and impatience crept in. "The least you could do is put your arms around me and hold me close when I kiss you. Just move your lips as I do." Her voice was high and Warbo could feel the sting of his pride.

"It is time for ride, come."

They moved to the big white stallion and he told her to speak softly to the animal to win his trust. She worked with the exquisite animal. He lifted her gently upon his back. He led her around the clearing slowly until the horse became accustomed to his new rider.

When he was satisfied he lifted her down from the animal and told her to pack the lunch and they would return to camp. He led the horse and the others to the small trail and made their way to the valley. When they left the timber, he let Janie have her turn to ride. He held her horse behind him and cautioned her to go slow.

Brave Warrior quickened his pace and Janie patted him gently. He quieted as they crossed the plain. When they reached the smooth prairie she gave him his rein and hugged him tight. His long legs covered the ground fast and she knew this was truly a magnificent animal. She was having a hard time just staying on, she was a little afraid of the power beneath her and she slowed him to a gentle trot. She put him through some simple tests and she could tell that he had been trained by an expert, as he turned with the slightest movement of her wrist.

Warbo's face beamed and Janie felt a strange desire to share his happiness. Her face turned red as they rode proudly into camp. As they walked down to his lodge, Warbo suddenly gave that blood-curdling yell she had heard so many times before. The Pawnees answered his yell and she asked, why do you yell like that and the tribe answer you?"

"When warrior face big challenge and he wins his battle, he gives the yell and tribe knows he has accomplished a great challenge. I capture wild stallion and train him. It is great feat."

Janie knew he spoke the truth because she had seen the wild animal before it was tamed. Now she understood that each time they heard the battle yell, she would know someone had worked very hard to face his adversary, whether it be man, woman or animals. Suddenly she wanted to make up to him for his inability to show his affection as she thought he should. She no longer wanted to hurt him and she regretted yelling at him. I'll teach him to kiss me if it's the last thing I do, she thought.

CHAPTER TWENTY-SIX

The camp was alive with activity when Janie rode in on the big white stallion. She stood proudly as Warbo helped her down and took the reins. He told them how he captured the horse and tamed it for the Wild One. If anyone wondered why he gave it to her instead of keeping it for himself they did not ask. They had all come to understand how much the Wild One meant to their Chief.

Little Dove came to see the beautiful animal. Her eyes were misty as she turned to Janie. "I am happy for you, Wild One."

Janie could see the sadness in her eyes and decided that Warbo no longer needed Little Dove. He didn't love her or go near her. It was time she was with Brave Arrow.

When at last Brave Warrior was bedded down with the horses, Warbo returned. They ate and Janie found herself watching his every move. Each time she looked at him, he was looking at her.

"I'm very happy tonight, Warbo. Thank you very much for the wonderful day. I would like to go there again."

"Your husband is pleased that you can speak the language of our people."

"Now I know why you refused to take me riding for so long. You were training Brave Arrow."

He smiled and she knew he enjoyed his devilment.

"Warbo, if I ask you something, will you promise that you won't be angry or make trouble for someone?"

His manner became stern and he said, "Do not ask me to let you go. Wild One. I could not bear to hear you hear you ask."

"Warbo, do you love Little Dove."

He was silent for a moment. "Many moons ago, I thought I cared for her. I wanted a son for my people. I have never cared for her as I have cared for you.

Janie moved to the pallet of furs and sat beside him. "I have learned from Morning Star that if a man no longer wishes to keep his wife he can trade her to another warrior for many fine horses or gifts."

"That is true."

"If another warrior loves Little Dove and you no longer summon her to your lodge, why don't you give her to another warrior?"

He smiled and pulled her to the pallet of furs. He laughed and his big arms pinned her down. He leaned over her, "You jealous of Little Dove?"

"Oh, for heaven's sake. Jealous? She should be jealous of me. I have stolen your love. I feel sorry for her. You can see the sadness in her eyes."

He let go of her and sat up abruptly. He knew she spoke the truth. It didn't seem to bother him to hear her say that she knew Little Dove didn't care for him. They had felt nothing for one another since the Wild One had entered his life.

"You want me to trade her to one of my braves?"

"Yes, I believe this would make Little Dove very happy. She knows she cannot make you happy."

He thought about it for a while. "Did Little Dove tell you this?"

"Oh, no Warbo. I have seen the look in her eyes for another warrior as I have seen the look of one of your braves for her."

His eyes flashed his anger. "You know of this."

"Warbo, you promised you would not be angry. You said you would make no trouble. They have done nothing. Little Dove is loyal to you and so is the warrior I speak of. I'll tell you what I saw and you can see for yourself but you must promise that you will say nothing to harm either of them. I just don't want Little Dove to be unhappy. She has been so good to me. If you no longer care for her, let her go. Let her feel the way you feel."

She put her hand on his and he could see the pleading in her eyes.

"I have done all you ask, Wild One., I have not forced my body on yours, although many nights I have fought with myself. It has been so hard not to touch you. I have taken you many places and let you ride with me. I tried to win your love the Indian way and now I have tried the white man's way. I brought you flowers and told you of my people. Today I give you fine present and yet you still do not love me. Still, you hold your body from me. Now you ask me to give my wife to another warrior. I can do no more."

He turned from her and her heart went out to him. He poked at the fire and threw small pieces of fat into it and the light lit the room. It turned her hair to a fiery red and he felt the hopelessness of his life. At Last, he spoke. "Who is warrior?"

"Give me your word, Warbo."

"Tell me, if Warbo think he is brave warrior and can take good care of her and her family, I will think about it."

"It is Brave Arrow."

He said nothing and left the lodge. Janie's heart pumped furiously. She was scared of what he would do. He had given his word he wouldn't harm Little Dove. She slipped from her clothes and huddled beneath the robes. Every vein in her body was contracting and she started to shake. Oh, Warbo, come back. I don't want to be alone. At last, he returned and slipped from his long breeches. He pulled the robe about him and turned to her. Never in his life had he felt so lonely. He felt her hand on his shoulder. It no longer mattered. He jerked away. "Leave me alone, devil woman."

"Don't you want me to sleep near you?" Why do you call me devil woman?"

He turned to her and his blue eyes were ablaze. "I wish the Pawnees had never brought you to our camp. Go sleep in the lodge of Little Dove. You do not belong with Warbo. I no longer wish to have you near."

His words were bitter and they tore at her heart. The tables were turned. She lay for a moment thinking about what he had said or if he meant it. There was no doubt left in her mind when the covers were pulled from her.

"I will teach you to kiss me," she said weakly.

"Go, I do not wish to kiss you or touch you. Leave my lodge now."

She wrapped her shawl about her shoulders and stepped into the night. There were few stars and the moon was hidden. The camp was dark, all were in their lodges. She sat on a log near the lodge and thought about the change in Warbo. He was sending her away. A few months ago, she would have gladly accepted this but now, Oh God, where would she go, what would happen to her... escape came to her and, she knew this was her chance. With Brave Warrior, she might make it. She got up and moved from the lodge. No one would miss her. He might not even follow, she thought, as she hurried through the darkness. Then she stopped. With each step, she could feel something pulling her back. She didn't want to leave his lodge. He was her protector but now she wanted Warbo. The desire spread through her body with an unsatisfying thirst.

She ran to his lodge and pulled the robe from him and covered his body with hers. "Warbo, please don't make me leave. I want to stay." She kissed his forehead, his neck, and smothered him with her lips.

Warbo lay still for a moment shocked at the young woman trying to win him over. He rolled her over on the pallet. His lips brushed her face and when he found her lips, he needed no more lessons. He kissed her as though he had been doing it for years. She answered his kiss and as his hand moved on her body she felt the door so long locked between them finally open.

As he kissed her, he wondered. Do I dare make love to her? It came to him that she had only accepted his advances when he acted like he didn't want her. He pulled away from her and said. "Sleep on the other side of our lodge." He turned his back and lay quietly.

Janie could feel the passion soaring in her veins. The need to be satisfied tore at her. Now when she wanted him and needed him, he was going to sleep. She was not about to be stopped. She stood above him and slipped the gown from her shoulders. It fell in soft swirls about her. She let her hair loose and it flowed around her shoulders in a fiery blaze. She pulled the robe gently from him and he turned. His eyes rested on her soft naked body and he could stand no more. She knelt beside him and her fingers found the strings that held the breechcloth tightly about him. She pulled it away and her hands caressed his body. His manhood took over and he pulled her into his arms as he lowered his head to bring the hard nipples into his mouth.

"Take me now Warbo, I need you", she whispered.

Their bodies melted in a sweet embrace and Warbo knew she was giving him freely the love he had fought for so long. He knew nothing was lacking now. When their bodies mounted in climax together he thought his heart would burst. He had waited so long for this day but now he knew she was worth waiting for.

Janie's body shook when at last she felt the sweet release of passion flow from her. She lay in his arms in peaceful contentment. For the first time, she knew the fulfillment of love. Warbo slept with her close beside him and he thought, "at last I've tamed the Wild One. She is mine and no one and can take her from me."

CHAPTER TWENTY-SEVEN

For the coming weeks, Janie lived in a dream world. For the first time in over a year, the white people were second in her mind. Gradually her guilt for submitting to Warbo slipped away. She realized herself to be a whole woman and her need for him mystified her and yet she let it bloom with the summer flowers. The selfish spitfire that had ridden into the camp of savages, no longer thought of them as her captors and escape took second place to her joy of living. I'll get back to my people in time, she told herself.

Brave Warrior became her prized possession and she never missed a day that she didn't comb his fine hair and go for her daily ride. Warbo always rode with her, even though he trusted her more now that she had given him the love he had longed for, something told him not to let her wander too far. At last, his life was complete, even though the thought of the white man's love caused him to doubt himself and he wondered what would happen if she had the choice. Would she stay with him? He pushed the thought from his mind. He had watched Little Dove and Brave Arrow and he knew that Janie spoke the truth, soon he would speak to Brave Arrow.

On a beautiful sunny morning, he decided to hunt for fresh venison. Janie wanted to pick some berries, so they rode out together. They rode to their special place in the high timber. He vowed no one would intrude into his sacred valley. It was here that he made all his important decisions of his office and here he felt the presence of the Great Spirit. Now he shared his garden paradise with her.

With clean swift strokes, he fashioned a long pole and sharpened the point until it was razor-sharp. He waded into the cool stream and waited patiently for his catch. It wasn't long before the campfire was covered with fresh trout impaled on wooden stakes. They ate in the shade of the towering evergreens and drank from the cool mountain stream. He made no venture from her side to hunt. He would do it another day. Nothing could draw him for the peaceful serenity of his hidden fortress.

The afternoon became hot and sticky. Janie slipped from her moccasins and waded into the cool water. "since this is your special bathing place, I think I shall use it too. Would you care to join me?"

His face reddened as he hadn't yet grown accustomed to his new way of life. "Soon," he answered.

The water grew deeper and she pulled her dress higher. She waded upstream away from the bank where he lay watching. She nearly slipped and fell and it reminded her of the time she was covered with moss. She laughed aloud and reminded him of what she was laughing about. He laughed with her and he felt the burdens of his manhood flow gently downstream.

The noise of the waterfall and her laughter covered the sound of the three men as they slipped silently through the trees and took Warbo by surprise. When he heard a twig snap he was on his feet in seconds but it was too late. He stood staring into the barrel of a long rifle. He said nothing and studied his position. Three men surrounded him and his eyes darted to Janie in the water.

A big man, heavily bearded, a felt hat pulled low on his forehead held the rifle on Warbo. "Well, look here, Jake, it looks like we got ourselves a real live Injun and his squaw having themselves a picnic."

The smaller man laughed nervously. "You keep an eye on him, Kirby, I'll fetch his squaw." He headed towards Janie who was watching her step as she waded through the rocky creek bottom.

"Ed, you better check around to see if there are any others," the big man ordered. The man as bearded and dirty as the others left to search the trees. Janie heard the shrill hideous laugh as she turned in the water. She stopped midstream and just stared. She couldn't believe her eyes, she thought she was looking at a white man instead of Warbo.

"You certainly don't look like a squaw, little lady." he said.

She saw the long shaggy hair around his ears and the dirty trappers' clothes. She knew she wasn't dreaming and she fairly ran through the water. She grabbed at him to see if he was real. "At last, at last," she cried.

"Now what's the matter lady?"

She ran to the closest man. Her chance had come! "He's held me captive for over a year now. I tried to escape but he caught me." She poured out her story breathlessly as the men stared at the beautiful girl in the deerskin dress. "Oh, how I have waited for this chance. Will you take me to the fort?" she asked in desperation.

They didn't answer and she felt herself becoming self-conscious of their stares. "He's held me prisoner; I tell you, please help me!"

"Why, that dirty stinking Injun," snarled Ed. "I think we can help the little lady, "

"She'd just be a lot of trouble. Let's kill them and get out of here."

Jake snickered and Janie wished he would stop his horrid gawking at her. "Now listen, Kirby, it would be a shame to kill something that pretty."

"I guess we could take her with us and if she gives us any trouble we can handle her in our way," he said as he took in each detail of her body as he spoke.

Warbo stood quietly, his eyes on Janie. He couldn't believe the change that had come over her in only a few short minutes. Was this the woman that had given herself to him just a few nights ago?

Janie grew nervous at their stares and tried to convince them, "I'm white. You just can't kill me. I won't be any trouble. Please." She was almost begging now and Kirby noticed the soft curves and he pictured having her close to him.

Ed put his hand on her shoulder and Janie drew away. She could smell the odor of his body. It was rank and sweaty. She surveyed the bearded man and she knew it had been a while since he had taken a bath.

"Now don't be afraid, little lady. We're going to take real good care of you, that is if you are nice to us." He grinned as he looked at her breasts.

"Time for that later, Ed. Let's get rid of this Indian before some of his buddies show up."

Janie's eyes shifted to Warbo. She had been too busy making her play for freedom to think of him. He stood there watching her and keeping an eye on the end of the rifle. She saw no fear in his eyes and he stood tall and proud. She had prayed for this moment and now that it was here she was uncertain what to do. She hadn't been prepared to watch him die. She looked at the three men, all equally dirty, and the fear balled in the pit of her stomach.

As she looked at Warbo, suddenly he was no longer the enemy. This savage was her protector. They just can't kill him, she thought. I know he wouldn't let me go without fighting to his death. She thought of the Pawnees. They need him; I can't let them kill him. When she looked at her rescuers, dirty filthy trappers, she knew they would have no respect for her. I would be lucky to see the fort. Ed moved toward Warbo, the knife glistened in his weather-beaten hand.

"Wait," she said.

"If you don't want to watch, just turn your head. I'll fix this Injun so he won't be taking anymore of our white women."

"I don't think you should kill him," she said.

"What's the matter squaw woman? You sort of like this Indian."

"You'll forget him soon as you know a white man again," Jake said grinning.

A plan formed in her head and she pulled the string from her deerskin dress. "Fond of him! I hate him! Look what he has done to me." She opened the dress and displayed the hideous scar still vivid on her chest.

"Let's cut him up and throw him to the fishes," Kirby growled. As their eyes rested on the scar they each, in turn, covered the rest of her body and Janie could see the lust in their eyes. Filthy savages, she thought.

"I have earned the right to kill him myself." She said hatefully.

They thought a moment and then Jake laughed nervously and said. "Yes, why not, let her kill him. I never saw a white woman kill and Injun before." You could tell he relished every minute of this. "Let's do the little lady a favor and maybe she can repay us, huh?" He moved about nervously and giggled all the time he talked and Janie wondered about his sanity.

"All right, give her the gun Jake. But let's get it over with now."

Janie took the long rifle and cocked the hammer back. She pointed it at Warbo. He stood tall and his blue eyes searched hers for a clue.

Janie spoke in Pawnee, "Trust me Warbo. Trust me," she said.

"What are you saying to that savage?" Kirby demanded.

"He doesn't understand English. I told him he was going to pay for capturing me." She moved to the side of where Jake was standing, keeping the rifle trained on Warbo. Kirby temporally lowered his rifle to watch the fun. Janie took advantage of the moment. She plunged the rifle into the ribs of Jake. "Put your hands in the air before I squeeze this trigger."

"What the hell!" he raised them slowly.

"I said up. Now you two drop your rifles or your friend is a dead man," she ordered.

"Do as she says," Jake yelled.

Kirby raised the rifle to fire but Warbo was on the big man in a flash. Ed went for his pistol but Janie squeezed the trigger and the man grabbed his midriff and fell to the ground. Jake fell to the ground whimpering like a baby. "Don't shoot, don't shoot."

As the two men rolled on the ground Warbo pulled his knife from the holder about his loin and held it high above Kirby's face.

"Don't kill him, Let him up."

"Warbo kill white eyes."

"They're still my people. Don't kill him."

Something in her voice stopped him and he let go. He picked

up the rifle and held it on him. "Now get your friend and get out of here," Warbo ordered.

They scrambled to the ground and dragged the dead man with them. Kirby yelled as he left. "You deserve to live with the Indians, you're no better than those savages."

As their hoof beats faded in the distance, Janie looked down at the rifle she still held in her hand. The barrel felt hot in her hands from being fired. She dropped it to the ground and it made a loud thud in the stillness of the afternoon. She couldn't explain her actions as they left she knew her chance for freedom rode with them.

Warbo put his knife back in its sheath and turned to her. As though he read her thoughts he could feel the sadness fill her body. He moved toward her.

Janie ran to him and he gathered her into his arms. She felt the tears streaming down her cheeks. "Oh, Warbo help me! I killed one of my people! Help me, I need you so!"

His lips found hers and he crushed her to him. She didn't want to think of what had happened or why she did what she did. "I couldn't let you die, Warbo." she whispered as she kissed his cheeks and forehead. He pulled her tight against him and kissed her hard on the lips. His kisses brought out the passion in her and she wanted him to make her forget.

"Take me Warbo, make me forget. Now!" her voice had urgency to it.

"You wish to return to camp?"

"Take me Warbo, make love to me, and take the memory away!" Her breath was short and her lips covered his bare chest.

"Now? Here?"

"Now, Warbo."

He lifted her in his arms and carried her to the blanket. Thereby the stream, the noise of the waterfall close by, he made love to her as he had never loved before. With each thrust of his body, his heart seemed to say, there's one more wall to break. Her body responded to his and he satisfied the need within her.

Afterward, as they lay on the blanket neither spoke. Janie was trying to sort out the events of the afternoon. She couldn't understand why she had defended Warbo and had killed one of her people for him. Maybe the chance will come again, she thought.

Warbo, too, was deep in thought. He remembered the happiness on her face when she had her chance for freedom. She will never truly be mine if she doesn't have the chance to choose. I can never trust her from my sight and there is still a wall between us, he thought. If she ever gets the chance again and they were good people, she would go with them, he told himself. I can't live from day to day in fear that she still wants to go back. He knew what he must do.

He stood up and said, "Come, Wild One."

She got up and straightened her clothes and folded the blanket. They walked in silence to the horses. When they reached the plain, Warbo struck out at a fast pace in the opposite direction of the camp.

Janie didn't question his direction as they often rode many miles before they returned to camp. After her ordeal, she longed for the tranquility of the tepee and her need to be alone and think. They rode at a fast gait and Brave Warrior kept stride until Janie could go no longer.

"Warbo, please slow down!"

He slowed the pony and let her catch up. "We have many miles to ride. It will be dark soon."

She was too weary to argue and she forced herself to keep up. As they topped a hill it was fast growing dark. In the valley below, she could see the lights.

"Where are we, Warbo? That isn't our camp. What is it?"

He slipped from the pony and lifted her down beside him. He put his arm about her.

She stared into the evening at the sight below. She could make out the high poles surrounding the fort. The lights weren't those of campfires. She was breathless. She thought she could hear her heart beating as it pounded and throbbed. She looked to him for an answer.

"Why did you bring me here?" Her voice rising and for a moment she thought he was just teasing her so he could gloat over her capture.

"Wild One saves Warbo from the guns of the white man. You have earned the right to return to your people."

"You mean, you'll let me go? I'm free. You won't stop me?" Her disbelief was clear and Warbo saw her face light up as it had earlier in the day.

"Warbo not let you go because you save my life. You saved my life before."

"Then why?"

"I thought Warbo had won your love but this afternoon when you have chance to escape, Warbo know he was wrong. There is still a wall between us. You must have right to choose between your people and mine." He moved from her and waited for her decision.

Janie stared at the big Indian standing so proud and looked to the fort. Her eyes burned and the lump in her throat swelled. She sat down on the big rock and her mind was torn in two. She never dreamed that she would be given the choice to go or to stay. A few months ago, the decision would have been so easy. As her eyes covered the fort she felt Carl's presence. She couldn't turn her back on Carl and her people. I'm white, I've got to go back, she reasoned. I love Carl, not Warbo, she told herself.

"Warbo, those are my people down there! I want to be with them! You knew I always wanted to be free," she tried to make him understand.

He knelt beside her. "Warbo will not forget the Wild One."

Janie could see the sadness in his eyes and she looked away. "You will forget someday and you and Little Dove will be happy as you were before I came into your life."

"Warbo will have no woman." He stood up and it was the Indian talking now. "I shall give Little Dove to Brave Arrow as you asked. Warbo wants woman with hair of fire."

"Oh, Warbo, I don't hate you. I was beginning to care but I don't love you like I do my white man. I'd always want to go back."

She moved away from him, afraid he would change his mind. She stroked Brave Warrior and kissed his soft neck. "Goodbye Brave Warrior." The tears fell onto his soft white skin and he nuzzled close to her.

"Keep Brave Warrior as a token of my love." He said.

"I can walk down to the fort. You need him. He is a fine animal."

Warbo brushed the tears from her face with his hand and lifted her onto Brave Warrior. "Someday Wild One, you will find that your heart is with Warbo."

He slapped the pony on the rear and sent her down the slopes. She stopped at the bottom and turned to wave. He sat on his spotted pony watching but as she waved he turned and pushed his pony into a fast run towards the hills.

Janie kicked Brave Warrior into a fast gallop and in her deerskin dress and moccasins, her hair blowing wildly, she rode to her people.

CHAPTER TWENTY-EIGHT

Night was falling fast as Janie approached Fort Kearney. She rode hard fearing Warbo would change his mind and come running from the hills. The tall wooden gates were shut and the sentry called out to her from his post-high in the tower. Janie trembled and she felt as though she were riding into the Pawnee Camp for the first time.

"Please let me in. I'm a white woman," she called and her voice quivered.

The gates swung slowly open and she entered cautiously. Brave Warrior reared on his hind legs and pranced wildly as a few soldiers gathered about her. She spoke softly and told him he wasn't the only one that was scared.

A tall man in his mid-thirties with wavy black hair and a thin pencil mustache came towards her. He ordered the men back and spoke, "I'm Lieutenant Marshall, ma'am."

Janie slipped from Brave Warrior. "I'm Janie West. I've been held captive by the Pawnees for over a year. Can you help me?"

"Come with me, ma'am. I'll have my men take your horse." As he stepped closer Brave Warrior moved back and fought the raw-hide rope.

"I think I better take him. He isn't used to white people." She felt foolish as she heard a quiet snicker from the group of men.

"Follow me, ma'am." He walked a short distance in front of her and Janie pulled her horse gently through the men. They moved away as they had already learned respect for this big animal. Janie felt their curious stares as she passed. She avoided meeting their eyes and patted Brave Warrior to reassure him.

The horses were quartered under a long roof. A few separate stalls were fixed at one end to accommodate any unruly horses. Brave Warrior was placed in one of these. Janie tied him securely and when she was satisfied he would remain calm she joined the waiting Lieutenant.

"I'll have to take you to the Colonel, ma'am."

"Yes sir," she answered.

They walked the length of the fort and stopped at a small log cabin. A short plump woman with soft gray hair opened the door. She stopped short and gasped audibly when she saw the white woman in a buckskin dress.

Colonel Dawson sat in a huge faded chair next to a wood-burning stove, puffing on a long-stemmed pipe. His brown hair was thick and had started to grey at the temples. His bushy eyebrows arched when he saw her and he stood abruptly. The faded cavalry uniform barely covered his short stocky figure.

"This is Janie West. She says she has been held captive by the Pawnees for over a year," Lieutenant Marshall said.

"How did you get here?" he asked.

"I was set free," she answered.

"Is Warbo still Chief of the Pawnees?"

"Yes, do you know him?" She was surprised that anyone would know of him.

"We know most of the Chiefs of all tribes, or have heard of them." He puffed hard on the pipe and his eyes stared through her. "Which brave set you free?"

"Warbo. He brought me here tonight."

"Warbo, you were his woman?"

Janie felt her face redden and she nodded in answer to his question. She heard the Colonel's wife gasp again.

"You will leave the fort at once," he said.

Janie was horrified at his words. "Leave the fort! I can't do that. I have no place to go. He may change his mind and capture me again."

"It's a trick. He is a very cunning Chief. He sent you to spy on us thinking we would trust a white woman." His face was red and he paced the floor.

"That's not true!" She cried. "He let me go. I'm Janie West, I'm white, I was captured last year and they killed Dr. Crowder and his wife Maria. I think our scout got away. Please can't you see I'm telling the truth?" She was sobbing now and felt the shock of his words.

Colonel Dawson's wife came to her. "You poor dear, come sit down. My name is Martha Dawson, don't be frightened."

"Colonel Dawson, don't you remember the scout that came in last year and told the same story. This must be the woman he told us about," it was Lieutenant Marshall talking on her behalf.

"But why would Warbo let her go? He doesn't do things like that. If he was through with her he would've killed her."

"I saved his life, sir. He told me I had the right to choose my freedom."

"How did you save his life?" he asked.

Janie gulped and thought how she would tell them of what she had done. She gathered her courage and spoke. "This morning, Warbo and I rode into the mountains. Three buffalo hunters came upon us and held guns on us. At first, I was so happy because I thought my chance for freedom had come. I begged them to bring me to the fort. The big one called Kirby wanted to shoot us both, but another man called Jake talked him into killing just Warbo. He said they could kill me later after I repaid them for freeing me." She stopped and watched their faces. They listened intently. "When they went to kill him, I stopped them. I told them I wanted to kill him for what he did to me. I convinced them to let me use their gun and they did. Then when I had the gun, I told them to let us go, but they started to shoot. I shot one and Warbo fought with the other. He could have killed Kirby but I stopped him and convinced him to let them go. They were scared and took the dead man and rode out. It was then Warbo decided to set me free."

"Was the third man named Ed?" asked the lieutenant.

"Yes, I think so."

"It sounds like the three we kicked out of the fort a couple of weeks ago."

"You killed a white man?" Colonel Dawson asked.

"They were dirty filthy trappers. They were no better than the Indians. They would have killed me after they used me. Don't you see? I had no choice."

"Where do you want to go from here?" the colonel asked.

"I was on my way to California to be married when I was captured. I just want to see Carl again."

The room was quiet and Colonel Dawson mulled the situation over. He went to his desk and searched through a large bundle of papers. At last, he brought out a dirty envelope and handed it to Janie.

It was addressed to Miss Janie West. The postmark was December. Time meant nothing to Janie. She didn't even know what month it was now. She had only estimated it was mid-summer.

"That is the last letter we received from Carl Downer. It was to be kept for you in case you ever escaped."

"From Carl, Oh dear God." she opened it with trembling fingers.

"My Dearest Janie, "

"It is hard to believe that something so terrible could happen to you. I blame myself for not bringing you with me. I pray that spring will bring some news of you if they haven't killed you by now. If by some miracle you ever escape, please send me a telegram and I'll send you the money to come to California. I live in the hope you will someday read these words. All my love, Carl Downer

She hugged the letter to her, and then looked to Lieutenant Marshall. "How did he know?"

"Your scout came to the fort and told us of your capture. He said they killed the Doctor and his wife and carried you kicking and screaming into the mountains. He said he couldn't help so he waited until they left and then returned to bury the Doctor and his wife."

"You mean Russ Fently? Then he did getaway! I've always wondered. Warbo told me he was alive. I lived in hopes, that he would bring help. Why, why didn't you come and rescue me?' She looked from one man to the other and her voice was bitter.

Colonel Dawson's face reddened and he spoke gruffly. "It would've been suicide to go after you. We have women and children at the fort to protect. We can't go gallivanting about the country for one woman and risk the lives of our people here."

"Lieutenant Marshall said, "We are sorry ma'am, but we wouldn't have had a chance against the whole Pawnee tribe. Warbo is a fearless leader and he could make life miserable for us.

"How well I know that," she said. "He is a dangerous adversary." She could see the truth in what they said. "Maybe you couldn't help me then, but you can help me now. Can't you take me to the next wagon train?"

The colonel studied her and decided she must be telling the truth. "You will not leave the fort for any reason. As soon as the detail goes to Chimney Rock to meet the supply train, you can go with them."

Janie breathed a sigh of relief. She looked at the letter, how long ago was this written? She asked.

"December" Colonel Dawson said.

"I mean, what day and what month is it now?" She felt embarrassed at the question.

"This is the 20th of July, ma'am, uh 1870, "the colonel added the year quickly.

"Then you wrote to Carl. How did you know his address?'

"The scout sent him a telegram from Omaha on his way back east. He wrote to us many times. We finally told him that in our opinion you were dead. It was then we received the last letter addressed to you."

"You told him I was dead?" It seemed incredible to her.

"From the description of Russ Fentley, we didn't believe you could survive in their camp. Few white women do, they are known for torture to their captives."

"How well I know," she said and her hand touched the scar on her chest. She was glad it didn't show.

"There's been enough talk. It's time this poor thing was fed and rested. She must have been through a great deal today." Martha said.

You have no idea, Janie thought. She got up and followed Martha to her room.

"Take her to Mrs. Keller's cabin. She has an extra room. I truly hope Warbo set you free and doesn't change his mind, we could lose a lot of good men," Colonel Dawson told her.

"The Pawnees are known to keep their word Colonel," the lieutenant remarked. "I will take you to your room."

Janie got up and followed him to the door. She thought about Warbo and then spoke in his defense. "If Warbo chose to set me free, I don't believe he would attack the fort."

They came to a small cabin and were greeted by a tall thin woman with black hair turning grey much too soon for her years. He introduced Janie to Mrs. Keller and explained the situation to her briefly and left them alone.

"My name is Agnes," she said, as she stared at the white woman dressed in Indian clothes. She was embarrassed and quickly looked away. "First, we better get you into a tub and clean the dirt off of you." She moved to the stove and filled the huge pot with water from the bucket by the door.

"I'm not that dirty. The Indians bathe every day." She said defensively.

"Just the same, it must have been a horrible experience."

"It wasn't pleasant," Janie answered. She wandered about the room and tried each chair. She ran her fingers over the wooden tables and stroked the pillows softly. She stopped when she felt the eyes of Mrs. Keller on her. She hadn't realized how silly she must have looked going from one chair to another.

"It's all right child, as soon as we get you out of those filthy rags you can try out everything. I have a nice soft bed I'm sure you will enjoy."

Janie went to the window and parted the curtains. She watched the sentry's walking slowly back and forth, she felt secure. If Warbo wanted me back, I doubt if even the sentries could stop him, she thought. She trembled slightly as she imagined she could see him now taking the high wall in his stride. She drew the curtains shut quickly.

Agnes fixed a tub for her and said, "Now hop out of those clothes and into the tub. I'll scout around and find you something to wear." She left quickly and Janie undressed hurriedly to enjoy the long-awaited bath. She pressed the soap to her nose and breathed the heavenly fragrance. It held a faint scent of perfume and Janie covered herself with its lather. At this moment she wished she could stay in the tub forever and relieve her body of her past. She poured the warm water over her shoulders and let it run down her back. Wash it away, she thought. She lingered only as long as she dared and then got out quickly. She wanted to have her underclothes, which were a trifle too large, on before Agnes came back.

The woman returned shortly and said," Donna Marshall the wife of Lieutenant said you could have one of her dresses until her voice stopped short and her eyes took in the deep scar on Janie's chest. She gasped audibly.

Janie saw the look of horror on her face and she took the dress and quickly covered herself. She felt the color rise in her face.

"I should thank God; it's not on my face. It's a little souvenir of my Wedding Ceremony." She tried to make light of the situation.

"Your wedding ceremony! Those horrible beasts made you marry one of them?"

"I was married to Warbo, Chief of the Pawnees." She said it proudly as she began brushing her long tangled hair.

"You can thank God you escaped."

"I didn't escape. He let me go," she said. She moved to Janie's deerskin dress lying beside the tub. She picked it up gingerly. "I'll burn these filthy rags."

Janie looked at the deerskin dress. "Burn it." She remembered the many weeks of hard work that had gone into making the dress. "I'll take care of it, and it isn't a rag. I made it myself."

"But-but" she stammered. The odor."

Janie laughed as she took the dress from her. She folded it carefully. "It's not so bad when you used to it. It is treated with soapweed to make it soft. Would you believe it took four deer skins and nearly four weeks to make it?"

"Just the same, I'd think you would want to be rid of anything that would remind you of such a shameful ordeal." She left the room and Janie could hear her in the small bedroom fluffing the bed.

Janie winced at the word shameful. It had been dreadful but somehow the word shameful left her fuming inside.

Agnes left and returned shortly with a warm meal of warmed-over potatoes and a small piece of steak. The food tasted so strange and different to her. Her appetite didn't go unnoticed as Agnes watched her intently. "Eat heartily, dear; it must have been terrible eating those savages' food.

"The food wasn't too bad. They have a lot of corn and beans and fresh meat, she paused. The look on her face stopped her. "Of course this tastes so much better." She finished eating and asked if she could retire early after her long day.

Agnes showed her the bedroom and went to great lengths to prove the bed was soft.

"We slept on many fine furs," Janie said and then realized once again she was defending herself.

Agnes Keller left her alone and when she was gone Janie tested the bed herself. She read Carl's letter once more before she turned out the lamp. He said to send a telegram. She must find out in the morning if it were possible. Clutching the letter; her mind a jumble of plans; when at last sleep overcame her.

CHAPTER TWENTY-NINE

The next few days were terrifying for Janie. She only ventured from the cabin to walk Brave Arrow. She decided if she was to ride him, she would need some long pants so her legs would be covered. She inquired of Martha and Agnes. They both looked at her with disapproving glances. They finally came up with some black material and told her maybe she could make some. The material was not too heavy, but Janie thought it would suffice.

She was in the stall talking to Brave Warrior when Lieutenant Marshall came by.

"He is a mighty fine horse. We could use him here at the fort. Would you want to sell him?"

"I don't want to sell him. He was a present from Warbo. He will make a fine horse for Carl's ranch." I must take him with me, she thought.

"Do you plan on riding him to California?" he asked.

"I will probably ride him for a while but they change horses from place to place and he will not have a lot of time to rest. I sure wish I had a proper saddle, it would be easier for me."

"I will look around, but it will take some training to get that powerful animal to take a saddle."

"If Carl sends money, then I could pay for it." she said."

Several days later when riding in from her ride, she was approached by the man that took care of the stables. "I heard you were looking for a saddle?"

"Yes, I think it would be easier for me to keep up with the other horses. Do you have one?"

"An old one, not real pretty, come look at it if you want," he said.

She slid down from her horse and followed him to the barn. It was an old saddle, worn and faded, but she was excited to try it. "My name is Janie West," she extended her hand.

"I'm Pete, glad to meet you, Miss West. He sounded so personal, she liked him immediately. He took her to the tack room and brought out the saddle. He was right, it was very old but Janie was thrilled to even try to use it. "How much?" she asked. "We'll wait until we see if he will even let you put it on him. I doubt very much that he will allow this. He is still a wild animal. I am surprised that you can even handle him."

"Warbo has trained him well, we shall see."

"We will start in the morning. I will try to help you," he said.

She thanked him and put Brave Warrior up for the evening. That night she worked on the material and cut out a pair of jeans. It took very little time and she smiled when she tried them on. They weren't beautiful but they were better than nothing. At least my legs will be covered, she thought.

The wagon train was due to arrive in Fort Laramie in two weeks. She spent most of her time in the corral with Pete working with Brave Warrior. They put the saddle pad on first and he didn't seem to mind. Janie was delighted.

"He is used to you and the blanket is not foreign to him. Just wait till he feels that strap going under his belly, and then we will know."

Several days later, the saddle went on and came off as quickly as it went on. They tried many different ways and one day, Janie got on with the blanket and Pete handed her the saddle. She scooted back on the horse and let the saddle drop slowly onto the blanket. She slid off the animal and left the saddle on with the stirrups hanging loose. She walked him around the corral for several times a day.

Finally, Pete said, "Let's try to buckle those straps today." he grinned.

"I used to saddle horses, it's been a long time but I think he will let me easier than you."

"That's a fact, girl. You handle him better than any man. Good luck." He moved away and watched as she gently tried putting the strap under his belly. He was fine until she started to tighten the strap and he began prancing in circles so fast she let go and watched him buck until the hated saddle and straps were lying in a heap. He bucked and finally settled down. She just stood still and spoke softly to him and soon he was nudging her with his nose.

They kept working with him for the next week and Brave Warrior finally decided that she was not going to stop trying to make him wear this contraption and he relented and let her tighten the straps. Getting on was a big challenge but she used the fence getting on and only used the stirrups when she got off. Gradually he finally accepted this new way of life and let his master win.

"I guess now it is time for the bridle," Pete said.

"He does everything that I want him to do with just this halter. Warbo trained him to turn with a gentle touch of the reins. I won't put a bridle on him; I don't think he needs one.

At last with her two new dresses and pants that she had made, she was ready to ride with the cavalry. She took the addresses of the ladies at the fort, and Pete the stableman and promised she would repay them for the material and saddle.

At last, it was time to leave the fort, and Lieutenant Marshall was assigned to escort her to Chimney Rock. With her deerskin dress wrapped tightly in her satchel, strapped behind the saddle she climbed on Brave Warrior. He pranced about in circles for a few minutes and then his newfound freedom kicked in. He rode with the soldiers and she pulled him back as the cavalry moved out. Janie knew he could match any horse in the unit and she rode proudly. An extra detail accompanied them and scouts checked the hills for signs of the Pawnee.

A short time after they left Fort Kearny, she wondered if Warbo was watching. When they neared Chimney Rock they could see the wagon train forming in the valley. They made their way down the slopes and Janie found herself scanning the hills, as were the soldiers. And there it was, smoke signals slowly rising on the far hill. Her heart pounded and there was no doubt in her mind as to who was sending them.

The scout saw the signals and raced to the Lieutenant. "I can't make them out, he said excitedly. The cavalry halted and the men concentrated on the smoke. The scout trained in reading smoke signals slowly moved to the front of the group. He watched intently and then turned to the Lieutenant.

"They keep saying the same thing, just one word."

"Well, what do they say?" the lieutenant asked? Should we be worried?"

"They are calling their warriors back to camp, I think."

"Are you sure?"

"The word they are saying is return, or come back", he said.

One of the soldiers yelled from the back of the line. "Is he going to attack us?"

If Warbo was going to attack us, he wouldn't send out a warning. He would have already surprised us several miles back. The lieutenant turned to Janie and said, "Warbo has been watching. He has kept his word," he smiled and Jane felt her face flush.

As she looked at the smoke softly billowing from the hillside she felt a lump in her throat and an ache in her heart. He isn't calling his warriors back, he is calling me. She felt a twinge of conscience as she thought of the effect her leaving was having on Warbo and his tribe. I suppose he is losing face today. After she thought about it, suddenly it wasn't so funny. The lieutenant handed her a few dollars and said, "You are a very brave woman."

The wagon master offered her passage to Fort Laramie in Wyoming. She rode close to the front wagon and ignored the curious looks of the people on the train. When at last they reached the Fort; she went in search of a telegraph. After hearing of her capture, a kind man and his wife offered her a place to stay until she heard from Carl.

She stayed by herself as much as possible. She had nothing to talk to these people about and each time the subject would come back to her capture. She didn't want their sympathy and refused to discuss her experience with them.

At last, the telegram arrived: Janie*had given up hope* am sending money* take stage to Sacramento.* Carl

It sounded so cold, so formal, she thought, but then telegrams were expensive and he couldn't say much. He had sent plenty of money so he must still care, she told herself. She bought some clothes and a small suitcase and in less than a week she left Fort Laramie by stagecoach. Brave Warrior was a problem and Janie always handled him as no one could approach him. She rode most of the time, but she felt she was tiring him with the extra weight. She tied him securely to the coach hoping he could keep up with the fast-moving horses. Brave Warrior never ceased to amaze her as he kept pace day after day. Even the stagecoach drivers were watching and Janie heard one of them say as she untied him from the stage," that is a magnificent stallion."

As the stagecoach moved through the country, Janie tried to put the thoughts of her past behind, but a day didn't go by that she couldn't see in her mind, the big Indian riding across the plains beside her. Memories of the night, she pushed to the farthest corner of her mind. The stagecoach driver never ceased to tell his customers they were riding with a special passenger.

Janie didn't mind telling her story but each time she watched for their reaction. It didn't take long to find out that everyone considered it a disgrace and nothing to be proud of. She finally asked the driver to quit telling everyone about it. When the men stared curiously at her she felt their eyes as she had felt the Indian bucks the day she entered the Pawnee camp. She decided there wasn't a great deal of difference between them.

It was nearing the end of September when the stagecoach left Donner Pass and headed for Sacramento. The mountains were beautiful and the valley stretched green and rich below. The steep grades slowed the stage and gave Brave Warrior a chance to regain his strength.

It won't be long now, she thought, as they left the mountains and headed to the relay station. How would Carl treat her? Did he still love her? She had thought of another woman. If he had forgotten her and married again, then why would he bother to send money? Fear nibbled at her and stamped unease upon her mind.

CHAPTER THIRTY

A small buggy was outside the relay station. An elderly man unhooked the horses while the driver attended his passengers. A young boy started to untie Brave Warrior and he lashed out at him. The driver yelled, "Leave that ornery critter to Miss West."

Janie moved swiftly to the horses' side and untied him. His spirits were high and he was thirsty. He pranced wildly and she spoke softly to him and calmly walked him to the big water tank. She let him drink and she patted him gently. He quieted.

A voice behind her said, "Janie". She whirled and her heartbeat rapidly. It was Carl. He looked older than she remembered. His black cowboy hat covered the black wavy hair. He wore a tailored suit and Janie knew immediately that Carl had done well in his new home. She moved toward him tugging Brave Warrior.

"You best tie him up. He looks a little wild to me," he said.

She felt her face redden and she hurried the horse to the small hitching post and tied him securely. As soon as she moved away from the animal, Carl swept her into his arms. She hugged him and tears were misty in her eyes. At last, he let her go.

"Oh, sweetheart, I thought this day would never come! Let me have a look at you." His eyes covered her body and then he winked. "Just as beautiful as ever, my sweet one."

"You were supposed to meet me in Sacramento. This is a surprise."

"This relay station is only about twenty miles from El Dorado Crossing and my ranch isn't far from there. This is much closer and I knew you would be tired of that stage.

The driver was taking her suitcase from the stage and heard Carl speak. "She isn't half as tired of the stage, as I am with putting up with that wild stallion."

"This must be your horse, Janie. Where did you get him?" Carl asked.

"Yes, Carl, "He was given to me by the Indians. His name is Brave Warrior."

Carl laughed, "You mean you stole him when you escaped."

Janie spoke quietly. "I didn't escape, Warbo let me go and he gave me this horse because he caught it for me and trained him. It was a gift."

"Who's Warbo?"

"He is the Chief of the Pawnees." She felt silly telling him this standing here beside the stage with so many people looking on. She had hoped he would wait until they were alone.

"Were you his woman?" he asked.

"Please, Carl, not here."

"Well, were you?" he asked with his voice getting louder by the second.

Janie felt her anger rise each time someone asked this question. She stood proud and answered, "No, I was his wife."

Carl's face flushed but he said nothing. He strode to the stage and picked up her suitcase and put it into the buggy. A middle-aged man joined him at the buggy. "Uh, Janie this is Morgan. He is my foreman."

"I'm very happy to meet you," she said.

"It took a long time getting you here, but I'd say it was worth the wait. It's about time we got us a cook." He smiled and Janie smiled at the big burly man. He looked as strong as an ox but Janie could tell he was a gentleman by his manner.

Janie took her horse and tied him to the back of the buggy. She stroked his mane and he nuzzled to her. "He's not wild, I ride him all the time. He just isn't used to white people yet." She spoke in defense of her prized possession.

They sat in the back of the buggy and Morgan moved the team

out slowly. At last, Carl spoke, "I'm sorry about what happened back there. You must understand it was a great shock to discover you were still alive."

"I realize it must be hard for you to still accept me after all that has happened. I was so worried that you might have…she hesitated.

"Might have what?" he asked.

"Gotten married," she said quickly.

"No, I'm not married. I have been going with a young lady." He paused for a moment. "It has been over a year, Janie. "I thought you were dead."

"I understand, Carl," she said.

"I explained to my friends what happened. It might take a while for them to accept you. In time this terrible thing will all be forgotten."

She nodded and turned to watch Brave Warrior keeping pace behind them. Carl turned and then he said, "He is a fine animal but we'll have to tell people I bought him." He hesitated, I mean, we just can't tell them he was a gift from the Indians. They would laugh me out of town."

"He is a fine horse. I thought you would be pleased. I brought him for your ranch. Each time the stage stopped for fresh horses, he kept going."

"You will have to change his name or else everyone would know he was your horse from and Indian. How could you bring him here? Each time you see him it will remind you of that dirty stinking filthy Indian. You will have to forget your past." he said angrily. You will have to leave your past behind."

"Please Carl, can't you wait until we are alone and I'll explain everything to you." As she could tell that Morgan was getting an ear full.

He nodded and a stiff silence fell between them. The valley was beautiful and Janie could see the mountains in the distance. They stopped and ate from a small lunch Carl had brought. It was nearing sundown when they entered El Dorado Crossing. Carl found a small corral by the stockyards. He had never been afraid of any animal so he approached with all the confidence he could find. Brave Warrior reared and took off running. Carl fell to the ground and finally let go of the reins. Janie wanted to laugh but she knew Carl wouldn't appreciate it. Several townspeople looked on as she walked slowly to Brave Warrior.

She whistled softly and it sounded like one of the Pawnee cries at night. The big horse stopped and walked slowly back to her. She stroked his mane and talked softly to him and he followed her back to the corral. Carl dusted off his fine suit and he wasn't in the best mood when they entered the small café to eat.

Janie looked radiant and the candlelight danced in her fiery red hair. Carl touched her hand and said, "You are still very beautiful, Janie, I'm glad you escaped."

"But I didn't...."

Carl interrupted her, "That's what we'll tell everyone. It will sound better." He smiled and squeezed her hand.

She resented his attitude but she said nothing. She was conscious of the stares of the townspeople. Few came to say hello. At last a young girl, Janie judged to be in her early twenties approached the table. She had pretty short black hair and was dressed neatly. She smiled gaily at Carl and his face colored as he stood to introduce her. "Janie, this is Marcella Parker. Marcella, meet Janie West."

Janie started to speak but Marcella said quickly, "I have so wanted to meet you. I have heard of your terrible experience. You must tell me all about it soon."

"Marcella's father owns the ranch next to mine," Carl said. Janie could tell he was trying to change the subject.

"I hope to see Carl's ranch tomorrow," she said. The country is so beautiful. I know I shall love it here." She avoided the subject of her capture as she noticed the increased nervousness of her fiancé.

"Bring Janie to the ranch tomorrow and I'll fix lunch and we can talk then," Marcella said.

Carl agreed and Marcella left but not without giving Carl a sweet understanding smile. Janie wondered if she wasn't being a little nice to someone she had just met. Something about the girl bothered her but she was at a loss to know why.

"Marcella is a wonderful girl, Janie. I hope you will be good friends," Carl said.

"I hope to be friends with all of your people." She answered.

"My people? You make it sound as though they aren't your people."

Janie had spoken so much about Warbo's people and her people during the last year that the word came naturally to her. "I'm sorry, Carl, it's just that after living with the Indians for a year, I guess I talk a little differently than I did. Warbo was the only one besides Morning Star and Little Dove that spoke English. I learned to speak Pawnee quite well." There I have done it again. Spoke about the Indians without thinking.

I'd rather not talk about the Indians," He said rising. I've made arrangements for you to stay in El Dorado. It is a small boarding house."

"But the ranch..."

"I can't take you out there just yet. People would talk." They left the café and he took her to a small white house at the end of the busy little street scattered with bars and saloons. Carl introduced her to a prim little lady with brown hair pulled severely back from her face and held tightly at the neck in a large bun. She showed Janie to her room and Janie fumed when Mrs. Harding quickly explained she wanted the room kept tidy. She knows all about me too, Janie thought. Probably thinks Indians don't keep their houses clean, and I've forgotten how.

"I'll be staying at the hotel tonight. I'll see you in the morning," Carl told her. He started to leave and then embraced Janie. "Tomorrow, I'll show you your future home." He kissed her lightly and left her to ponder his behavior.

All Janie could think about the rest of the evening was, why didn't he ask about my capture? Somehow it would be easier if he knew how hard I tried to get back. She slept little and was up waiting for him. She grew impatient and she decided to check on

Brave Warrior. He came running to her and she patted him gently. How she loved this big, wild animal. Janie knew he wanted to ride and she could control herself no longer. Forgetting the saddle she climbed on from the fence and left the corral. Janie knew he had been exhausted each day after keeping pace with the stage horses. When she rode him bareback, the towns' people stared curiously at her but she didn't care. This was the first time she had ridden for a long time. She pulled her skirts over her knees and left town.

When they reached the road they had come in on, she let him run free. Janie had learned to love riding and she felt her troubles slip away as though she were leaving them in the trail of dust she left behind. She turned him around and headed back slowly. Carl would be looking for her and she better not be gone too long. He was waiting by the corral and she could tell he was very unhappy.

"Now, you've done it!" he said angrily.

"Done what?" she asked as she slid from his back.

"You've just proved to the town that I didn't buy that damn horse. After that episode, last night and now you ride out calmly on him. They know whose horse he is."

"I'm sorry, Carl, it's just that I haven't ridden him since Warbo set me free..."

"You mean when you escaped," he interrupted her.

Janie felt the sting of pride. She had forgotten he wanted her to tell everyone she escaped. She bit her lip and suppressed the desire to tell Carl she wasn't ashamed. She put Brave Warrior back in the corral and they walked back to the cafe in silence. Janie knew she was here with Carl but for some reason, he seemed to be a million miles from her reach.

CHAPTER THIRTY-ONE

They took Brave Warrior to the ranch because Carl didn't want him left in town. She put him in the corral and they toured the ranch. It was set on the open prairie with only a few shrubs and bushes planted around the house. A small white picket fence enclosed a yard full of rose bushes and flowers. The cabin was small but was built quite comfortably.

They left shortly for the Parker residence. They talked about the ranch on the way and Carl told her she could come out anytime. "I'll have to come and take care of my horse. He would only let War--- she stopped. "He doesn't like men to well."

"Not white men anyway," he replied curtly.

The remark hurt but she ignored it. She didn't want anything to spoil this day she had waited for so long.

"You hated this Warbo?" Carl asked and he looked straight at her for her answer.,

The question surprised her and she found she didn't know quite how to answer him. She thought for a moment and then she said, "In the beginning, I hated him with every fiber of my being, but then I learned to understand the Indians and Carl. I had no choice but to accept their ways. I guess I don't hate him anymore."

"No, I guess you don't hate him or you wouldn't have kept the horse. Janie that animal doesn't know how to be penned up and he isn't used to fences. How are we going to keep him anywhere?"

"In time, he'll adjust, give him time, Carl"

"I guess we all have a little adjusting to do," he answered.

The Parker Ranch came into view and the subject was dropped. Marcella was sweet and Janie could tell that she and Carl had grown quite close. She served tea and delicate cookies on beautiful gleaming crystal. Marcella watched Janie's reaction to the dishes. Never had Janie held such delicate dishes.

"I suppose these are quite different from the dishes you've been used to," she said and Janie saw her sly smile.

"No, they're quite different," and Janie thought of the first time she drank from the buffalo pouch. She laughed aloud and then became aware of the strange look on their faces. She stopped abruptly and said, "Excuse me, I was just thinking of the first time that I drank from the Pawnee' water pouch. It has a small opening and I squired it all over me." She laughed again but they failed to see the humor of it and Janie sobered.

Carl cleared his throat and moved to the window. Janie knew he was nervous so she changed the subject. She was glad when he finally announced it was time to go.

Marcella said, "Do come back again, I would love to hear more of your adventure."

On the way back to the ranch she asked Carl if Marcella was the girl, he had told her about.

"I've dated her for the last several months. She is an attractive girl, Janie, and I thought you were dead.

"Are you in love with her?"

The question surprised him and he stopped the horses abruptly. "Janie, you're the one that wears my ring. A lot has happened but as soon as we get to know each other again, we'll be married."

"I hope so, Carl, The ranch is lovely. It's like a dream come true. I waited so long and I thought I'd never be free. I even escaped once but he found me."

He hugged her close, "Oh, damn it, Janie, why did it have to happen to you?"

"Carl, my love for you kept me alive. It's the only thing I lived for."

"In time you'll forget," he said as he started the horses again.

"I'll forget but will you?" she thought.

During the following weeks, Carl came often to see Janie. He showed her the country and she believed he was happy. He was nice enough to her but Janie sensed a lack of emotion when he held her. Does he feel responsible for what happened to me? Is he trying to make up for my capture or does he care? The questions went unanswered and Janie could feel no warmth in their relationship.

With Carl's permission, she got a position in a small dress shop. She couldn't decide if the woman needed her help or considered her a drawing card for curious shoppers. She wondered if they accepted her or merely tolerated her because she was Carl Downer's fiancée. They were pleasant enough but more than once she caught them talking behind her back.

Her job gave her independence and she was glad not to have to depend on Carl for her support. She ate in the small café and became friends with one of the waitresses. Neva Dickens was a pleasant girl with rather plain features. Janie could tell she had little schooling and her clothes were faded and much too large for her. Neva moved to the same boarding house and when Carl didn't come in from the ranch they would often visit in the evening.

Late one night as Janie prepared for bed, Neva knocked on the door. Janie let her in although she had on only a light gown. The night was hot and sultry. Janie sat on the bed and let the gentle breeze blow through the room. The gown parted and the scar stood out vivid and deep.

Neva looked at her in horror. Janie was tired of always hiding it so she pulled the gown open and said, Take a good look. Some wedding ring wouldn't you say?"

"Oh, Janie, I'm sorry. I heard about your capture by the Pawnees, but I didn't know they had done this to you. I didn't mean to stare."

"It's pretty awful, isn't it?" Janie had grown so used to it that it was now part of her. Only the look of horror on everyone's face that saw it reminded her of how bad it was.

"I'd like to hear about it if you don't mind."

They talked far into the night and Janie never realized how good it felt to voice her thoughts that had been so well hidden. Until now not even Carl had asked her about what had happened. Neva listened and her eyes became wide with interest.

Long after she left Janie lay thinking about her life. I should be telling my story to Carl, she thought. Maybe then he will know how hard I tried. She decided to tell Carl the first chance she got.

Janie thought about Carl and Marcella. She was sure Carl felt a deep attraction for the woman. Marcella was always more than polite and Janie had heard she usually got what she set out for. She wondered if the politeness would wear off when she and Carl were married.

She went to the ranch in her spare time and rode her beloved horse through the rich green foothills. Carl was right about Brave Warrior, as each time she rode him she saw the big Indian waiting to help her on. She wished Carl would ride with her as Warbo had. She waited patiently for him to ask her to marry him. His embraces were warm but somehow he never to tried to take her as he had before he left for California. She thought of Warbo when he took her the first time. Not good, she thought. Then her face flushed and her heart skipped a beat when she remembered the day at the river before he let her go. Could it ever be that good with Carl? She pushed the thought from her mind and said to herself. Don't think about it, it is much too hard.

Marcella offered to buy the beautiful white stallion but Janie refused.

"What's his name?" She asked.

"Brave Warrior," she answered before she could think.

"But that's an Indian name. Then he is your horse?" she asked sweetly.

Yes, he was a wild mustang and Warbo caught him and tamed him for me. It was a gift from him. "I love this horse she said, I could never part with him."

"Maybe in time, he will get used to white people."

"I guess it doesn't matter, as long as he is with me," Janie told her.

Marcella left her then and Janie wondered if she detected a smile on her lips.

It wasn't long after that Neva began coming to her room more and more frequently. Always she brought up the subject of her capture. She was getting quite used to their names and now she asked questions about Warbo.

Janie told her of the times he had staked her out in the sun and nearly cut the clothes from her body before she surrendered. She told of her escape and how good he was when he found her. When she told him how he painted the picture of her on the lodge, her eyes grew misty and she was at a loss to explain why.

"How did you get Brave Warrior?" Neva asked.

"How did you know his name?"

"You've talked of him many times, Janie." Neva colored but Janie thought nothing of it.

"Oh, I suppose I have, I just didn't remember telling you about him."

"Everyone has talked about the animal and how afraid he is of white people, so I assumed he was yours when you lived with the Indians."

She told Neva of the time they had first spotted the beautiful stallion and how much she thought of him. He said he named him Brave Warrior because he was brave and wild and dressed in white like the Wild One."

"Who is Wild One."

"That was my Indian name. Given to me because I fought so bravely and was so hard to tame."

Janie related the encounter in the mountains with the white men, but she didn't tell Neva she killed one of them. She just said she decided she was better off with Warbo instead of the filthy trappers. "It was because I saved his life that he let me go."

Long after Neva left, Janie lay thinking about the day she was set free. Why had she given herself to Warbo only a few short weeks before he let her go? As she drifted to sleep she wished Carl would take her with the passion that Warbo had the day she left him. Her body trembled when she remembered that day and she longed to have the same pleasure with Carl.

Janie didn't see Neva after that night. A note was delivered to the store late in the afternoon. It read: "I'm sorry Janie, but I needed the money. Please forgive me." Neva. Janie's brow knitted into a frown. Whatever was she talking about?. The note left her puzzled and she went in search of the woman. She learned that she had boarded the evening stage for San Francisco and no one seemed to know why. When the weekly addition to the El Dorado News came out Janie did not need to wonder further.

There in bold headlines: THE TRUE STORY OF THE CAPTURE AND RELEASE OF MISS JANIE WEST!! She took the paper and left the store quickly. She walked in short pronounced steps and entered the newspaper office. An old man sat studying some papers and only glanced in her direction.

"Where did you get this story?" She shook the paper at him. The tone of her voice brought him from his work to face the angry young woman.

"It was a human interest story submitted to me by Neva Harding. Of course, we also had Miss Parker's approval."

"It's a rotten, filthy lie! Human Interest?" She yelled at him as she slammed the door loudly behind her. As she stepped on each crack of the boardwalk she wished it was Marcella Parker she was stepping on. She took the paper to her room and read the story. The tears burned her eyes as she read: Janie West known to the Pawnees as" The Wild One." Her wedding ring, a vivid scar on her chest. Love slave to an Indian. And in conclusion, Janie West picks Warbo over white people. She was released only because the Pawnees had no further use of her. Janie slumped to the bed. For a moment she sat as though paralyzed with shock and then slowly bitterness and hatred of Marcella Parker brought her to her feet. Pulling out the jeans and boots and clutching the newspaper in her hand she headed for the stable.

She rode out to the ranch to look for Carl. Morgan told her he was out on the range. She mounted the stallion and kicked him into a hard gallop towards the Parker residence. Morgan chuckled to himself and he couldn't recall ever seeing a madder woman than Janie West. At this moment he was glad it was not he that she wanted to see.

As she neared the ranch her breath came rapidly and her body shook with uncontrollable anger. If she noticed Carl's black gelding hitched outside she paid no attention. Her jaw set in determination and her eyes narrowed she knocked hard on the door.

Marcella stepped aside in surprise as Janie burst into the room her hair flying in all directions. "Janie, what a pleasant surprise."

"Marcella, what a pleasant surprise." She purred and her eyes blazed. "The Wild One is here and you better do some explaining."

"Whatever do you mean?"

Janie was in her face and flung the paper at her. "How much did you have to pay Neva to get all the information out of me? Then take what I said and turn it around to make it look filthy. How Much?" she was screaming and Carl grabbed her and shook her.

"Janie, stop this. What are you talking about?"

Marcella handed him the paper and Janie could see the hidden smile on her face. He took the paper and his eyes lit up when he read the headlines. "OH, my god, Janie! How could you?"

"How could I?" This bitch of a girlfriend of yours paid Neva to get all the information she could about my capture and then turned it around to make me look bad. I should pull her rotten hair out of her head, she said as she started to Marcella.

You could see the terror in Marcella's face as Janie started towards her. "Stop her Carl," she whimpered.

Carl grabbed Janie and held her back from Marcella, "Is this true?" he asked.

"Neva was just telling me about it one day and I suggested that she might be able to sell the story. I didn't think she would." She smiled sweetly and Carl turned on Janie.

"I told you not to tell anyone. How could you do this to me?"

"I didn't do it, Carl; your lousy bitch did it. She started to defend herself and suddenly it didn't matter. She wanted to get away. Tears blurred her vision and she ran from the house. Brave Warrior carried her far and fast into the foothills. She stopped and let him rest. She buried her head into his neck and cried softly. Oh, Janie, what have you come back to? Her question went unanswered and she quietly rode back to the stable. She pastured the animal and slipped to the seclusion of her room.

Mrs. Andrews told Janie she could keep her job and that anything she did in the Pawnee Camp must have been done out of fear. Janie appreciated her kindness but inwardly she fumed because no one knew the real story.

Carl downer didn't come to El Dorado Crossing for several weeks and Janie could contain herself no longer. She decided to ride out and get the matter settled once and for all. Morgan told her that Carl was at a small roundup camp at the foothills of the Cascade Mountains. She begged him to take her there. After much deliberation, he smiled and agreed. He had grown accustomed to this little spitfire and he decided she was much more of a woman than that snooty woman, Carl was going with. She rode Brave Warrior in her pants and boots and they entered the camp at sundown. Carl was surprised to see her, and his face reddened in guilt as he helped her down.

"Oh, Darling, I had to see you. I have missed you so much." She wrapped her arms around him and planted a kiss squarely on his mouth.

Carl couldn't resist her and pulled her to him. He answered her kiss and Janie felt his love return. They ate supper cooked over an open fire and Janie felt right at home sitting on a log for a chair.

"Janie, I'm glad you came but it's going to be mighty rough sleeping out here. For a woman I mean."

"It's too late to return to the ranch, and besides I've slept on much worse, Carl."

Carl looked embarrassed and was glad Morgan had left them. "I guess I had forgotten."

"That's the trouble, Carl, you haven't forgotten. You don't even know what there is to forget. Not once have you asked what happened. You believe that story in the papers, don't you?" Her voice was higher now and the tears mounted in her eyes.

He came to her and put his arms around her and said, " I was afraid to ask."

"It's just that, if you knew what happened, maybe it would change things," Janie said as she wiped the tears on her sleeve.

Carl knew she wanted to talk about it so he said quickly. "What kind of a bed did you sleep on?"

"Warbo had a lot of soft furs and they used them for a mattress. They were quite comfortable especially when he put soft leaves beneath." She stopped and held her breath. "Why did she make it sound so easy?"

"You always slept in a tepee?" he asked.

"For many moons after my capture, I slept in a lodge with Little Dove, Warbo's wife, and her mother and sister." As she scraped the plates she threw the meat onto the fire and watched it sizzle and light up the darkness.

"Why did you do that?"

"Makes more light. Warbo always used to do that at night."

Carl's eyes flared and he grabbed her and shook her. "You even talk like an Indian. Can't you forget that stinking Indian?"

"He wasn't a stinking Indian. At least he treated me like a woman."

Carl kissed her savagely and for the first time, she felt the passion in him. He pulled her to the bedroll and kissed her again and again and his hands felt the soft curves of her body. "I want you, Janie. Now."

She had longed to hear those words but now she knew it couldn't be good between them until he accepted her past. She pulled away from him. "You must hear my story, Carl." Then if you still want me, I am here."

Carl sat up and lit a cigarette. "All right Janie, I'll listen.

She started at the beginning and left nothing out. She told of her capture and the killing of the two braves. "I tried to kill myself, but I had no courage." She told of their fights and how much they had hated each other in the beginning. Carl felt her love as she talked about their fights and her torture in the sun. Her eyes softened when she spoke of the lodge and Warbo bringing her the sweet peas. It was as though he was there with her now and Carl could feel her love slipping away to Warbo as she talked.

She paused for a moment and she saw him sitting on the willow rod backrest smoking his pipe. "He isn't so different from any other man," she said. He tried to make me surrender to him the Indian way, with meanness, but I never gave in. I suffered so much. It would have been easier to let him have me than take the torture he put out. I refused to sleep in his lodge. She told him of her escape and how hard she tried to outfox him but her fall from the horse ruined her plan. I had a severe concussion and I would have died if he had not tracked me and taken care of me. Then he started being nice, bringing me the flowers and catching the wild stallion. Oh, Carl, you don't know how hard I fought him for you. She left nothing out and told of the fight with Sharitarish. I would be dead if he had lost that fight.

"He must have been a very brave and tough Indian." I just get so jealous every time you mention his name." he said.

"Jealous, of an Indian?" The thought had never crossed her mind.

"He's still a man and I don't think you'll ever forget him. I think you have a lot more to forget than I." He pulled her to him and for the first time in months she felt free to go to him. He unbuttoned her dress and pulled it from her shoulders. He stopped when he saw the scar. His eyes opened wide and he moved back from her and stared at the horrid flesh.

She pulled her dress open for him to see and watched his astonishment.

"My God, Janie! That's horrible!" He stopped himself and moved to her. He put his hands on her shoulders but Janie felt her blood run cold.

She pulled the dress about her and said, "The scar will not go away, Carl."

For the first time, Carl realized what she had gone through. "I'll make it up to you, darling. Just give me a chance."

As he moved to embrace her she pulled away and went to her bedroll. She couldn't bear to have him touch her. Not yet, she thought.

CHAPTER THIRTY-TWO

anie nestled in the huge bedroll. The sounds of the night reached her ears. She could hear the valley quail as they chirped crossly to their playful offspring. The crickets sang in perfect harmony and an occasional croaking of a frog lulled her to sleep. The campfire dimmed and cast its shadows into the night. Suddenly Janie found herself back in the Pawnee camp. She could see the firelight flicker on the painting of a red-haired woman. A man sat cross-legged in front of a fire and sent smoke signals from the lodge. She could see the words spelled out across the sky. Return Return. His eyes were blue and cold. He didn't smile and the sadness filled his every feature.

The night air was chilly and Janie felt herself moving to the big Indian and she saw the snow gently fall about the tepee. She reached out to him. She felt his arms strong about her and she kissed him tenderly. She anticipated the thrill of his touch and she heard him say. "Someday the Wild One will find her heart is with Warbo." She moaned and tossed in her sleep and cried out, "No, no, let me go."

Her screams awakened Carl and he was beside her in seconds. "What is it, Janie?"

She hugged him tight and looked into the darkness waiting for Warbo to appear and drag her away. She realized where she was and sighed heavily. "Oh, Carl, I guess I was dreaming. It was so real."

He stroked her hair and spoke comfortingly to her. "I'm here darling. It must have been terrible. In time the dreams will go away."

"Oh Carl, they won't go away until I am no longer his woman, but yours. Can't you see, you must make me forget?"

"I wonder if you can ever really be mine again, Janie." He covered her gently and returned to his bedroll.

She thought about what Carl had just said and his words only added to her frustration. Damn you Warbo. You must be stopped. Carl's ring will hide yours' Warbo! You've lost.

Janie persuaded Carl to let her remain at the camp for a few days. She couldn't bear to be alone. She rode with Carl and helped him round up the strays. Her memories rode with her and it seemed she could see Warbo standing proud and tall in the silent hills that surrounded them. She stopped to water Brave Warrior. She could see her reflection in the water as she cupped her hands for a drink. She heard his laughter and she turned quickly. She realized she had once again imagined it, but she knew he was with her. She remembered him standing by the river and how his laughter had filled the air when she stood covered with moss. She smiled. He had a really good laugh, she thought. Now it was her laughter that rang from the willows along the small river bed.

She thought being with Carl these few days would bring her closer to him but she could feel them growing farther apart as each day went by. She grew silent and Carl knew she was a troubled soul.

"Janie, I know something's been bothering you, do you want to tell me about it?"

She said nothing and he put his arms about her. "Maybe you should set our wedding day. It might make you feel better."

"When do you want to get married?" she asked.

"I would have married you when you returned but you're not the same girl that I knew and loved in the East. I don't think you still love me."

"Carl, how can you say that? I only lived for the day to be with you. That's all that kept me alive for over a year." Tears stung her eyes and the world turned blurry.

Sometimes a person only thinks he wants a certain thing and then when he gets it, he doesn't want it." Carl told her.

"But I do want you Carl, I love you."

"Then set the date."

"All right, let's get married as soon as possible. I want to be free of his memory."

"It was probably the fact you were sleeping outside and the campfire and all that reminded you of him and everything."

Janie convinced herself Carl was right and she determined to block Warbo from entering her mind. They returned to the ranch and pastured Brave Warrior. Carl took her to town.

But Warbo was not to be stopped. He plagued her dreams until she awoke and paced the floor. She saw him running in the snow, playing fox and geese. A red-haired woman ran with him but each time he reached for her she disappeared and he fell to his knees in the snow.

The dreams saddened her and she tried without success to understand why. She couldn't bear to return to the store. She would be married soon, so she bought some material for a wedding dress and spent her time in her room and worked on a beautiful gown. Even this brought no pleasure into her life.

She remembered her first wedding to Warbo. Her hand darted to the scar. The scar, always the scar. A constant reminder that will never go away. I will never get him from my mind, she thought. She remembered the words she had spoken when she saw the mark of Warbo. "A snake for a snake." Somehow it wasn't funny.

She held the dress to her and stood in front of the long mirror. Before she realized it, she threw it on the floor and pulled the deerskin dress from the closet. Holding it to her she danced about the room. She saw Warbo smile as she stepped from the lodge wearing it for the first time. Suddenly she stopped and realized what she was doing. She threw the dress to the floor and the tears were not to be stopped.

When Carl came that evening he noticed her eyes were red and swollen he didn't say anything. He talked of their wedding plans and Janie listened but she didn't seem to hear. As he left he embraced her warmly. She didn't respond. He hugged her tighter and kissed her fiercely on the mouth. She pulled away.

"Janie, our wedding is only a few days away. You better decide whether you love me or that damn renegade Indian. He stomped out of the room before she could answer.

Long after he left she thought of his words. She remembered the first time she had made love to Carl. She thought she had enjoyed it then. What was stopping her now? Will I ever respond to Carl as I did to Warbo? Do I love Carl? For the first time, she knew there was doubt in her mind.

For the next two days, Janie sat staring out the window, her mind in constant torment. Will it be any different when I'm married? She thought. Will I ever forget him? The doubts seemed to grow larger as her wedding day neared. A knock on the door brought her back to the present. She was surprised to find Morgan outside.

"We've had a little trouble with Brave Warrior. Carl wants you to come out and see if you can quiet him down."

"He's alright, isn't he?" Her voice registered her concern and she felt her pulse quicken. She couldn't lose him.

"I think he misses your rides. He's been acting strange for about a week. He's going wild and he keeps looking for you."

"I know I haven't been riding him, Morgan, but I've had my reason."

"I can't understand that, Miss West. You seem to look very happy when you ride out."

Janie felt guilty as they rode to the ranch. She had neglected Brave Warrior but only because he reminded her of Warbo. Carl waited for her outside the corral. "Don't go near him, Janie. I think he's gone completely wild."

She had never seen the horse so angry. He pawed the ground with his feet and whinnied in fierce short snorts. He looked as he had the first time she had seen him.

"We should've gotten rid of that ornery critter right from the start. He's been nothing but trouble," Carl said.

Janie felt her temper rise to full force for the first time in months. "Get rid of him. I can't do that!" she screamed at him.

"Well I can't tame no Injun pony or its master either for that matter!" Carl yelled back.

Janie crawled over the fence and said. "Just shut up. I'll handle him." She called to Brave Warrior but he made no move toward her. He circled the corral in short running leaps. She spoke in Pawnee and he stopped and listened. As she slipped from the fence she heard Carl mutter, "I think she's part Injun." She ignored him and moved slowly from the fence. She spoke softly to him. He stood still and let her advance. Gradually she worked her way to him and patted him gently. Slowly he nuzzled to her. She slipped the halter about his neck. He hopped wildly as she led him to the fence. She patted him gently and slowly mounted. She sensed his anxiety and motioned for Carl to open the gate. He shook his head in disgust and steered clear of the opening as he did so. Janie let him run free and had a hard time staying on. He gradually quieted and they walked slowly up the valley. Golden Poppies were in full bloom and the meadow was full of their beauty.

She started picking the flowers while Brave Warrior grazed peacefully in the rich green grass. She took the bouquet and placed them beside his nose. He nuzzled to her. "Oh Brave Warrior; you don't belong in this country. You belong with your people in a land that is free with no fences to bind you." The tears stung her eyes as she smelled the Poppies. It wasn't Poppies that came to her but the rich fragrant smell of sweet peas. She looked to the mountains and the small white clouds that hovered above them. The clouds with the apricot lining came to her and then she saw the smoke signals coming from the sky. They seemed to say, Return, Return. For the first time the words served their impact.

"He wasn't calling his braves back to camp. He was alone when he let me go. He was calling me! He followed me to Chimney rock after watching the fort for nearly two weeks. He wanted ME! To return." She said aloud. "Could I? she thought. A thrill swept through her when she thought of Warbo. This time she didn't push his memory aside. She sat in the field of flowers and she knew that her heart was back in Nebraska with a proud, fierce, and gentle man. NO ONE HERE WILL COME UP TO HIM OR MAKE ME FORGET HIM.

Suddenly she jumped up and yelled, "I don't belong here

either." She ran to Brave Warrior. "We're going back!" She told him and tears of relief streamed down her face. She felt a heavy burden lift from her shoulders. She had been so deep in thought she hadn't heard Carl ride up.

He looked at her for a moment and then he said, "Back where, Janie?"

She whirled and stood up proud and straight. "I'm going back to Warbo"

He looked shocked. He dismounted and came to her. He saw the radiance in her eyes and he knew her decision was made. "I knew you'd never forget him. But to go back, Janie, do you know what you're saying?"

"I think for the first time since I left Warbo, I know what I feel and what I want."

"You want to go back?" It seemed incredible to him.

"Carl, you remember the nights in the mountains. You said you didn't think I could ever really be yours. You were right. It's so hard for you to understand but he is with me. A day hasn't passed that I haven't thought of him."

"I guess I knew from the beginning, Janie. Every time you talked about him I saw the light in your eyes."

"But I fought him so hard for you. I lived for this day."

"You fought him when you loved me, but when I heard your story, I knew when you stopped loving me. You didn't realize you loved him, did you?"

"He was so good and he tried so hard. Why couldn't I see things the way I do now? Why did I come back and ruin your life?"

He put his arm about her. "You haven't ruined my life. Just knowing you are alive and happy relieves the burden I've carried this past year knowing I let you die a horrible death."

"Then you don't hate me?"

"I could never hate you. I believe our love died together. Yours in a Pawnee camp and mine when I received that last letter from Colonel Dawson."

"Oh, Carl, I've wasted so much time. I want to go home."

"He'll take good care of you, won't he Janie?"

"He'll protect me with his life. He proved that when he fought to his death twice for me."

"Come with me, Janie. You must see something before you leave." He helped her to the horse and they rode silently to a small meadow below the ranch house. Beneath a huge weeping willow tree, a small cross stood and the letters now beginning to fade said, Janie West, beloved fiancée.

"We've both lost something, Janie. But I think maybe we've found something better."

"Then you and Marcella---"she broke off. In time, Janie. In time. You could not forget Warbo and I doubt that I will ever forget you Janie, but my life will go on. If you stayed, I would never know who you were thinking of each time I took you to my bed.

He turned away and they rode silently back to the ranch. Janie looked at the countryside and felt no remorse. Her mind became a jumble of plans for her return trip.

CHAPTER THIRTY-THREE

C arl consented to let Brave Warrior stay until the stage lines opened with the promise that Janie would keep him calm. She went back to work to earn her passage. Calculating the months, she knew it would take many months to return, and she felt the excitement in her body as she contemplated Warbo's reaction.

She spent a lot of time with Brave Warrior and lived on the memories of her past. She thought of all the little things she would be giving up but the vision of Warbo kept overriding her doubts.

She saw little of Carl but nothing bothered her now. She let her hair fly and longed for the day when she could ride her great stallion into camp. She chuckled when she saw the curious stares of the townspeople. By now they knew that she was going back and Janie laughed at the conversations that must be going on about her sanity. She bought a beautiful bracelet for Little Dove and a new bible for Morning Star. For Warbo she chose a long keen hunting knife with a beautiful red and white pearl handle. If he thought the doctor's scalpel was something, he'll really like this, she chuckled. She found a telescope and as she purchased it, she envisioned the look on his face when he looked through this foreign object.

Carl dropped in occasionally to see her and Janie wondered if he was concerned or just wanted to make sure she didn't change her mind. She felt no grudge toward him and she knew nothing could stand in the way of her decision. One night he waited and walked her back to the boarding house. "I can tell you haven't changed your mind. Have you covered every part of going back? One thing I don't understand. If you hated him then, how do you know for sure you love him now?"

"I only hated him because I wanted to be with you. That was all I had to come back to. I had to be free and away from him to realize how much I loved him. You were always in my way."

"I will never forget the times when you loved me. I shall miss you very much. Do you have enough money? I will help you with anything you need. I want you to be happy with your---he hesitated, "husband."

Janie blushed, "Yes, he is my husband, renegade or not. Oh, Carl, I am so sorry but I can't wait until I see him again."

"He's a mighty lucky man." He said.

When he left, Janie wondered if Carl wasn't a little shrewd. I bet he might not be so nice if I changed my mind.

She mapped her route so she could arrive in Fort Laramie well ahead of the supply train to Fort Kearney. She imagined how it would be when she returned and she pictured the lonely man sitting so proudly on his horse the night she rode away. How could I have left without a backward glance? She wondered.

Janie worked out a plan to enter the Pawnee camp. She thought about the Pawnee scout at the fort and wondered if he would guide her back to the camp. It was late in March when she finally met the stage. She thought the stage driver would have a heart attack when he saw the big pile of luggage and her tie that ornery stallion to the back of the stage. " I wish you would make up your mind, lady," he grumbled as he put her things aboard. She had purchased some blouses to wear with her Levis and boots. She rode Brave Warrior with his new saddle that Carl had purchased for her to take the load off the horses pulling the stage.

She felt no remorse as she waved goodbye to Carl and Morgan as the stage moved out. It seemed so many years since she stepped from this stage and waited for Carl. Now she was on her way to a new life.

The trip was exhausting and they encountered many delays before they finally reached Fort Laramie. It was nearing the end of May. She grew impatient waiting for the cavalry but Brave Warrior welcomed the rest. She bought warm blankets and added them to her growing pile of luggage. At last Lieutenant Marshall rode in and Janie ran to meet him.

"Hello" she yelled as he approached. "Remember me? "

"How could I ever forget you and what on earth are you doing back here?"

"I am going back to Warbo," she said, as she waited for his response.

"I guess you've had a long time to make that decision. I won't try to stop you," he said.

As the familiar hills came into view, she felt her skin tingle with excitement. Janie proudly rode her stallion into Fort Kearney. She watched the stunning looks she received and remembered how frightened she was when she rode in a year ago. She recognized a few of the faces and she knew they certainly hadn't forgotten her.

As she unloaded her luggage, Mrs. Keller approached her. "Lord, Lord, if it isn't Janie West. What on earth are you doing back here?" she asked.

"I'm going back to my husband," she said.

"Going back! Sakes alive girl. They might kill you!"

"Maybe so, but I'll take my chances with Warbo," she answered as she dragged the heavy bags with her.

Colonel Dawson looked dazed when she asked him to escort her to the Pawnee camp. He proceeded to lecture her until she finally stopped him.

"I'll not change my mind. Perhaps your Pawnee scout will take me? I will pay him."

"What about all that luggage you are dragging with you?" he asked. You will need pack mules with all that junk. How am I going to get them back?"

"Warbo will return them," she spoke confidently.

Colonel Dawson snorted. "You've got more faith in that Indian than I have."

Lieutenant Marshall came to her aid, "He kept his word last year when he let her go. I know he watched the fort until she left and all the way to Chimney rock. You remember I told you about the smoke signals?"

"Then you take her, and don't lose any of my men," Colonel Dawson said gruffly.

Janie spent a sleepless night. It didn't bother her to think of the things she would leave. It suddenly came to mind that maybe she could establish a truce with the Pawnees and the Fort. She asked the lieutenant the next morning at breakfast.

"In what way, Miss West?" he asked.

"If I was desperate for medicine or some dire supplies, could I come to the fort to see if they were available?

"The only thing that you can do is convince Warbo to meet with the Indian Agency when they meet to establish a peace treaty between the Pawnees and our people."

"I will think about that." She said.

As the Lieutenant helped her pack the mules, he said, "There will be one happy Indian tonight." He winked at her and gave the order to move out.

When they topped the hill in the distance she looked back but without misgivings. Nothing could stop this impelling force that ran in her veins and she knew her decision was right. The closer she got to Warbo, the more she wanted to feel his strong arms about her.

The small company rode for the better part of the day. Janie's heart pounded when at last a smoke signal slowly rose from the far hill. Lieutenant Marshall drew up short. That's what you've been waiting for. This is as far as I go. That's Pawnee country, ma'am." The Pawnee scout took the reins of the two mules and told her he would go as far as possible.

As they moved through the tall aspens she could feel the presence of the Pawnees about her Brave Warrior pranced wildly as he sensed too that they were in familiar territory. She pulled the scarf from her hair and let the wind blow it gently about her.

She smiled when she heard their long low whistles through the trees. She answered them and laughed at their confusion. They moved in silently and at last jumped from the trees and from behind bushes. They shouted to each other and from the excited voices and triumphant smiles on their faces, Janie knew they thought they had once again captured the Wild One.

The Pawnee scout handed the reins of the mules to one of the braves and Janie thanked him for bringing her back to the Pawnees. He agreed to meet her in three days with Warbo to get the mules back to the captain. He waved and gave the sign of peace and left the group. She breathed a sigh of relief when Brave Arrow and Twisted Hair joined the small hunting party. She was happy to see him, she hugged him tightly. His face reddened and she knew he was embarrassed. She spoke in Pawnee that was nearly forgotten and told him to take her to the camp. Brave Arrow smiled and his face beamed proudly. The group moved silently through the trees.

Suddenly Janie felt sick. Where was Warbo? Why is he not here? She wondered. Her heart sank at the thought he might have been killed during the past year. He always rode with the hunting parties, she thought, and the fear increased as they rode. Brave Arrow led the party and Janie called to him. When she tried to make him understand her Pawnee, he only smiled when he heard Warbo's name. When at last they entered the camp, the women, children and dogs came running to meet them as they had so long ago. Janie slipped from Brave Warrior and extended her arms to the people. "I have returned," she said in Pawnee.

The women looked at each other and talked for a few minutes. Then their faces registered the pleasure her words brought. She smiled and went to look for Warbo. She saw his lodge sitting in the center of the camp. The shield and Warbo's poles were crossed in front. No smoke came from within. Her knees grew weak and she trembled. Little Dove's tepee no longer stood beside of Warbo's.

At last she spotted Little Dove coming from the river. She ran to her and embraced her. Tears stung her eyes and she asked, "Where is Warbo. Is he—"She stopped short and her eyes dropped to the stomach of Little Dove. Janie gasped, "You are with child." Janie hadn't expected this and she couldn't explain the dread that crept into her being.

"Warbo will be proud," she said feebly.

"Little Dove is carrying the child of Brave Arrow. When you went to your people, Warbo let Brave Arrow have me. We are very happy."

"You are not married to Warbo?"

"No woman has entered the lodge of our Chief since the Wild One leave."

"When will he return?" she asked.

"Soon. I am glad you have returned."

Janie told the braves to unload her things outside behind Warbo's lodge so he wouldn't see them. She asked Little Dove to tell the camp that she wanted to surprise Warbo, so please do not give her away. They grinned as Little Dove spoke and Brave Arrow hurried the mules and Brave Warrior to a hidden pasture. She was surprised how happy they were and how they too wanted to participate in her surprise. As Janie headed to Warbo's lodge, Little Dove stopped her. "No one enters his lodge without his permission."

"Do you think I've forgotten? I'm not waiting until dark to get it ready. Something tells me that I will be forgiven." She said. She took down the shield and hung it on the tripod. Opening the flap, she went in and smelled the musty stale air. I'll fix that she thought. Her eyes rested on the picture of her still painted on his lodge. Beneath the painting was her cloth bag. She opened it slowly and found all her old clothes still intact. The tears came to her eyes when she thought how hard it must have been for him to see these things every day. They were faded and ragged with the bible still tucked inside. They were placed beside his prized possessions.

She shook the hides and cleaned the floor with the tiny broom she had purchased for just this occasion. She gathered fresh leaves and made a nice comfortable bed for them. She grinned when she thought of the many times she had hated to sleep here. Her pulse beat faster as she worked. She started a small fire as the evenings were still cool. Little Dove brought food for their supper.

She put the new blankets on the hides. When at last everything was ready, she went to the river and had a quick bath. She changed clothes and when she started to put on the pantaloons and cami-sole, she thought, that will be a waste of time and she dropped them back into her bag. She put on the wedding gown that she had made for her marriage to Carl. As she looked at the dress she thought, I was making this gown for Warbo, not Carl as it had the same V neck with the black ribbon running down the front, the same as in the painting. This is truly my wedding day, she thought as she left the long row of buttons unfastened. She combed her hair and let it fall softly about her shoulders.

She heard Little Dove call to her and she went outside. She held a small bouquet in her hand. "These will make your lodge smell as it did so long ago."

Janie's eyes lit up. She took the flowers and breathed their sweet fragrance. "Now all is complete. Thank you, Little Dove" It had bothered her to think of sharing Warbo with another woman. Now he will be all mine, she thought.

I pray his love hasn't turned to hate. She stepped from the lodge and checked the camp. There was no evidence of her coming and she smiled at the squaws cooking supper. The braves sat around sharpening their weapons but their eyes moved frequently to the lodge. They would not give her away.

Brave Arrow had been watching for Warbo and he signaled to her even before the hoof beats broke the stillness. She hurried inside and she knew her heart was beating as loudly as the horse's hooves.

Warbo entered the camp and Brave Arrow took his pony. He started for his lodge and as Janie peeked from the lodge she could see the droop of his shoulders. His body registered the pain he had suffered. As he approached the lodge he saw the smoke slowly rise and he stopped short. The shield hung on the tripod. His war lances stood to one side.

Anger flashed in his eyes and his shoulders came up straight and proud. That's my Warbo, she thought. His voice was loud and demanding. "Who dares to enter the lodge of Warbo?"

Janie watched and giggled as the braves stared straight ahead as though they hadn't heard. She shivered at the sight of the big man standing there so angry. His chest was bare and he wore only the soft moccasins and the long breeches trimmed with fringe. He carried his bow and quiver. He dropped them on the ground and headed for the lodge. He could get no answer here, he would see for himself. When Janie saw him coming she stepped back to the wall in front of the painting. She looked to be a part of it as she waited for him to enter.

He entered the doorway letting the flap close behind him. His knife glistened in the firelight. The smell of fresh sweet peas penetrated the air and his heart pounded. His eyes searched for his aggressor. When his eyes found Janie standing in front of the painting, he thought he was dreaming. He blinked and rubbed his eyes for a moment.

Janie's heart was pounding," Welcome, my love," she said softly.

The firelight danced in her red hair and it shone above the beautiful white dress. He slipped the knife in its holder and went to her. He gathered her into his arms and ran his hands through her long fine hair to convince himself that she was real. She heard a joyous moan as his lips found hers and his kiss made her body tremble. Her hands caressed his neck.

"Oh Janie, what took you so long?" His hands roamed up and down her body, not wanting to let her go. Then moving to the door of the lodge, he stepped outside and she felt the chills run up her back as she heard the Pawnee war cry of victory come from his lips. In turn, the braves answered his call and you could hear its echo throughout the camp. He stepped inside, closed the flap, took off his moccasins, and long breeches, and pulled her to him.

"And what great battle have you won today, my husband?" she asked.

"The hardest won I have ever fought. The Wild One is mine at last."

"And all brave Warriors must have their reward, she said as she loosens the tie to his loincloth."

THE END

CPSIA information can be obtained
at www.ICGtesting.com
Printed in the USA
LVHW011044281220
675216LV00002B/328